The Face of Evil

An Allie Bishop FBI Mystery Suspense Thriller / Book 2

EVA SPARKS

Chapter One

Residence of Helen Mercer
Tacoma, Washington

The electric tea kettle whistled happily on the stove. Helen bent to switch it off, surreptitiously inspecting her reflection in the shiny metal. She gave her front teeth a quick swipe, clearing off any stray lipstick that may have lingered from after this morning's church service. She ran a hand through her neatly bobbed black hair. It was stylish but understated, without a hint of gray, just how she liked it.

Thankfully, she had stayed in her best yellow sundress and cork sandals—she typically changed into her slippers the minute she got home. At fifty-three, Helen enjoyed wearing heels, but only when someone else was paying attention. Today, she had a handsome house guest who had stirred an unexpected response in her with his lingering scent of sunshine and woodsmoke.

The sound of the doorbell had been a welcome surprise, as well as the young man standing on her doorstep holding a plate of freshly baked banana bread. A gentle summer breeze danced through her pink hollyhocks that stood watch at her front gate. Helen smiled at her orderly garden, and the vibrant flowers seemed to nod their approval of the clean-cut visitor.

Glancing around her tidy kitchen, she was glad she had taken the extra time to wash the breakfast dishes. It was so easy to grow lax living alone, but she generally took the same care with her home as she did in her appearance, though no one really dropped by anymore, not even her grown daughter.

Stephanie always called before she stopped by. Conscientious to a fault that girl was, Helen mused to herself. She poured hot water into the glass cylinder that held the freshly ground coffee. Maybe that was why her daughter was still single. Helen carried the tray of coffee and sliced banana bread to the counter, where her guest was perched on a stool.

"I hope it was all right to drop by," he chatted casually. "I had a small bunch of bananas that were starting to turn. I thought I'd bring you a loaf and then run one up the street to Mr. Williams. He's been pretty lonely since he lost his wife. Did you know her?"

"Oh yes, Gigi was special. But I'm afraid I haven't seen him since the funeral."

"I walk his dogs every other Thursday so he can take his mother to play bridge."

"I didn't know his mother was still with us." Helen poured coffee into two Le Creuset mugs. Picking hers up, she cradled it in her hands and leaned against the counter. It was her favorite corner of the kitchen for gossip.

Her companion poured milk into his coffee and gave it a stir. "Mrs. Williams will be eighty-two next month. You don't like banana bread?"

"Oh, I was enjoying the conversation." In truth, Helen was somewhat fanatical about her diet. She didn't eat sugar unless it was a special occasion.

"You're not gluten free, are you?" Remorse welled up in his face, and Helen's resolve melted like butter. "I'm sorry. I should've asked."

"No, no." Helen took a big bite. She didn't have to fake the look of pleasure that washed over her face. It was delicious. Over the next few minutes, she finished the slice and eagerly accepted a second slice. "This was your mother's recipe?"

"Yes, Mrs. Mercer. Chocolate banana bread was her specialty."

His eyes lit up when he talked about his mother. It was cute. "Please, I've told you before, call me Helen. Mrs. Mercer was my mother, and she's long gone."

Did he blush? That was sweet. His hair stuck up in a trendy way, like the barista at her coffee shop and the guitarist at church.

He smiled. "Yes, ma'am."

"Ma'am isn't much better," she teased. "Your mother obviously taught you manners. First, you helped me clean out my gutters—not many people would stop their workout to help a neighbor—then you made me that delicious pot pie when I had a cold. Now banana bread? I don't deserve this attention."

He beamed at her. She felt a little flushed and adjusted her necklace. It had been a while since anyone looked at her with such adoration. She felt a little flustered. "You don't have anyone at home to bake for?"

"Just me and my mother."

"Really? Well, I should introduce you to my Stephanie. She and I have dinner most Sundays. Either she comes here, or I treat her somewhere. Tonight, we're getting sushi. Do you like sushi?"

He shook his head. "Actually, I've never tried it."

"Well, there you see, that would be my way to say thank you." Helen's eyes sparkled with the idea.

"That's very kind of you."

"We would love it. It's hard to be new in town. That's why I'm glad we'll be walking together more often. I remember when my late husband and I moved up here from Virginia. I was so lonely. You know, my pastor was just preaching on the importance of loving your neighbor in service today. Do you and your mother have a community of faith?"

He shook his head. "I'm not all that religious. I prefer to take life in my own hands."

Helen blinked at the odd turn of phrase. "Do you mean…?" but then she waved it away. "My Stephanie isn't religious either, but I personally find church to be a comforting ritual. It reminds me of my childhood. I took my daughter too when she was little, but…" She shrugged and trailed off. "I guess it didn't take."

She liked the idea of the two of them together more and more. Her daughter's fair complexion would complement his pale eyes and darker hair. As Helen studied her fine-boned neighbor, the room tilted slightly. She blinked, and the kitchen began to swim around her head.

Beads of sweat broke out on her lip. It must have been the sugar, she scolded herself. She lifted her cup to her lips, but her hands trembled, forcing her to set it back on the counter. She tried to continue, but the words stretched uncertainly in her mind.

"It's obvious you're a very loving mother." He gently laid his hand over hers on the white marble counter. Helen could feel his calluses on her bare skin. Her heart thudded violently in her chest. She needed to get control of herself.

"Thank you." Helen started to object to his compliment but then let the words sink in. She had been a good mother. She had poured everything into her only child, and it felt good to have that effort acknowledged. The ever-present guilt of being a mother and getting it wrong was a specter that made it hard to accept praise.

"Honestly, Helen, being in your home, I can feel the comfort, beauty, and love," he said, nodding to the elegant kitchen. "I think that was obvious when we first met. You have a generous spirit, and you remind me of *my* mother. I think that's one reason why I feel comfortable coming to you for help."

Helen lifted an eyebrow and started to ask a question, but the kitchen felt hot and stuffy.

Her arms and legs felt heavy, and stars danced before her eyes. She had read about strokes and heart attacks, but oddly, she wasn't in any pain, just a growing numbness that slowly filled her with fear.

She swallowed and tried to focus. "You need my help?" Helen rasped and took a deep breath, but it was a struggle.

There was a weight on her chest. She gripped the counter as the kitchen swayed wildly.

"Yes, Helen." Suddenly, the young man hovered at her elbow, his mouth very close to her ear. "But you've already done enough. Now all we have to do is wait." His breath was sweet as it fluttered past her face. She blinked rapidly.

The gnawing unease turned to terror as her legs buckled. She slumped toward the floor, but she didn't land on the hardwood. With alarming ease, he lifted her small frame into his arms, then carried her through the dining room into her tidy living room, where he laid her gently on her pristine, slip-covered sofa.

Wild-eyed, she surveyed her beloved objects—the antique bookcase that held her husband's first editions, the silver-framed photos of her daughter, the ornate candlesticks she found in a flea market, a Chinese vase that she liked people to believe was a family heirloom. The modest home was filled with treasures Helen had curated and cared for.

But now, each piece sat stoically, watching her suffer in silence.

She gurgled and choked, but not a sound escaped her suddenly constricting throat. Helen tried to arch her back. She heard one of her sandals land with a hollow thud on the rug, but she didn't feel it fall. She tried to wiggle her toes, but nothing. Her fist wouldn't clench, her hands were of nothingness.

She tried to scream. Only a muffled gurgle came out.

"Sssshhhh, sweet Helen." He knelt on the floor next to the sofa, face close to hers, watching her gasp in silent agony. "You know, your face is so lovely." He studied her carefully and traced her brows with a single finger. You've taken excellent care of yourself, Helen. It was the first thing I noticed when we met."

He brushed raven locks of hair off her face and admired her well-nourished skin. "There are none of the worry lines here." He touched the spot between her brows. "Or age spots, or jowls. It's the jawline, you know, that often ages a woman. As if gravity itself is getting its revenge." He gently prodded her cheek, fascinated by the spring in her plump, dewy skin. "But you've defied them all."

Helen's hazel eyes watched him in horror. She was incapable of movement. Drool began to fill her slack jaw and dribbled out the side of her mouth.

He watched her carefully, seeming to take pride in her fear. "I promise, the worst part will be over very soon."

Helen watched the young man reach for the pocket of his cargo pants and remove a scalpel. She tried to scream, but this time, her eyelids barely fluttered. A tear slipped down her powdered cheek.

He carefully flattened her out on her back until all Helen could see was the ceiling fan above her. It spun lazily in the summer heat, indifferent to her terror. The stone fountain on the table gurgled passively as he examined her face.

He poked and prodded, but she couldn't even feel his fingers along her jawline, across her brow, chin, or her nose. She was a paralyzed observer as the scalpel appeared in front of her face.

He placed the tip at her hairline and pressed into the skin. Her mind was screaming in terror as she heard the blade cut across the top of her forehead and move down beside her ear. A wave of nausea flooded through her at the sound of skin separating from bone. Her attacker paused to admire his work and adjust his instrument, now covered with a sheen of bright red blood. *Her* blood. Helen moaned.

Suddenly, his head snapped up, and he was frozen stiff as he listened to a new sound in the house. Helen's eyes widened and rolled to the edges of her vision. But she couldn't hear or see anything but the cotton weave of her couch.

The sound came again, and this time, she recognized it. Her cell phone chirped sweetly from the kitchen. The refrain lilted through the house. "Brown Eyed Girl" was Stephanie's song. The one Helen had sung over her crib when she brought her home from the hospital, the one she and her father had danced to in the backyard on summer evenings.

A shudder of foreboding washed over Helen's soul.

Her attacker disappeared for a few moments and returned with her phone. He looked at the caller ID with obvious pleasure. "You're right, Helen, I should meet your daughter. Very soon." He glanced at the photo of the girl on the screen and then at the frames of her childhood. "She's beautiful, just like you."

He bent over Helen, the scalpel disappearing out of her line of vision again. The ungodly sound was the only witness to her tragedy.

A sudden desperate rage welled up in her spirit, and she finally felt her body respond. With a jerk, she flailed once and, unaided, slumped precipitously off the couch. Her right shoulder slammed into the floor with a violent thud.

"*Nooo!*" He stood over her, screaming in a primal rage. "No

—no—*no*! You *ruined* it." The scalpel was still in his hand. Helen could hear the gurgle of blood leak out of her wound, and something made it difficult to see out of her left eye. Her head lay tipped to the side on her beautiful hand-tied rug. The rich wool fibers drank up the blood that spread out across the ornate pattern.

"Dammit, Helen!" The young man flew into a rage. He paced her living room, jamming his hands into his hair and muttering to himself in frustration, calling her vile names. He bent toward her head, examined her face, clutched his hair, and howled again. Helen now understood that his trendy hairstyle was simply the wild result of madness. His eyes were glassy, a vein throbbed in his forehead, and blood was speckled across his chin.

But Helen's one good eye looked past him. Stephanie's cracked graduation portrait had fallen off the coffee table. She stared lovingly at her beautiful daughter for a moment until her mind finally understood the horror looking back at her in the reflection in the broken glass.

A long red slice ran across her nose and cheek, and her left eye socket appeared melted off her skull. Half her face hung detached from her body, but the mask had been torn in her desperate attempt to escape.

Her face was marred, practically sliced in half. She stared at her reflection in horror. A moment later, resignation and defeat descended upon her. She fixed her eye back on the beautiful image of her daughter.

In a final act of defiance, she would not look up at the crazed killer standing above her.

She didn't watch as he cradled the hefty stone bookend in

two fists and raised it high above her head. And she didn't hear the sickening crack as it smashed into her skull, nor the sound of her body being wrapped in the elegant hand-knotted rug and dragged toward the door.

Later, as Stephanie's portrait lay alone on the living room floor, her cell phone rang once again with "Brown Eyed Girl."

Chapter Two

Madame Vaughn's Lounge
Tacoma, Washington

Special Agent Allie Bishop's thighs burned as she hunched behind a lime-green dumpster in the dark alley. The scent of cigarette smoke and rotting food clung to the brick surface at her back. Allie watched a rat scamper across the glossy concrete. The street light glistened off a shallow puddle.

Unlike the rest of the damp state of Washington, rain wasn't a constant in Tacoma. The rare summer shower curled Allie's shoulder-length hair. A trickle of sweat slipped down between her shoulder blades, past the gun holstered at the small of her back.

The radio crackled. "Driver is approaching. Bishop, King, take your positions and wait for the subject to exit."

Allie watched headlights flare at the mouth of the alleyway, behind the luxurious watering hole of the rich and notorious. She steadied her breathing, trying to still her pounding heart and steady her nerves as she considered how she had ended up here.

The success of her first case, capturing a serial killer preying on her hometown, had led her to this assignment. Her boss, Special Agent in Charge Finnigan Marze, had developed a diverse team to look into a complicated string of shell corporations accepting funds as consultants, advisors, and strategists for the looming senatorial election. She had been tapped to investigate the suspicious movement of funds out of the capital.

Fresh out of Quantico, Allie relished the opportunity to learn the finer points of embezzlement by studying shady financial transactions. Illicit funds seemed to move like water into offshore accounts and into the pockets of wealthy men and women who sought to curry favor with government influence.

"If the FBI shows up on your doorstep, they've been watching you for months, possibly years." That was how her partner, Special Agent Jason King, explained it while they painstakingly combed through a complex web of aliases and relationships, all of them leading back to Washington's lieutenant governor, Adam Lowe Sandberg.

Allie's work ethic, sense of justice, and addiction to the legal stimulant that was Snapple Iced Tea helped her reveal a consistent pattern of behavior in Mr. Sandberg's busy schedule as a public servant. On the last Thursday of every month, Sandberg would spend the evening at a corner table of Madam Vaughn's with his former Stanford roommate Michael Wong, a senior member of the Yin Investment Group based out of Shanghai.

Sandberg's credit card receipts testified to copious amounts of liquor and marathon sessions of karaoke as the primary entertainment. However, they had uncovered an alarming pattern. For over nine months, funds were released from government coffers on the last Friday of the month. One day after each of these meetings. Many of the earmarked funds were funneled into advisors, pet projects, and initiatives that benefitted Yin's strategic partners and a handful of Sandberg's largest campaign supporters.

Working in conjunction with the Washington State Public Disclosure Commission, they were now ready to confront Sandberg. Agents stationed inside Madam Vaughn's were surveilling the conversation, and Allie listened for the signal that the FBI had the evidence it needed to move in.

Sandberg's car service had a standing order to pick him up at the back alley at midnight. If everything went according to plan, they would pick up Sandberg, present him with the incriminating evidence, and get him to give up his partner, Michael Wong.

A voice whispered in the earpiece she had tucked under her loose curls. "Bishop, King, you are cleared to approach. Subject heading in your direction."

Allie stepped out from behind the dumpster and fumbled with a weighty Zippo lighter. She didn't smoke, and the gesture was awkward, but she needed a reason to loiter in the abandoned area behind the club. She didn't want to spook Sandberg back into the lounge and alert his partner of their presence.

The door of the back entrance sprang open. The lieutenant governor swayed drunkenly in the silhouette of the doorway. Allie clicked open the lighter and brought the flame to a cigarette in her mouth. She cupped it in her hand and inhaled the smoke, nursing it to life. Only then did she lift her head in time to nod at Sandberg as he slid past her into the alleyway. His easy stride was lubricated by song and top-shelf tequila.

She waited until the door clicked closed. "Mr. Sandberg?"

"Mmmmm?" He turned unsteadily on his feet and gave her an obnoxious once-over.

"Special Agent Allison Bishop, FBI. May I have a moment?" She tossed the cigarette aside and straightened her shoulders.

The two locked eyes. Allie watched the wheels turn slowly behind the fog of spirits as she steadily closed the distance between them.

For a moment, she thought she had him. Then she watched the flicker of contempt flash across his face, and he bolted away from her and toward the car waiting for him at the curb.

"We got a runner!" She spoke into her earpiece and sprang forward in pursuit, pumping her arms as she tried to match his alarming speed.

Allie was only a body length from her subject when he grabbed an oversized recycling bin. Pulling it down between them, glass bottles skidded across the concrete, and a stack of wooden pallets toppled into the fray. Allie shielded her body from the falling tower, but glass sprayed across the alleyway, forcing her to slow her steps as Sandberg neared the edge of the lonely alley.

At the last moment, he threw a glance over his shoulder at her, and a smile tugged on the edges of his mouth, the neon sign above his head lighting his wicked grin. Sandberg was so busy smirking that he didn't see Jason step out from the darkness. Her partner lifted an arm and caught the lieutenant governor

The Face of Evil

under the chin in an expert clothesline they didn't teach at Quantico.

The force of the collision lifted the crooked official's feet off the pavement and deposited him onto the slick sidewalk. A loud grunt escaped his chest.

Jason straightened his suit jacket with ease and bent to his quarry. "I believe my partner requested a bit of your time, sir."

A groan was the only response the inebriated man offered as Jason rolled him over and placed a set of handcuffs on his wrists. Then he hoisted Sandberg to his feet.

"Suspect is in custody," Allie breathlessly spoke into her earpiece as she joined Jason at the edge of the alley. SAC Marze and two other agents stepped out of the waiting sedan that had been masquerading as the governor's car service.

"I'm gonna be sick," the middle-aged man grumbled. The three agents stood quickly to the side while he emptied the contents of his stomach into the gutter.

Allie winced at the sight and turned away.

"Mr. Sandberg, you have the right to remain silent. Anything you say can and will be used against you in a court of law." Jason continued to read him his rights. When he was done, a team escorted the woozy politician toward the waiting car.

"Well done, you two." SAC Marze ran a hand over his military-grade mustache while the team of agents tended to their capture. "I wasn't worried about getting him into custody, but getting him to resist arrest is a secondary win for us."

"Ego is a ruthless mistress," Jason laughed.

"Exactly." Marze gave Allie a rare smile. "We didn't need him to admit anything at face value, but by underestimating

Bishop, he played right into our hand. Between this and the footage, we got two tonight. It should make the next part easier—getting him to turn on his partner."

Allie winced and inspected her left forearm. She noticed blood collecting on the band of her watch and traced it to a neat tear in the sleeve of her green silk shirt.

"This is my favorite shirt," she groaned.

Jason handed her the red pocket square from his suit coat. "I know an excellent tailor. I'll text you his address. He works miracles, even fixed a bullet hole for me once in a vintage Armani dinner jacket."

"Seriously. A bullet hole?"

"Well, I wasn't wearing it at the time," he grinned. "We ran a sting on a dry cleaner over in Yakima Hill. A little place on Proctor Street was laundering much more than shirts. The Russian mob, to be precise. I must have had everything in my wardrobe cleaned twice during surveillance. When we raided the place, the grandmother came out with a Glock, and my dry cleaning took a direct hit. Incredibly tragic."

"Thankfully, it was the only casualty that day," Marze added, and looked at Allie. "Bishop, I have an ambulance on standby around the corner. Stop by and get that cut cleaned up. I need you both at the office first thing in the morning. Sandberg's lawyers make more in an hour than we do in a day. We don't have much time before he's back on the street."

Marze got into his ride and drove off. Jason went for coffee across the street while Allie got her wound cleaned and dressed. She was relieved to hear the cut on her arm didn't need stitches, just antiseptic and a clean bandage. She begged a plastic bag off the medic. Slipping out of her silk shirt, she folded it neatly and tucked it into the bag in hopes of salvaging it. Then she pulled a clean denim shirt from her satchel. Hearing something hit the pavement, she looked down to see a well-worn journal lying open.

Allie felt her pulse quicken at the sight of her mother's delicate script staring up at her. She scooped up her treasure. She had foolishly been carrying it with her everywhere since it was delivered to her three weeks ago. Somehow its nearness was comforting.

Her mother had disappeared when she was seven years old. Very few of her belongings had been handed down to her only daughter. Her mother's final words had haunted her ever since she read them:

If you're reading this now, then I have left this journal here for a purpose. I don't know what my future holds, but I fear that I don't foresee us together in it.

Whatever happens, Allie...

Find the truth.

Keeping the journal close seemed to quell the growing unease those words had sparked inside her. She had yet to tell anyone about the journal, Grams included. She wasn't sure why, but she wasn't ready to just yet. In a way, it felt like something that only she and her mother shared. Their little secret.

Jason appeared and handed Allie a styrofoam cup of coffee. "Marze just called. He wants us to head over to Veterans Park off Fifth Street."

"In the middle of the night?" Allie asked. She stowed the last of her belongings and shouldered her satchel.

"They just pulled a body out of the Puyallup River."

Her eyes brightened.

"Don't look so excited," he said as they headed toward his Charger. "It's bad form."

"What?" Allie smirked. "Come on. After weeks of financial spreadsheets and credit card receipts, it will be nice to be back in the field."

"That's true. I even picked up a pair of readers last week because I was going cross-eyed. But still, you're way too giddy about a washed-up corpse."

Chapter Three

Veterans Park
Tacoma, Washington

"Where did you get this coffee?" Allie asked as she took a sip from her styrofoam cup.

"Pretty bad, isn't it?"

"Terrible."

Jason turned off 5th Street and parked next to the flashing lights of the medical examiner's van, where a handful of police cruisers huddled along the edge of the river. They grabbed their windbreakers from the trunk, and Allie changed into a pair of boots. She tossed the coffee onto the grass, stuck the cup in the door of the car, and grabbed two Snapples off the back seat.

He leaned over her shoulder. "You keep Snapples in *my* car now?"

"Do you want one or not?"

"Yes, please. He twisted off the cap and took a long pull on the bottle. "We're looking for Officer Corrigan. He's our point of contact with the Puyallup PD." The two made their way down the path toward the line of yellow crime scene tape illuminated by two industrial-sized flood lights. The hum of a generator purred in the background, and a handful of staff and uniformed officers busied themselves on the fringes.

"No Snapple for me?" A burly bald man with a red braided beard tucked into his official white jumpsuit lifted the yellow crime scene for the pair to slip beneath.

"Tiny!" Allie was thrilled to see her old colleague, the night manager at the ME's office.

He smiled. "I'm starting to like seeing you on a regular basis. Wasn't sure I would see you much at all after you left us. I heard you were coming and decided we could wait to let you see the body *in situ*. If there's a psycho out there carving up women, I'd want you hunting him."

"Ahhh, Tiny. That's so kind." She blushed and motioned to her partner. "You remember my partner, Agent King."

"Indeed." The two shook hands. "It starts with the Snapple," he warned Jason. "Soon, she'll get you addicted to Thai food, and you'll be as big as me."

Allie cocked an eyebrow. "Wait. What did you say about carving up women?"

"I'll let Corrigan fill you in. He's busting a gut to work with the feds." He lifted his chin to an officer in uniform standing on the bank of the river. "Let me know when you're done, and my team will finish up."

The body had been pulled from the river and now rested under a white plastic sheet. It was obvious to Allie's trained eye that the crime scene had been processed, that they had been invited to the party as a formality. All her former experience working at the ME's office made Allie feel naked without her camera at a crime scene, but she reminded herself she was there to observe and assist.

The two agents approached the uniformed officer. "Evening, I'm Special Agent King. This is my partner, Special Agent Bishop. What do you have for us?"

The slim officer looked down at the sheet. "The body was discovered by a fisherman late this evening."

"Pretty late for fishing," Allie said.

"He works the late shift and knew they'd be biting after the rain. He snagged much more than he bargained for. I have his statement, but they had to take the old guy out on a stretcher."

"That bad?" Jason asked.

"See for yourself."

Allie slipped on a pair of gloves and bent to lift back the sheet. Over her shoulder, Jason winced.

"According to the ME, the victim was killed before she was thrown into the river," Corrigan narrated. "Time of death is subject to change due to the warmer temperature of the river this time of year, but it's possibly one to two days ago, but maybe earlier."

"Blunt force trauma to the head," Allie pointed out. "Could have been hit by debris in the river, maybe a boat if her body didn't stay submerged for long." Allie clicked on her flashlight to take a closer look. "Middle-aged woman, medium height and build."

She noticed a fishing hook and bobber tangled in the woman's black hair. Her skin was pale, and her lips were a bluish-purple. A cut ran from the corner of her right jaw, up her cheek, and across part of her nose. The left side of her head was badly gashed. She studied the cut. "This cut here, it's too thin, too precise to have been any common instrument."

"Hunting knife?" Jason asked.

"Maybe."

Jason grimaced at the bloated body. "Pretty gruesome."

"Tiny said someone's carving up women? Is she not the only one like this?" she asked Corrigan.

"In the past six months, we've pulled two other bodies out of Puyallup, not far from here. That's why we called you."

"Someone's using the river as their own personal dumping ground?" Jason asked.

"With today's rain and the height of the river right now, the crime scene could be from anywhere between Mount Rainier and Puget Sound." Corrigan sighed. "Each victim fits the same general description—medium build, middle-aged woman with hazel eyes and black hair."

"So our unsub has a type?"

"And a thing for pain. The other two bodies washed up without faces."

"Excuse me?" Jason said, alarmed.

"The two previous victims had their faces removed, very carefully, with surgical level precision."

"So something happened with this one." Allie was intrigued. "Could it be possible that our victims are alive when the perpetrator removes their face?"

"Lovely. Thanks, Bishop," her partner quipped.

"Something like that," Corrigan confirmed. "The cause of death was poison in both previous cases."

"Same poison both times?" Jason asked.

"I believe so. We'll have to run tests on this subject before we get a clearer picture of the pattern, but if I was a betting man..."

Allie snapped a couple of pictures with her phone before finishing up her assessment and laying the sheet back over the victim.

Jason handed his card to the officer. "We'll need a copy of the complete report of the previous two victims."

"Absolutely. We could use some help on this one." Corrigan's shoulders sagged, but he looked relieved. "Tiny speaks highly of you, Agent Bishop."

"Don't believe everything you hear," Allie chided him with a smile.

They made their way up the riverbank and said goodbye to the ME's team. The moon had already sunk out of sight, and a cool breeze swept off the water. Allie shivered as they headed back toward the car. She considered the implications of the case as they stowed their gear and finished up for the night. As a rookie, she was still learning to trust her instincts. "What do you think?"

Jason got in behind the wheel and started the car. "I don't like it," he sighed. "We either have a serial killer with a thing for the faces of middle-aged women—"

"Or a copycat who couldn't finish the job?" The car grew quiet, and when Jason spoke again, he spoke for both of them.

"Whoever we're dealing with, he's one sick bastard."

Chapter Four

FBI Field Office
Tacoma, Washington

Allie fussed over a large houseplant in the corner of her cubicle. Grams had given her the luscious plant for her new apartment after she returned from Quantico. The purple ceramic pot held a healthy Pacific bleeding heart. It was the same lovely flower Grams cultivated on her beloved family farm in Gig Harbor, just outside Tacoma.

Allie loved the reminder of her grandmother, her anchor and best friend.

But she brought it to the office today because it was quickly becoming apparent that she spent far more time at the TFO than at her apartment. Allie gave it a healthy drink of water and nudged it a little closer to the daylight. She couldn't bear to watch the tender pale pink flowers wither and fade. She had her grandmother's work ethic, but she was pretty certain she had not inherited her green thumb.

"Something's different," Jason said as he entered her cubicle in a quiet corner of the bustling floor. "Don't tell me." He scanned the space. "New case board." He pointed to the empty whiteboard they used as command central.

Allie's cubicle served her well. She enjoyed the natural light from the sprawling bank of windows an aisle away. Jason appreciated the space as well and the two had fallen into an unspoken pattern, doing most of their collaborations from here. Last week, he had pulled in a comfortable office chair, and it was becoming a permanent fixture in her cubicle, alongside the small bust of Abraham Lincoln her grandfather carved.

"And let's see. A new French press, a new candle, and a potted plant. Are you moving in?"

"You tell me." She plucked two shriveled blossoms off the plant. "I'm the rookie here, but the preliminary evidence from last night made me think I'd better clear my schedule."

"Sadly, yes." Jason stretched and sighed. "What's up with your poor plant?"

"Grams said it would take a little while to adjust after moving it inside. But yeah, I'm worried."

Jason snapped a picture with his phone and sent a text. Allie's phone chirped in response. "Let's ask Victoria. That woman can grow anything." The pride in his wife was one of his most endearing qualities.

"How's she feeling today?" Allie asked, genuinely concerned.

Jason's wife had been battling breast cancer these last few months. She had good days and bad. "She's amazing, but my apartment is starting to feel like Jumanji. Her plants are nearly out of control."

"You poor thing," Allie teased.

He nodded at the coffee pot. "May I?"

"Be my guest." Allie opened the two new files on her desk as he topped off his Yeti. "The initial lab report from last night's crime scene just came in."

Jason opened another file. "Your friend, Tiny, was able to identify our victim from last night."

"That was fast."

"That's what I thought. Our victim had a knee replaced last year. He was able to find a serial number on the joint and match it with a medical database provided by the medical device manufacturer."

Well done, Tiny. "Who was she?"

"Helen Mercer, age fifty-three. No previous criminal record. Her husband, Gerald, died four years ago." Jason pinned a copy of her driver's license photo on their crime board. "Owns a home in Ruston. Next of kin is a daughter, Stephanie Mercer, unmarried. Listed at an address in Old Town. Officer Corrigan and his team went to her house late last night."

"Time of death?" Allie asked.

"Difficult to ascertain due to how much time Ms. Mercer spent in the water, but Tiny is officially placing it at or after noon on Sunday."

Allie was jotting down details. "Cause of death?"

"Inconclusive."

"I'm sorry. What?"

"I'm just reading what it says." Jason shrugged.

"The woman had a giant gash on her head, and her face was ripped off. How can it be inconclusive?" She grabbed the file from his hand and scanned it. "What time is it?"

"Nine a.m."

"Good. Tiny may still be up." Allie dialed a number on her cell phone.

"It's not my fault, Bishop," the familiar voice on the other end of the phone offered.

"Your standards are slipping, my friend."

"The minute I wrote it in the report, I knew you would call," he chuckled over the line.

"And?"

"Your victim was poisoned, had her face sliced open, bashed with a heavy blunt object, and dropped in the Puyallup. It made my job a little difficult."

"And you're making mine difficult by not giving me a way to track down her killer."

"The answer you want will be in the toxicology report, but you have to give it time."

"Why?"

"She was poisoned by something nasty. The toxin in her system was fast-acting and powerful. It paralyzed her entire body, limbs, lungs, liver, and heart."

"Is it synthetic?" Jason asked.

"Too soon to tell, but Ms. Mercer would have died an agonizing death while this sicko carved off her face."

"And by leaving the death inconclusive..." Allie's mind raced. "We can link her death back to the other two victims if the poison comes back as a match."

"Bingo."

"You're a saint, Tiny."

"You owe me a Snapple," he laughed, and hung up.

"So our unsub is a chemist? Or a scientist?" Allie mused aloud, making notes on the whiteboard.

"Maybe not." Jason objected. "Lots of poisons are plant-based. Possibly a horticulturist or a naturalist?"

"Either way, he's smart."

"Hey now." His voice held a warning. "Don't be sexist. Statistically speaking, poison is a weapon preferred by women."

"Fine. But why use the poison only to smash in her skull?"

"Two unsubs?"

Allie sighed and leaned back in her chair, frustration coursing through her.

"What else do we know?" Jason handed her one of the files Officer Corrigan's office had sent over.

Allie flipped it open. "Rhonda McTavish, age fifty-two. Hers was the first body discovered in the Puyallup back in January. Decomp was pretty bad by the time she surfaced, but according to her driver's license, she had hazel eyes and black hair."

"And no face." Jason grimaced at the autopsy photos. "Tamara Heathers, age fifty-four, was found further downstream in April."

"I can see why Corrigan thought there was a pattern."

"The no face thing is a bit of a no-brainer, Allie."

Allie rolled her eyes and pinned the photos of the victims on the case board. "Look at them side by side." The victims could have been related. They were beautiful women with similar coloring and features, including black hair, high cheekbones, hazel eyes, and thin lips. "They look like the cadavers I used in my anatomy classroom that displayed the layers of tissue in the human body. It's clean, precise, and methodical."

"Medical practitioner?" Jason asked.

"It's possible, but why only take the face? All their vital organs are intact."

"True. Kidneys, liver, and even human hearts fetch a small fortune on the black market. But they haven't been touched."

"Different addresses, different jobs, different backgrounds. These women are being targeted because of their appearance. But for what?"

It was Jason's turn to show frustration. His jaw clenched, and he shook his head. "What's next, rookie?"

"Corrigan sent me the daughter's number, and I reached out to her requesting a meeting."

"Stephanie Mercer?"

"Yes." Allie glanced at her watch. "She's agreed to meet us in half an hour."

Jason nodded, drained the French press, and grabbed his suit coat. "Let's go."

Chapter Five

Les Davis Pier
Tacoma, Washington

A salty breeze tugged at Allie's fine brown hair and threatened to pull it loose from its ponytail. The midday sun was warm on her face, and the light reflected brilliantly off the water. Mount Rainier towered in the distance, the capstone of a beautiful day.

Allie savored the rare moment of fresh air as they left the car and headed toward the wooden walkway that jutted into the sound. Paddle boarders clustered along the beach, and serious squid jiggers swapped stories over coolers and tackle boxes. Tourists paused for selfies while children happily tossed french fries to feisty seagulls. She strode with Jason toward the spot Stephanie had requested they meet, taking in the scene behind their mirrored sunglasses.

"Everything all right?" Allie asked as she surveyed the crowd gathered along the popular fishing pier.

"Yeah, why?"

"That's the fourth time in fifteen minutes you've checked your phone."

"Sorry. Marze has me working a missing persons case tonight with Eastman, which means I won't be home till late."

"Don't apologize. I got this if you need to be somewhere."

"No. It's just... Victoria had an appointment with her medical oncologist this morning."

"Yeah, she texted me. We were supposed to have coffee."

"The side effects of this latest chemo were rough. They wanted to meet and talk through her options."

"You didn't want to be there?"

"Victoria didn't want me to be there."

Allie frowned. "Because?"

"I think the guy is kookie."

"Ahhhh." She dodged a persistent seagull as they continued down the pier.

"He has a whole list of ways to alleviate her pain—meditation, yoga, herbal tea, massage, chakra cleansing, acupuncture."

"What's wrong with acupuncture?"

"I just don't think humans were ever meant to be porcupines. But I suppose if it helps Victoria, I don't care."

"Liar."

"What?"

"You've given up sugar, processed meat, and red dye for this woman. You brew your own kombucha and have a supplement for every day of the week. You've even got *me* on vitamins. My hair and nails have never been healthier."

"Your point?"

"If someone told you licking a frog would help V, you'd track down every breed of toad and tree frog in three counties."

"So?"

"He's cute, isn't he? Her medical whosie-whatsit?"

"Oncologist. And who told you that?"

She grinned. "He's a dreamboat doctor, and he's helping your wife. That's tough."

"Dreamboat? What are you, eighty years old?"

"I'm right, aren't I?"

"I am not comfortable with this conversation anymore," Jason bristled.

Allie shrugged and shaded her eyes. "Stephanie said she would meet us at the last bench on the pier. That's her over there. If you need to make a call, please. I got this."

"Nope. I'm good. I'm respecting V's wishes." He paused. "She told you he was cute?"

She took pleasure in ignoring him, walking the last few steps to a lone woman who sat looking somberly over the ocean. Allie's stomach clenched. Meeting grieving families was never easy. "Stephanie?"

The young heavy-set woman lifted her tear-stained face to greet them. Her brown eyes testified to the love this daughter had for her mother. She didn't stand, just nodded and looked back out over the water.

"This was our spot." She pushed a greasy strand of pink-streaked hair off her face. "She would meet me here after I got off work at least once a week. We would go for a long walk. Mom was in great shape and wanted me to get in my steps."

Jason sank onto the bench next to her. He offered her a

Kleenex in silent solidarity. Stephanie accepted it and gave each of them a weak smile.

Allie considered opening the conversation with many of the platitudes they had been taught in training, but she followed Jason's lead, and they sat for a long moment in silence. Finally, she started to squirm. A list of questions rattled through her mind, but she refused to break the moment.

"We played tennis on Saturday evening." Stephanie finally said, her lower lip trembling. "I don't play much anymore, but Mom loved it. I would humor her. Now I'm so glad I did. If I'd known..." She held back a sob and sniffed.

"When was the last time you spoke with her?" Jason prodded gently.

"Sunday morning. She was in good spirits, heading to church in the morning like always. We made plans for sushi that night."

"Nothing seemed off?"

"No." A long, heavy sigh escaped her. "Mom was beautiful and charming and made new friends so easily. I hated it as a kid. She talked to every server, barista, even knew her butcher's name. I think she even gave him a Christmas present. She didn't have to work after we lost Dad, so she volunteered in every cause the church organized and took great care of herself." Stephanie ran a hand over her cargo pants.

"Any information you can provide is helpful to our investigation," Allie finally said.

A flicker of excitement passed over her round face. "I love true crime podcasts," Stephanie admitted. "So did mom. It was our escape, trying to figure out the puzzle before the big reveal. I never imagined being on this side of it."

"You and your mother were very close," Jason noted.

"Yes. Gerald was my stepfather. Mom had me when she was a teenager. In some ways, we practically grew up together. I know it was hard when I moved out, but we talked almost every day. Mom was so much more outgoing than I am. She was always making plans with people. She loved the outdoors, gardening, shopping, and hiking. Me? I'm an introvert. I prefer my online gaming community." She shook her head. "That never made sense to Mom."

"Do you have a partner?" Allie asked.

"No. Just me and my two cats. Want to see a picture?" Stephanie offered up her screen to Jason. "That's Bunny, and that's Alex. They're my fur babies, and they drove Mom nuts."

"They're pretty," Allie said. "You mentioned an online gaming community. Do you play a lot of video games?"

"You could say that."

"Was Helen supportive of your...hobby?" Allie struggled for the right word.

"Actually, she was. She was very proud, and it's a bit more than a hobby." Stephanie narrowed her eyes at Allie. "I'm a UX/UI designer."

"A what?" Allie asked.

"A gameplay developer with Infinity Games out of Bellevue. We just got acquired by Microsoft last year. I've been with them for a few years now."

Jason looked impressed. "Nice. Would I know your work?"

"The Elder Scrolls."

Jason looked even more impressed. "On PS? I'm a Gran Turismo man, but my nieces love that game."

Allie observed the conversation, a little confused and out of the loop.

"Did you ever play Skyrim as a kid?" Stephanie asked her.

"No, she grew up in a time machine," Jason explained.

"Oh." It was Stephanie's turn to look awkward. "Home-schooled?"

"Something like that." Jason moved on. "What do you play for fun?"

"Depends on my mood. Overcooked. Extraction, but you'll mainly find me on Overwatch."

"Tough game."

"My team swept Tacoma Con this spring. It's our city's version of Comic Con. And Mom, she was right there in the midst of the whole scene." Stephanie laughed softly at the memory.

Allie took in the woman's anime T-shirt, Vans, and cargo pants with new respect. A professional woman passionate about her work.

Stephanie blew her nose and straightened her shoulders. "But you're here to talk to me about Mom. What can I do? How can I help?"

"We could use a list of your mother's friends or associates," Jason said. "People she spent time with this past month. Did she have an online calendar?

Stephanie huffed. "Not Mom. She was old school. She had a planner, but it would be at the house. I can probably find it for you, no problem."

"That's not necessary. We can coordinate with the police department."

"Please." A look of desperation grew in Stephanie's expression. "I need something to do. Work gave me a leave of absence this morning. After Gerald died, Mom drew up a detailed will, funeral arrangements, and the whole thing. It's all done. The church secretary already called me." Her voice trailed off. "But I can't put Mom to rest, not like this."

A furrow creased Allie's brow. "This is a very difficult situation for you, I understand. But we have strict procedural guidelines we have to follow."

Stephanie's voice rose. "My mother's killer is out there, stalking women. The Puyallup Police have found three victims. That we know of! How many more are out there that we don't know about?"

"I understand your pain, Ms. Mercer, but—"

"Do you?" Stephanie spat and glared at Allie. "Do you know what it's like to have the police show up at your apartment before the sun comes up to tell you they pulled your mother's body out of a river?"

Jason took over, leaning into Stephanie's line of sight. "Anger is a justifiable response right now, Stephanie."

Allie was grateful for his presence. He had a kind way of comforting hurting people.

"You have every right to be enraged by what happened to your mother, but I promise you, we're on your side." He glanced at Allie. "Agent Bishop and I will do everything we can to find the person who did this to your mother." He pulled a card from his pocket. "Here's my email. And you already have Allie's number. You can send us anything that comes to mind, anything that might be helpful. But you can also rest. You're not alone. This is what we do for a living. Trust us."

The Face of Evil

"Thank you." Stephanie nodded quietly, mollified by his words.

The agents said their goodbyes and headed back down the pier.

"What do we do when she goes all Mable Mora on us?"

"Who?" Jason gave her a look over his sunglasses.

"*Only Murders in the Building*? Three strangers create a podcast to solve a crime in their apartment."

He looked amused. "Look at you with the pop culture reference."

"It's got Steve Martin and Martin Short in it."

"There it is." They walked on in silence until they stepped off the pier. "I don't know. I guess it reminded me of what Victoria's oncologist said."

"Dr. Dreamboat."

"Exactly." He laughed, then added seriously, "Pain is harder to bear without a purpose."

Allie considered the statement. "Yeah."

Jason continued as they walked. "If helping track down her mother's murderer eases her pain, who are we to argue?"

Chapter Six

Helen Mercer's Residence
Ruston, Washington

Helen's pink hollyhocks greeted the agents as they unlatched the gate to the white picket fence surrounding the Mercer home. The light blue bungalow was tucked into a bed of matching blue columbine and lupine flowers. A butterfly flitted across a manicured bed of dahlia, vinca, purple phlox, and sweet woodruff.

Black-eyed Susan flourished next to yellow snapdragons, and tufted grasses waved happily in the gentle breeze. The scent of lilac drew Allie's attention to the stone path that wove toward the back of the house. A stone bird bath and a set of wicker rockers sat invitingly in the corner, clashing wildly with the yellow caution tape strung between the porch columns.

Allie recognized the neighborhood. Ruston was a cozy suburb on the northern tip of Tacoma that grew from the historic roots of the city's first Western settlers. She often enjoyed a long evening run off Owen Beach and the miles of preserved nature trail where she could glimpse the lights of Gig Harbor across the sound.

Allie hadn't been much for fitness growing up and had simply relied on the intense physical labor of the farm to keep her healthy. But the FBI's regular fitness requirement had given her a new sense of discipline that she had grown to appreciate. As a runner, she got to explore a different side of her community. She was starting to love the long, meandering treks through neighborhoods, along the Puget Sound, or through the urban sprawl of Tacoma. The movement stripped away the mental and emotional weight of a case and allowed her to feel at home in her skin again.

In front of Helen Mercer's home, Jason and Allie checked in with the black and white cruiser stationed in the driveway. Helen's murder had made the papers, and the cruiser was a deterrent to curiosity seekers who might be inclined to enter the premises.

Allie slipped a set of booties over her boots before they entered. A riot of color greeted them when they opened the door, coming from a massive bouquet sitting in a cut glass vase on an antique table in the sunny entryway.

"Did Stephanie say if her mother was dating anyone?" Jason asked.

"These are cut flowers," Allie explained, pointing but not touching. "Dahlias, snapdragons, hydrangea. She brought these in herself. Based on what I saw in the front yard, she was a master gardener." She felt a pang of sadness at the thought that these beautiful flowers would never be appreciated by their owner again. The fleeting fragility of their petals tugged at her heart. The way a normal moment could shatter and splinter so unexpectedly always hit her hard.

"Her purse and keys are right here." Allie used a pen to open the flap of the Louis Vuitton sitting on the front table. "Wallet's here too."

Maybe it was her inexperience that made her extra tender. Or maybe it was the stolen moments frozen in time. Allie clicked several shots of the personal effects with her camera. Her gaze moved to Jason as he made his way into the kitchen, and she silently scolded herself. He didn't seem unsettled by stepping uninvited into the space. Allie, however, trod lightly into the home as if Helen Mercer would step around the corner at any moment.

It was obvious that their victim had refined taste. The home was small but charming. The cabinets were a rich maple gleaming with quiet elegance. The appliances were high-end stainless steel. Every other inch of the tiny space was white marble.

Allie framed a shot of the scene laid out on the counter. An empty serving plate with a handful of crumbs sat next to a carafe of coffee and two mugs.

"She had excellent taste in coffee." Jason pointed at the bag of beans that sat next to the stove. It was roasted locally at a coffee shop downtown.

"Two cups?" Allie took in the scene.

"She had a guest."

"Fingerprints?"

"Doubt it. The cup is full. May not have been touched."

Allie opened the trash and peered inside. "Baked goods are gone. No packaging, no box. So what does that mean?" She asked aloud and continued her conjecture. "It was homemade? But where did it go? Did they eat it? Or..."

"Her guest got rid of it?" His voice carried in from the dining room.

"Because it was poisoned?" Allie leaned over the measly crumbs.

"I've got blood spatter," Jason announced.

Allie moved through the dining room and stood on the threshold of the living room. The room was as neat and luxurious as every other part of the house, but Allie's gut warned her that something about it was off. She snapped several photos while she searched for the culprit of her unease.

"It's dark in here." She looked up from the back of the camera.

Jason nodded and pointed to the light switch, where a faint streak of blood barely stood out. He pointed to a thin line of blood along the edge of a heavy damask silk drape. Slowly, he gazed across the broad picture window covered in fine ivory dressing, then used gloved fingers to pull the cord. The luxurious material glided back to reveal a horrific scene.

Dried blood peppered the leaded glass and the wooden frame that overlooked the back garden. Allie let out a faint gasp in surprise.

"That's a lot of blood," she breathed. Light flooded into the living room, revealing tiny bits of blood that speckled the bookcase, the couch, and the picture frames clustered in the room.

"Almost what you would expect from blunt force to the head." Jason examined the first editions on the bookcase. "Someone tried to rearrange the scene, gave it a crude wipe down. Nothing here is symmetrical." He pointed to the orderly cluster of books. "I think one of these bookends is missing?"

Allie's eyes adjusted to the sunshine pouring into the room. She noticed the slight variation along the floorboards. "I think there was a rug too," she added, pointing to the faint outline of pale wood.

"Good eye."

Allie drew the two scenes together into a narrative. "So she knew her attacker."

"Invited him inside, made a cup of coffee, and had something to eat."

"Her daughter said she went to church that morning. Did she meet someone and invite them over?" Allie steadily moved around the scene.

"It's possible, or she met them afterward. Maybe they stopped by with a treat."

"I haven't seen her planner yet. It may give us a clue. But the poison must have been slipped into her food or coffee. It kicked in fast, but they were here in the privacy of her home."

"She lives alone, no one to interrupt. It's a good place as any to carve off someone's face."

Jason used his pen to lift a throw blanket tossed over the corner of the ivory sofa. It concealed a large pool of blood that had sunk into the cushions.

"But something went wrong." Allie pointed to the spatter. "Instead of letting her die a slow painful death while he worked, he gave up and smashed her skull."

"Did Helen put up a fight?"

"Was someone else here to force his hand? What caused him to make a mistake?" Allie asked. Her eye caught on something metallic sticking out from under the edge of the couch. She silently pointed it out to her partner.

After she snapped several pictures, Jason lifted the skirt of the sofa and tapped at the object. He pulled a heavy silver frame out into the light, shards of glass making a grinding sound with the movement as it rolled into view. The glass was cracked completely, but the smiling face looking up at them was unmistakable. A vibrant, younger, thinner version of Helen's daughter clad in a black graduation gown and cap smiled at them.

"It's Stephanie," Jason said.

Allie pointed her camera at the frame on the floor. "Obviously."

"Not there." Her partner pointed out the back window. *"There."*

Stephanie Mercer's head poked over the top of the back gate as she slowly edged it open. She paused to make sure no one was in the yard before entering her mother's property from the back alley.

"Where is that damn officer?" Jason barked under his breath. "Probably still sitting on his ass in his cruiser." He marched toward the front door.

Allie stood frozen in the middle of the living room. Her natural curiosity compelled her to wait and see how the scene played out. She watched as the victim's daughter tiptoed past the recycling bins and up the narrow sidewalk. *Would she notice the blood?* Allie held her breath and clicked away from inside the living room waiting for the young woman to approach the scene.

Stephanie stopped at the back window. Her gaze paused on

the glass then she moved her head to study the dark stain. Allie zoomed in on her face looking for the faintest reaction.

Just before Allie got a clear answer, she heard a shout and a commotion from the side of the house. Jason had harangued the lanky uniformed officer, who was tailing behind. The officer wasted no time and grabbed the plump woman's arm, but Jason raised a hand in protest. Then he led the two out of view and back down the side of the house to the front.

Allie opened the front door to a vastly different scene. Stephanie was bent double, hands on her knees while the officer uncomfortably shifted his weight from foot to foot. Jason had a supportive hand on her back.

"Here?" Stephanie asked as she stood up quickly. "Mom was killed here, in her house?" She placed a hand over her mouth, and her knees buckled. The two men grabbed each elbow and led her over to the cruiser for support. Allie hurried over.

"I'm afraid so," Jason said. "We'll have to get a forensic crime unit in here to officially process the scene, but this appears to be where your mother was murdered." Allie watched the muscle under his beard flex.

"I want to—" Stephanie took several deep breaths and bent double again before she caught her breath. "I want to apologize." She motioned to Allie. "For my outburst."

"By sneaking into your mother's house?" Allie asked.

"I came to water her garden." Stephanie protested, but one look at Allie's furrowed brow made her cave. "*And* see if I could find anything that might help." She looked genuinely stunned. "It never dawned on— I can't believe this is a crime scene now. Mom loved this house." She burst into tears. "I'm sorry. It's so difficult...all this."

Allie softened toward the woman. "I understand." She hesitated to share her grief, but Stephanie looked disoriented and lost. She was staring glassy-eyed at the house, the place that had held so much of her mother. To lose a mother *and* have the sanctity of her home violated in the process was a significant blow.

Allie leaned against the cruiser next to Stephanie. "My mother disappeared when I was seven," Allie admitted into the fading afternoon sunshine. "I know what it's like to live in the dark, all the questions, the conversations you'll never have."

"I feel so selfish," Stephanie said after a long moment. "She had always been there. Somehow I just thought she always would be." She took a deep breath and glanced at Allie for the first time, seemingly with a new appreciation. "How do you... find a way to move forward?"

"Unfortunately, there isn't much of a choice," Allie added simply. "The sun keeps coming up, seasons change, time marches on. A piece of you will never be whole." She shrugged. "Birthdays will keep ticking off, though it will feel like they shouldn't. It's strange. The days just pull you forward, whether you like it or not."

Stephanie absorbed the thought in silence while Jason and the officer moved to the end of the driveway. "How can I help?" she finally asked, and handed Allie a piece of white notebook paper with a list of her mother's contacts.

"Let us do our job here," Allie said. "As for the house? Eventually, you're going to need a professional cleaner. I can send you a name. He'll know someone who can handle her belongings, too, if you don't feel up to it." The thought seemed to add another weight to Stephanie's reality, and a heavy groan escaped her lips. "Find a good counselor and a support group. You don't have to go through this alone." They were true and right words, but Allie felt the pang of her own hypocrisy.

It had been three weeks since her mother's journal was discovered at their family's old vacation cabin. There was so much to process, so many emotions to work through. Every time she considered finding a counselor, the idea of having to say it all out loud to a stranger made her teeth ache and gave her a blinding headache.

The FBI provided its agents with a list of reputable professionals specifically equipped to listen to painful case-related trauma. They were there to advise law enforcement for the betterment of their mental health. But the honest fact was Allie didn't trust anyone with the tangled parts of her life, no matter the education or the motive.

As a young girl, she had been the prosecution's star witness in her father's trial after she watched him bludgeon a naked woman to death next to their vacation home. Allie knew her complicated past could be a liability in this work, but it also gave her purpose, something she needed daily.

It was too much of a risk to let in someone who wanted to dig up all her wounds. Especially if that person had the power to remove her from active duty. And for the first time, she had a thin string to pull on in the tapestry of her mother's life. At the very end, Johanna Bishop had sensed that something ominous was at hand. What it was, and why she had felt it so strongly, Allie didn't know. But she certainly intended to find out.

"I'll think about it," Stephanie replied. "Thanks for the

advice." She nodded to the paper she had given Allie. "I hope some of those names help. She loved people. They loved her."

"I'm sure this will come in handy," Allie assured her. "Thank you for getting it together for us."

Stephine stood up straight and took in a deep breath. "I'll get out of your hair and let you do your job. My car is parked in the back alley. Okay if I go back down the side of the house?"

"Of course. We'll have Officer Bentley escort you." Allie waved the officer over and watched as the two of them disappeared into the backyard.

"So," Jason said. "What now? Forensics should be here any minute."

Allie popped her hands on her hips and surveyed the street. "I guess it's time to talk with the neighbors."

Chapter Seven

Neighborhood of Helen Mercer
Ruston, Washington

Allie knocked on the large front door and took a step back. The air held the faintest hint of salt from the waterfront, and in the distance, seagulls cried. She waited a full minute for an answer, but none came. Not even a dog barking.

"Can I help you, young lady?" A reedy voice called out as she stepped off the stoop.

Allie lifted her head, searching for the owner of the voice in the bright glare of a perfect summer afternoon.

"I don't need a new lawn service or a different cable provider. I already have both, thank you. My husband is on a pension, and we don't need any more insurance."

Allie finally located the source—a slight, steely-eyed woman with cropped hair the color of a battleship, staring down from a second-story balcony of the house next door. She wore a pale blue house dress, and a pair of spindly legs were tucked into bright pink socks.

"Actually, I'm not selling anything," Allie called up to her. She pulled out her badge. "I'm with the FBI."

"Merciful heavens." Allie watched the woman clutch her gown. "John, the FBI is here," she called over her shoulder.

"May I have a moment of your time?"

"Of course." She nodded to the house behind Allie. "The Rileys are out of town. Have been for a week. But come on over. I'll meet you at the door."

Allie walked down the driveway and started for the house next door. She caught sight of Jason several houses down, moving farther down the street. It was the middle of the afternoon on a weekday, and they weren't finding many neighbors at home.

The sunshine was full and fair, so Allie unbuttoned the front of her green blazer and slipped it over her arm. Then she untucked her white blouse over her holstered gun and started up the next driveway, admiring the sprawling yard. The house sat on a sloping corner lot with a wide second-story patio to maximize the view of the water and the Point Defiance ferry.

"You're with the FBI?" The face that greeted her at the front door was only slightly less suspicious, but the woman opened the door wide. "Please come in. We live upstairs, and I have to be close if John needs me."

"Thank you." Allie stepped inside. "John, that's your husband?"

"Yes. I'm Grace. Grace Turnbull." The two climbed a wide staircase with a small chair lift attached. "John has Parkinson's," she explained. "But we're still getting along all right."

"Have you lived here long?"

"Fourteen years." Grace led Allie into a large living room with a vaulted ceiling. She motioned for Allie to take a seat on the leather sofa, and she sank into an easy chair across from it. "This was John's parents' lot. His father was a mechanic for the ferry after World War II, and John always loved it here. He used to climb up on the roof as a kid and watch the ferry for hours. He doesn't have any siblings, so after his folks passed, we bulldozed the original house and built this."

"It's beautiful." Allie glanced out the picture window. She couldn't help but admire the cluttered neatness that seemed to come with a certain stage of life. Potted plants flourished across every occupiable space. The rest was covered with the detritus of a well-lived life. Vacation curios, birthday cards from grandkids, and black and white photos of beloved family, all of it tenderly curated to remind the housebound pair of happy moments.

"He can still enjoy the view, which is a small mercy." Grace nodded to a closed bedroom door at the end of the hall. "We have a steady support of live-in nurses that stay on the floor below." Grace lifted a hand. "I'm sorry, you didn't come to chitchat with a little old lady. How can I help you?"

"Yes, Helen Mercer, your neighbor. Did you know her?"

"Oh yes. Helen is a dear. Everybody knows Helen. She always visits John if he goes to the hospital, and I wander over regularly if I just need to get out of the house. She always has time for a cup of coffee. So thoughtful. You know, she brought over a new crossword book from the drugstore last week. I didn't get to see her—she left it at the door. I've been a bit holed up here with John the last couple of weeks. He's been in a rough patch. But Helen understands the nights can get long as a caretaker. So she helps me stay active some days. We take walks, or she bugs me to help her in her flower garden. Acts like she needed my advice, she never does..." Grace trailed off, and a frown pulled on her lips. "Did something happen to Helen? You asked if I knew her, but I just realized you asked about her in the past tense."

"Yes, ma'am." Allie suddenly wished Jason were here. He was so much better at this kind of thing. "I'm afraid she's passed away."

Grace sucked in a quick breath. "Oh dear. No. No, not Helen. I saw a police car over there this morning. I had a bad feeling, especially after I called her and she didn't answer. But I've always been of the opinion that you don't poke around with police business. I'm a curious old lady, but I won't go down there just to satisfy my curiosity." She reached up and wiped a tear from the corner of her eye. "That's so terrible. But if you're here about Helen..." she trailed off. "Was it bad?"

"Unfortunately, it looks like she may have been killed in her home this weekend."

"No!" Grace clutched at the neckline of her house dress again, and a worried expression flooded her gaze. "Was it a robbery?"

"We don't believe so. That's why I'm here," Allie explained. "I was wondering if you've noticed anyone out of the ordinary in the neighborhood? We believe that Helen knew her assailant."

Grace sighed. "I can't believe it. Not Helen." Allie let her continue to process the bad news before repeating her question.

"There's plenty of people in and out of the neighborhood,"

the older lady replied. "But it's pretty quiet on the weekends, thank heavens."

"I'm specifically curious about any activity around lunchtime on Sunday, maybe a little after."

"Oh no. I'm so sorry, dear." Grace looked crestfallen. "John had a terrible night Saturday, kept me and Betty, the nurse, awake till dawn. So we weren't much good on Sunday. I kept the blinds drawn and tried to rest."

"Did Helen mention anyone new in her life recently? A friend or boyfriend?"

"I don't think so," Grace pondered. "No one likes being a widow, but it suited her. Helen made the most of her time and never mentioned dating."

"What about anyone new to the neighborhood?"

"Let's see...Helen did invite me to lunch with that cute couple on the opposite corner." She waved a hand toward the front of the house. "The one with the Subaru and all the toys in the driveway. Brittany and what's his name? They moved in a few months ago and asked Helen to help them redesign the flower garden in their front yard."

Allie nodded. "That's helpful. Anyone else you can think of?"

Grace snapped her fingers. "Yes, actually. I've never met him officially, but he runs past the house most evenings. I saw him chatting with Helen last week when we took John to the doctor. Helen said he recently moved into a house a few streets over."

"Do you know his name?"

Grace shook her head. "I don't. I have seen him speaking

with her while she works in her garden a couple of times. But I didn't want to pry. He's a young man. About your age."

"Mid-twenties?"

Grace nodded. "If I had to guess. Of course, my vision isn't what it used to be."

"Any chance he visited her on Sunday?" Allie asked.

"I have no idea."

"Did Helen mention if he lived with family or friends?"

"No, I think they were talking about trimming her hydrangea when I stopped by."

"Can you describe him?"

"A little rugged. He reminded me of a Kennedy."

"Which one?" Allie asked.

"Robert. I always like him better. I don't trust a pretty face."

"Did he have the same build?"

"Yes. And he has a good smile. Athletic-looking man, with medium-length brown hair."

"Did I notice you have a doorbell camera?" Allie asked politely.

"We do. My son-in-law's idea, so I don't have to go up and down the stairs as much."

"That was nice of him."

"Except that he makes me use the iPad. Can't figure out the dernblasted thing. It's not that hard to go to the front door, but I think he just likes to keep track of all the comings and the goings. I can't blame him."

"Any chance I could get a look at the footage?"

"Be my guest. I'll have my son-in-law send it to you." She accepted Allie's card with the email on the back. Her shoulders slumped. "I can't believe Helen was murdered. And in her home. My son-in-law is going to have a fit when he hears about that. And I am so going to miss our talks." Her head snapped up. "Do you think we're in any danger?"

"No," Allie assured her. "We don't think you're in any danger." She decided it would be best not to tell her why, that her face did not match the kind preferred by their unsub. "We'll certainly tell you if that changes. But you don't have anything to worry about."

A sound down the hall interrupted the two, and Grace stood to check on her husband. Allie thanked her for her time and let herself out. On the way, she studied the doorbell camera, hoping its line of sight went all the way to the street. She doubted it, but at least she had a new line of thought to follow. Not many people were home during the day in the understated middle-class neighborhood, but that didn't mean someone wasn't lurking.

Allie knocked on several more doors without any luck. But soon, she discovered the Subaru with the stroller parked on the porch. No one answered when she rang the doorbell, but she was pleased to see the camera staring back at her with a direct line of sight out to the street.

She showed her badge to the camera and left a note with her card tucked into the doorjamb.

If Helen had been spending time with a young runner, perhaps one of the neighbors' doorbell cameras captured him.

Retracing her steps back up the street, Allie studied each home from the sidewalk, paying special attention to porches with a front door camera. Most of the older homes had yet to be updated with the modern convenience of communicating with guests, watching kids, and slowing package theft.

Allie reached Helen's and went inside to have a final look around. She was certain that Helen had known her attacker. It could have been anyone. Right now, they didn't have enough data on Helen's social life to zero in on anyone in particular. But this younger man who went on runs and chatted with Helen sounded like a possibility. They needed to find out more about him, starting with his name.

Allie looked up when she heard a noise in the backyard. Jason was pacing the rear walkway, talking on the phone. She strode to cross the room but caught the sound of his tone, so she stopped before reaching the back door.

"I'm sorry, but no. I don't think it's a good idea," Jason said aggressively. His voice held an edge that Allie had never heard. His shoulders were tense, and he was stripped down to his shirt sleeves, his coat draped over the porch rail. He placed a hand on his head as if frustrated, if not angry. She watched as he grabbed a cloth handkerchief and mopped his brow. Jason was always cool and calm. But something had him riled up.

"No. Again, it's not a good idea," he snapped. "Listen, I don't care. I'm sorry. I understand that it's a part of our past, but that's where it needs to stay. It's time to find a way to move on. Please."

Did he sound...guilty? Allie felt wrong listening in, but she had never witnessed this side of her partner. She couldn't help but wonder what he wanted to keep buried in the past. She suddenly thought of Victoria, who was at home staring cancer in the face.

Allie's stomach soured, and the horrid realization dawned on her that she may have misjudged her partner. Trusting people had never come easy for her, not after her father's betrayal.

Jason paused for a long moment, listening. "Fine," he sighed, "but this is the last time. I mean it. Text me the address and I'll stop by tonight."

A shiver of dread crept up her spine as Jason hung up. She swallowed hard and moved out the back door and onto the porch, her gaze on her notebook.

"There you are," Jason barked. "You done?"

"For now. Find anything?"

"No. An old man who was hard of hearing and a couple of nannies who tried to flirt with me. Do I look like an Encyclopedia salesman?"

Allie glanced at his seersucker suit and orange bow tie without comment.

"I heard that." He started down the side of the house to the car. "I need sugar. Let's get out of here."

Allie followed with a frown creasing her features. It was obvious whatever had rattled her partner was even worse than she suspected. He always ate like a health nut, for Victoria's sake. Allie got into the car, and as they pulled away from the house, every one of her pores tingled with curiosity, and even a little anger.

Chapter Eight

University of Washington Tacoma
Tacoma, Washington

Allie sprinted her last hundred meters and slowed to a stop in front of the University YMCA, disturbing a fat pigeon from its perch as she finished pushing herself to the edge of her endurance. Checking her time on her sports watch, she started her cool down in front of the large yellow complex on the edge of campus.

After Jason's emotional ice cream stop on the way back to the office, Allie finished up her reports and decided to stretch her legs. She needed to shake off the sugar and enjoy the rest of this delicious summer evening. Jason left early to help another agent, and Allie was waiting to get the official reports back from the tox lab as well as the forensic lab that was still combing through Helen's life.

In front of the Y, Allie leaned over and stretched on the steps, enjoying the relative quiet of the city. Most of Tacoma's evening commuters had escaped downtown, and the sun hung low over Mount Rainier. The delicious scent of BBQ wafted over from a nearby restaurant, and Allie's stomach growled. A plan entered her mind fully formed. Slipping out her phone, she texted Victoria.

I'm craving panang curry from Thai Pepper. Can I grab you anything from there?

Yes, please! No. 7 Hot Pot Ginger Rice. Please! Thank you. You're a lifesaver!

On it. I'll swing by soon. Running home to shower and change.

Allie placed the order on her phone and grabbed her gym bag from her locker inside the Y. The run had cleared her mind, but it hadn't displaced the questions.

Her thoughts kept altering between the case and Jason's phone call. Even after ice cream, his mood remained unsettled for the rest of the afternoon. Jason had earned her trust over these last two months, something Allie did not give away freely. And if anyone understood a desire for privacy and uncomfortable skeletons in the past, it was her. Still, the entire tone and the wording of the phone call made her uncomfortable.

Allie picked up the food and made her way to Victoria and Jason's apartment. She knocked on the door and waved to the camera. "Hey, it's me," she called out as she stepped inside.

She knew the doorbell alert went to Jason's phone. But tonight, she was here to support a new friend who had just completed a grueling round of chemotherapy. The curated poison had left Victoria a startling shell of herself. She was honored that her partner and his wife had invited her into their lives at such a delicate time.

Growing up, Allie did not have many friends. So friendship surprised her when it seemed to come naturally. She had found that in Darcy Hunt, her mentor back in Albany. And now to have found it in her partner and his wife felt rare.

It helped to have a friend who understood the FBI, a whole new world for Allie. On top of that, Victoria was open about her own grief, and Allie found it remarkably refreshing. Allie had always maintained an innate sense of self-protection that typically kept people at arm's length. Victoria's friendship was like having a big sister in the FBI world.

Morbidly, Allie wondered if Victoria's illness forced them into a deeper friendship. Time was something neither of them took lightly, and strangely, it helped Allie enjoy the human connection. These last couple of months, she had chosen to ignore her personal warning system that told her she was getting too close. After all, if you put something over the dashboard warning light, is it still on?

"Okay, so what are we thinking tonight?" Allie asked as she shut the door behind her. "Music or movie? I've got *The Very Best of Nina Simone* on vinyl or *Some Like it Hot* with Marilyn Monroe."

Victoria's voice sounded from the gray recliner in the corner of the living room. "That's a tough one. Nina is a supreme diva, but it's Monroe, *the* supreme diva."

"I guess that's the theme of the evening," Allie replied as

she entered the living room and placed the paper containers on the TV tray in front of the couch.

It was painful to see Victoria curled up in the chair under a heavy quilt. She had seen her on a bad day before, but Victoria was such a natural beauty that anything else was jarring. Allie used her best poker face, but Victoria's cheeks looked sallow, her lips gray, and the circles under her eyes suddenly made Allie feel a pang of grief.

She fled to the kitchen to pull herself together. "Can I get you another kombucha? Tea?"

"No thanks. They're pumping me full of fluids up here." Victoria pointed to the IV bag that hung above her chair. "Any more, and I'll float away."

"Anything good?" Allie came back with napkins. Finding a seat on the couch, she opened her chopsticks and unpacked her dinner, inhaling the delicious scent of coconut.

"Vitamins and good wishes, I think." Victoria sat up and reached for a plastic fork. "I'm still having trouble keeping anything down, and the only thing that sounds appetizing is ginger rice and turmeric tea. That's weird, right?"

"Not at all. Thankfully, you have a friend who has a slight obsession with Thai food. I'm just glad to see you trying to eat."

"I'm afraid I'll never get my tastebuds back. I miss pizza, but the thought of tomato sauce or cheese makes me want to vomit. Poor Jason."

Allie tried not to roll her eyes. "He's a big boy. He'll survive."

"He's going to be a big boy. He's literally eating for two right now. Everything my mother brings over for me has tomatoes and olives in it. I can't stomach it, but my mother is Spanish, and feeding me is her love language. I can't turn down food, so Jason eats it off my plate when she's not looking."

"You can't tell her?" Allie chuckled.

"I think her head would explode."

"Seriously? You have cancer. You could ask for the moon, and I'm sure your parents would give it to you."

"I don't think there's a category of language in that part of her brain that would understand, 'No, thank you.' I could say the words, but she would just hear, 'Please bring me more.'"

It felt good to laugh, but just as suddenly, the mood shifted, and Victoria looked pensive. "It's her way, you know. She can't heal me, but she can cook for me, so she goes all out. I get that. I'm everything I am today because of her cooking."

Allie listened in silence. She had learned years ago that sometimes the best gift you can give a friend is a willing ear.

"The first time we came to the United States when I was a kid, it was to work in my grandfather's bakery. I loved that place. It was always warm and smelled like prosperity. Baking bread is the most hopeful scent in the world. 'Flour, water, yeast and salt, heat and hard work. That's it. And with it, *you can feed a nation*,' my grandfather used to say."

Victoria looked up wistfully. "We baked in the good times and the bad, all day every day—food was our life, and our lifeboat. I think the physical movement healed us, and the ritual, it gave us purpose. When my grandfather got sick and couldn't come to the bakery anymore, that was the worst day of my life. It was the beginning of the end..." she trailed off. "We all knew it. He knew it most of all.

"That was when I started teaching lessons." Victoria waved a hand at her music corner, where an acoustic guitar and a baby grand piano stood looking neglected. "My grandfather was sick, and the bills were piling up. My father fell into a depression. It was like the bread absorbed the sadness, and it didn't taste as good. Not as many people came to the store, and it was a very scary time for the family." Victoria stared past Allie at the memory, lost in thought. "I had been trading my mother's food for music lessons for several years with a man who lived in our apartment complex. My brother thought he was a pervert, but it turned out, he was just hungry."

Allie snorted in surprise.

Victoria gave a weak smile. "He was. He played some with the Tacoma Orchestra, and he let me practice in his apartment at night while he was at work. He could smell my mother's cooking, but he was very shy and never accepted our invitation. We are such a big, loud, overstimulating cluster. I think we scared him, but he craved her food. I brought him a plate after dinner, and we made a deal. I'd bring him a plate of paella, and he'd give me a lesson on the piano."

"That's beautiful," Allie said, and slurped down a noodle.

"He got me a teaching gig at the church on Pacific Crest Avenue. My parents had no idea how to make money outside of the bakery. Everything I earned kept us afloat that year. It fed us. It was the proudest moment of my life."

"You are one of the most resilient people I know," Allie said.

"I have a lot of time on my hands now. I've always loved time alone. In a big family, it was such a luxury. So time to practice was never wasted. It was precious. Now I just sit here for days and watch the dust settle on my beautiful piano."

Allie watched a tear slip down Victoria's face. Her heart hurt for her.

"I don't mind hard work," her friend continued. "I don't mind pain. It's not the hardships that bother me, Allie. It's not even the inconvenience. Not the acupuncture, dieticians, the doctor's appointments, or the treatment. The hardest part is losing my independence. Being cared for twenty-four-seven, I feel like a baby all over again. Some days my legs don't work. I don't have the energy to read, eat, or even watch TV some days. I fade in and out when Jason's telling me about his day." Her voice cracked. "I can't cook, can't bake, can't even play my music."

They sat there for a long time. Allie finally stood up and placed a record on the player. The melodic static filled the room as the needle found the groove, and Nina Simone filled the air with all the comfort Allie didn't know how to say out loud. The strength in the woman's voice washed over Victoria in the same way it had when Allie was younger, searching for meaning amid senseless suffering. Finally, after a long while, the needle came to the end of the record and whispered into the empty air.

"You may not have the energy to make music right now. But that's the best part—music is magic, even when all we can do is absorb its life-giving goodness." Allie reached out and squeezed Victoria's hand.

"Thank you," she said sleepily.

Allie felt drawn in by the softness of the night, Nina's bold, tender music, and Victoria's honesty. She felt an unexpected urge to tell her friend all about her mother. She picked up the chopsticks, the napkins, and the empty takeout containers, trying to stifle the need to confide in someone.

But the urgency pressed into her heart. She wanted to share her thoughts and questions with her wise, brave friend while there was still time. Allie sat back down on the couch, reached for the journal from her bag, and laid it on her lap.

"V?" Allie asked, but no response came from the recliner. She was fast asleep.

Allie smiled tenderly. Standing up, she draped another blanket over her friend, turned off the light, and slipped out the door.

Chapter Nine

FBI Field Office
Tacoma, Washington

"I've had six months to get used to the idea that she's gone. But it hasn't gotten easier. I wake up in the night and still reach for Rhonda."

Rhonda McTavish had been the first victim found in the river without a face. The local police had previously handled the case, but now that it was in Allie's lap, she wanted to get the widower on the phone herself. He had expressed his remorse upon learning that a third victim had been discovered. Allie had inquired about a friendly neighbor who may have befriended his wife in the weeks before she disappeared, but Henry McTavish could offer no useful information.

She was starting to feel a little awkward in the conversation, not knowing exactly what to say. She was a trained agent, not a therapist, after all. "How long were you married?"

"Thirty-four years. We were planning a trip to Greece this

summer to celebrate. I have the tickets here. I can't decide if I should go or cancel. I just sit and stare at them. But now you tell me that the person who killed my wife may have been hanging around the house?"

"I apologize, Mr. McTavish. I don't mean to cause you any more pain." Allie searched for the right words. Inwardly, she wished that her time at Quantico had prepared her more for dealing with situations like this. Some days it felt like half her job was playing a therapist to grieving people. Definitely not up her alley. "I only hope it helps to know we're diligently hunting the person who did this to your wife."

"Thank you." His voice broke as he spoke.

"If you remember anything out of the ordinary, please call me and I will update you with any progress."

"No," he barked. "No offense, Agent Bishop, but I can't live like this. You can ask me anything about Rhonda, but I don't want to know about any more victims. Please. Every time this sicko strikes, I fall apart all over again. It makes me wonder if I could have done more to protect her. I can't sleep, I can't eat, I can't work. Hearing from you makes it feel like she just died all over again. Call my daughter if you need to. She is stronger than I am. But the next time I hear from you, I beg you. I want this to be over. I only want to hear that you've arrested the sonofabitch. Or better, yet, that he's dead. Then I can go piss on his grave."

His words weighed heavy on Allie's shoulders. After the line went dead, she looked down and realized she had snapped a pencil in half while she listened to his impassioned plea. She opened the bottom drawer and tossed the pieces on top of a growing stack of broken No. 2 pencils lying splintered at the bottom.

Allie cracked her knuckles and settled her gaze on the bust of Lincoln, thinking. She had begun combing through properties bought and sold in Helen Mercer's neighborhood in the past several months. But after a while, the search failed to turn up anything productive.

Allie grabbed another pencil, tucked her hair up into a bun, and speared it. It was an effortless gesture, but it helped her concentrate while she looked over her notes. She opened another file on her computer and began sifting through doorbell camera footage Helen's neighbors had sent over.

She played the footage at high speed and swept through hours and hours of comings and goings, the occasional spider walking across a lens, and countless deliveries from Doordash, UPS, and Amazon. It was clear she was looking for a needle in a proverbial haystack, searching for a brown-haired man in running shorts. But nothing matched the profile Grace had given yesterday. Unfortunately, the analysts had done their job well.

Standing to stretch, Allie wiped crumbs off one of the signature literary T-shirts she often wore to work beneath a suit jacket. Today, she sported her favorite Langston Hughes's "Shakespeare in Harlem" top. She had fallen hard for his poetry back in Mrs. Crompton's American Lit class.

Deciding that she had ingested enough coffee this morning, she thought it was time to hydrate. She wandered out of her cube holding her mug and went in search of one of Jason's fancy herbal teas.

"I see you, Ms. Langston Hughes." Special Agent Ryan

Eastman greeted her at the doorway of Jason's cubicle. Allie blushed. She never liked the spotlight, but it was hard not to fall under Eastman's charismatic spell. With dark skin, a firm jaw, and piercing eyes, he was cute.

"You've read him?" Allie's eyes sparkled.

"Have I read him?" He clutched the collar of his crisp white Oxford in mock agitation. His piercing green eyes grew wide, and he looked at her partner in surprise. "She wants to know if I've read him?"

Jason shrugged and took a bite of yogurt.

Eastman stood to his full height and began to recite.

Hold fast to dreams
For if dreams die
Life is a broken-winged bird
That cannot fly.
Hold fast to dreams
For when dreams go
Life is a barren field
Frozen with snow.

Allie hushed under the spell of his baritone voice. He stood for a moment, one elegant dark hand raised for emphasis as the words hung in the air. Applause erupted from beside the water cooler, compelling Eastman to take a mock bow. His shiny curls glinted under the fluorescent lights as he stood to his full statuesque height with a look of obvious pride.

"I thought you said you used to be a firefighter," Jason asked, his crossed ankles showing off his bright green socks.

"I was." Eastman nodded. "It gave me time to read between shifts. And let me tell you, the ladies love a fireman-poet."

"Yes, please!" a female voice called from a nearby cubicle.

"There has to be more to this story," Allie pressed. Eastman was the office jokester, but the easy laughter meant he rarely shared much about his life. Allie often watched his showmanship with envy. He charmed his way through difficult scenarios with one-liners and antics that broke any tension swirling around the office.

"My parents are intellectuals," Eastman grinned. "My mother came from Nigeria to study at Berkeley and met my father there. Growing up, they were passionate about poetry. Still are."

"I had no idea," Jason admitted, stunned. "Didn't you play football in college?"

Eastman smirked. "Don't judge, my friend. I may be big, but I am a poet at heart."

"What did your parents think?" Allie asked. "About you joining the Bureau."

"They knew the FBI was the closest I'd ever get to law school. I guess they've made their peace with my life choices. It rankles my father's sentiments a bit. I enjoy that. But Mama, she's still an immigrant at heart and will probably never forgive me for not becoming a doctor."

Allie grabbed a square sachet of tea. "How was the stakeout last night?" she asked Jason as she poured hot water into her mug.

"I don't want to talk about it," Jason grumbled.

Eastman grimaced and ran a finger across his throat, motioning for her to kill the line of questioning. He jumped to her rescue. "Miss Allison Bishop, I believe you are the next contestant in our trivia quiz for the morning. Today's subject is Nobel Prize Literature."

"Really?" Allie perked up. She'd been expecting something a little more mundane.

"Seriously, Eastman." Jason pouted. "Give it a rest."

"We are never going to beat those DEA snobs if we don't practice, my fine fellow."

"It's Tuesday night trivia. In a bar."

"If you took as much pride in your mind as you did in your appearance, we would never lose," Eastman said. "Winner gets to use the microwave first at lunch."

Allie was fully invested now. She had leftover panang curry from last night.

"Today's question. Who won the Nobel Prize for Literature in 1953?"

"I have paella in the fridge today," Jason grumbled. "I was really looking forward to it."

"Ernest Hemingway!" Allie snapped. "*Old Man and The Sea.*"

"Nice." Eastman wagged his eyebrows. "You are very close. We need to have you join us."

"Whatever," Jason snorted. "She's terrible at pop culture. I'll warn you."

"Right? Do you have a guess? Nobel Prize 1953?"

"J. K. Rowling?"

"Is it any wonder why we lose?" Eastman sighed, and stalked away.

"Will he tell me the answer?" Allie asked hopefully.

"Oh, don't worry," Jason smirked. "He'll need to gloat. He enjoys being the smartest in the room. But he has a thing for a girl on the DEA team. So he wants us to do well as a unit. You made him very happy. Better clear your Tuesday nights."

Allie picked up her steaming mug. "Have you heard from Stephanie Mercer at all?"

"Stephanie? No, why?" He tossed a wrapper in the trash and leaned back in his chair.

"I wanted to run the mysterious neighbor thing past her, but she hasn't returned my calls. She seemed to like you, and so I wondered."

Jason gave her a once-over. "Don't take it personally. She's probably at home catatonic. Grief hits like a bulldozer sometimes."

"Don't I know it." She leaned against the wall.

"Hey, thanks for stopping by last night. That was good for Victoria. She felt bad for falling asleep on you."

"Of course. I adore V." She hesitated but decided to pry open what had bothered her from yesterday. "Hey, I, uh...just needed to tell you. I overheard some of your phone call yesterday. The one on Helen's porch."

Jason's face clouded over. "You shouldn't be eavesdropping on other people's conversations."

"I know! It was an accident." She nervously shifted her weight. "That's why I wanted to say something now, so you don't think I meant to snoop. I just want you to know I'm here if you need anything."

Way to go, Bishop. You should have kept your mouth shut.

She was flustered now. "Do you need anything?"

"I'm fine." Jason swiveled around in his chair, his back to Allie, but then added, "Just a lot on my mind right now. Nothing I can't handle. You can forget you heard anything."

Allie was relieved to see Eastman reappear. "You uneducated people do not deserve microwave privileges today. Be warned! I brought a huge portion of seafood stew," he announced to the office. "It's going to smell *great!*" He winked at Allie. "Hey, would you believe Hagan was fully convinced it was Stan Lee? You were the closest. Microwave's all yours."

Allie gave him a wry smile. "So, who was it?"

"Churchill. For *The Second World War.*"

"Have you read it?" Allie asked.

"Yes, I have," he gloated. "I own the audiobook. You have to try it. I put it on, and bam, I'm out like a light. Works every time."

Allie made a rapid retreat to the kitchen. After her food was heated up, she returned to her cubicle and grabbed her laptop. She needed to do a little personal investigating on her own time.

She climbed the stairs and grabbed a spot on the roof where a couple of lawn chairs were stashed. Finishing off yesterday's leftovers, she thumbed through her mother's journal. It was a tiny bit of comfort in the sea of heaviness that was her current case. Stephanie's conversation from yesterday had inadvertently stirred up old feelings regarding her mother.

As a kid, she'd had so many questions about her mother's sudden and complete disappearance, but then, after the trauma of what her father had done and losing him, Allie had buried her questions. She decided she didn't want to know any more about her broken family. Grams had filled the maternal hole in Allie's heart, and that had always been enough. At least, until this journal showed up. Now the questions roared to life, and Allie searched the handwritten pages for any hint of what had happened. There hadn't been much from her past except for a single name. Sadie Talbot.

Allie turned to the page and touched the name. It was a link to her mother. She opened the file she had discreetly started on her laptop. The records were sparse. Ms. Talbot either purposely kept a low profile or was simply of a certain age and didn't feel strongly about social media. It included a very old article in the Seattle Times with a picture of Ms. Talbot cutting the ribbon at the launch of Blackburn, her first real estate office.

Now Blackburn employed several hundred people and bought and sold property for several sizable trusts, legal entities typically employed by celebrities or corporations interested in preserving their privacy. This information strengthened Allie's idea that Sadie abhorred the spotlight. It was a sentiment she could appreciate. But she was frustrated to find so little about the woman. Sadie was the only connection Allie currently had to her mother.

She picked up her phone and dialed. "This is Allison Bishop calling for Ms. Talbot. I left a message last week to see if I could get an appointment? Yes, I left a message that time too, but I'm happy to give you my number again. Please have her call me at her convenience. Thank you." She sighed and hung up.

Allie was undaunted. She had no problem chasing down dead ends and dark alleys. She was insatiably curious, patient, and determined. It was her one real talent in life. She desperately wanted to know why Johanna had written such a cryptic, dire message in the last entry of her journal.

When her phone rang suddenly, Allie fumbled it in her hands. She was nervous, reaching into a shadowy past.

"Special Agent Bishop?" a man's voice answered.

"Speaking."

"This is Weston Heathers—Tamara Heather's ex-husband. My office said you'd called."

She thanked him for calling her back. "Has the Puyallup Police Department updated you about the latest in Tamara's case?"

"Yes, and I was saddened to hear about it, but thankful that it's finally warranted more resources. Has the FBI made much headway?"

"We are working very hard to apprehend the suspect, but I'm afraid we're not at liberty to disclose much at this stage.

"Tell me how I can assist."

"Your ex-wife listed you as her personal contact and the executor of her will. Is that correct?"

"Correct."

"I don't mean to pry into your personal life. I wondered if it was an oversight on her part or if it meant she still trusted you to handle her financial affairs."

"Tamara was a very good paralegal. She worked in my office. She wouldn't have made a mistake. She asked me to do it after we divorced. I could never say no to her. Neither could anyone else for that matter. Tamara was a force of nature, but I still cared for her, even after it was obvious she never desired monogamy."

"Thank you, that's why I called. Is there any chance you knew who Tamara spent time with? What I meansis, do you happen to know if she had been getting close to a male neighbor? Anyone posing as someone new in town?"

"I knew the ins and outs of Tamara's financial assets, but I wasn't privy to who came and went from her house. That was the reason we divorced after all."

"Would she confide in you if she felt uneasy in a relationship?"

"If you asked me a few months ago, I'd have said yes. But after everything that happened, I think the facts speak to the contrary. I'm sorry...do you think it was someone she knew?" He asked, stunned.

"We're currently hunting down every possible connection. Did Tamara have any contact with Helen Mercer or Rhonda McTavish?"

"No, I explained this to the police. I'm sorry I can't be more help."

By the time the call ended, Allie was dejected. She stared at the case board. Helen Mercer's neighbor had witnessed an unidentified male hanging around. Was it a coincidence, or her killer? If only Allie could find someone in the victims' lives who could corroborate the pattern, they would have a tangible lead. Allie crossed her arms over her chest. She hated having nothing to show for her time spent on the inquiry. For the moment, at least, it looked like the dead would keep their secrets.

Chapter Ten

Residence of Stephanie Mercer
Tacoma, Washington

"Seriously, Allie, we're FBI, not social workers. We don't make house calls." Jason peered over the dash of his Charger, looking for the address his partner had rattled off.

"You're the one always telling me to trust my gut." She pointed to a small white house on the corner of a neighborhood overlooking a quaint town center. "And it's telling me something's off. Stephanie Mercer couldn't leave the case alone for two hours after they discovered her mother's body. It's been three days now, and I've been trying to get her to return my calls, but nothing. Not even a text or an email. I don't buy it."

"There could be one of a hundred reasons why you haven't heard from her. It could be the flu, or grief. She could have had a work emergency."

"She designs video games, Jason. How much of an emergency can there be?"

"Tech start-ups can be a wild ride. You think our day is unpredictable, try one of these venture capital launches and then say that with a straight face."

They parked behind Stephanie's car and made their way up the sidewalk to a brick Dutch Colonial with black shutters and a red front door.

"You're hungry." Allie pointed to the Oooh La La Burger across the street. "If we knock on the door and we find Stephanie on a conference call, I will buy you a burger."

Jason grumbled but gave the spot a good long side-eye. The tantalizing scent of french fries floated across the street. The walk-up window had a bright yellow awning and shared the storefront with a local market selling organic meat and produce. An afternoon crowd lingered on the open patio, enjoying the sunshine.

Allie's mouth watered at the thought of a late afternoon pit stop. "Come on, their Portabello burger is supposed to be amazing," she said, trying to tempt his conscience and his stomach. She noticed he had given up sugar again and was back on his strict health regimen.

She had also noticed that no one in the office questioned his motives or teased him about it. Allie loved that about her coworkers. Most of them had quietly joined his quest to will Victoria's cancer away through clean living and exercise.

"Fine," Jason caved. "But I'm getting V something too."

"You have to get fries." Allie smiled and set her attention to the doorbell, and her body went cold with dread. The red door hung slightly ajar, and the keypad above the knob looked like it had been kicked in forcefully. The wood was splintered where the lock had busted the jamb.

"Jason!" Allie said in alarm, and pulled her gun in a fluid motion. Wordlessly reading the situation, he followed suit, pointing his sidearm low and taking a quick peek into the house via the window.

"No one in the front room. I'll go first, enter, and go left. You go right. Stay close. Understood?" He was on high alert.

"Got it."

"On three. One, two, three."

Jason pushed open the heavy door with his foot. It creaked open while he swept into the room and cleared the sight lines. Allie followed after, using her weapon as an extension of her arm as she surveyed the living room.

"Clear," Jason announced.

Keeping her back to the wall, Allie advanced into the next room and swept the space until she was satisfied it was empty. Her senses were on full alert for any sound or movement. Not knowing what or who might be around the corner was the epitome of an adrenaline rush.

Jason made swift work of the bedrooms while Allie advanced into the backyard and checked the sides of the home. Soon, the entire house was clear, and they rejoined in the kitchen.

"Looks like there was a struggle." Jason pointed to a kitchen chair that lay on its side and a broken glass that was shattered across the floor. "And there's a weird setup in what looks like her office." He pulled out his phone and called in local backup.

Stephanie's belt bag was slung over a hook on the coat hook by the back door, and her keys hung next to it. The sight sent Allie's heart into her gut. She pulled on a set of gloves and began to search the small house methodically.

"I told you I had a bad feeling," she finally said. "But no blood."

"Yet," Jason added as he continued to look around. "Try her cell again."

Allie punched in the number, and they waited. A buzzing noise led them deeper into the house, past the first bedroom and into a small room with a map of Tacoma pinned up above a rugged desk. Jason located the phone in a desk drawer.

The oversized map took up the bulk of the wall space. Stephanie had tacked up pictures of all three victims, including her mother, and the location where each body had been discovered. Several newspaper clippings about the murders had been arranged on a makeshift case board. The red yarn had been threaded between the location of each victim and their home.

Jason flipped the pages of notes on the desk. "Looks like she went and got an alibi for every single person in her mother's contacts. Impressive, if not a little annoying. She was triangulating the distance between the victims' homes. Did you say our suspect was a runner?"

"Yes, but how would Stephanie have that detail? I learned that from Helen's neighbor. Did we ever find her mother's planner?"

"I didn't see it on-site or on the list of evidence we recovered." Jason flipped another page. "Why?"

"Because it's right here." Allie thumbed through the small black binder.

He frowned. "How?"

"No idea. Unless she entered her mother's home before we got there and didn't realize it was a crime scene. Remember, she turned up with a list of contacts hours after I asked her for it."

Allie clicked her tongue. "I thought it was fast, but I just figured she was motivated. Look at this." She pointed to a printout of the text conversation between Stephanie and her mother.

3.4 miles today on Owen Beach with my new walking buddy! It was followed by a happy face emoji.

The phrase "new walking buddy" was circled several times in red.

"Doesn't look like Stephanie knew the name of her mother's friend." Jason bent over the page.

"Why wouldn't Stephanie have told us about someone new in her mother's life?" she asked, feeling a little irritated.

"Did you tell her about the friendly neighbor?"

"I tried." Allie sighed. "But she never called me back. I didn't have the planner. This was information that would have been helpful. It's evidence that helped her make the same connection I did, eventually."

"She's cross-referenced every single person in her mother's planner with the date they last interacted," Jason noted.

"You think she got too close to her mother's killer? Maybe he broke in and kidnapped her to shut her up?"

"It's a possibility," he agreed. "Stephanie doesn't fit his victim profile. There's a strong chance that we're dealing with the same person. But we might not be. He didn't take her phone or look hard enough to find this information. If he was trying to shut her up and shut down what she discovered, I would expect all this to be gone. The fact is, we don't know much about her. It could be something else entirely."

He pointed to lists carefully marked off one by one on the wall. "I might hire this woman. She'd make an excellent analyst."

"We need to find her first," Allie reminded him, and started to bag the evidence. They returned to the front of the house just as local law enforcement arrived. Once they had the scene locked down, the agents stepped out to canvass the area.

Jason longingly eyed the burger joint as they headed next door. "I'm hungry."

"Easy cowboy. Facts first, then food," Allie repeated his mantra to him as she knocked on the door of a faded home with a scraggly, unkempt lawn. "Don't you have a protein bar or something?" A dog barked inside, and they waited for someone to answer. Allie could hear kids giggle and shout in the backyard, and a television blared a cartoon theme song. A shadow crossed behind the glass, and a small head peered up at them from the window.

"*Mommm*," a little voice shouted. A scuffle ensued between mother, dog, and child until the door finally creaked open.

"Yes?"

"Afternoon, ma'am," Allie nodded a greeting. "I'm sorry to interrupt. I'm Special Agent Bishop, and this is Special Agent King, with the FBI."

"*Cooool*..." the little voice interrupted.

The corners of Jason's mouth tweaked slightly beneath his beard.

"Have you seen your neighbor today?" Allie asked, indicating the house next door.

"Stephanie?" The woman wore sweats and a tired frown, but her brow creased even deeper with the question. "Has she done something wrong?"

"Not at all. In fact, we were just checking on her. She was assisting us in an investigation."

"Are you really with the FBI?" A small head popped out from around the door. "Like, do you shoot people?"

"Decklan!" the woman hissed, and stepped out onto the front porch, shutting the door to the children behind her. Immediately, little faces filled the window.

"What did you say your name was?" Jason asked, pulling back his jacket to give the faces in the window a good look at the badge he wore on his belt. Their wide-eyed wonder was epic.

"Emma." She crossed her arms tightly around herself. "Emma Kawalski."

"Emma, have you seen anything out of the ordinary in the past forty-eight hours?"

"Stephanie isn't very social. Kind of keeps to herself." Emma looked thoughtful. "Her mother is over there quite a bit. Nice lady. But now that you mention it, I did notice someone the day before yesterday. Older vehicle, dark sedan. I only noticed it because I almost hit it backing up. I'm not used to a car being there. I ran to the store, and it was still there when I got back, but by the time I got the groceries unloaded and into the house, it was gone."

"What time of day was this?"

"Let me see. Coby fell asleep in the back, and I had to take him straight in for his nap. Maybe two p.m.? Decklan turned on the TV, which was playing Sid the Science Kid on cable. So that would make it mid-afternoon before three. That's when I let him watch Magic School Bus."

Allie jotted down the details in her notebook.

"Is Stephanie all right?" Emma asked, and glanced nervously at the faces in the glass.

"I hope so," Jason said. "Unfortunately, it's too soon to tell."

"Would your doorbell camera pick up movement on the street?" Allie asked hopefully.

"No, it only goes to the sidewalk. Someone stole D's bike last year, and the dumb thing didn't even register."

Jason handed her a card. "Please reach out to me if you hear from Stephanie or if you recall anything else."

"You might check Dave's," the woman added, pointing to the organic grocery. "He had a break-in about the same time as the bike disappeared, and he got a big ole security system put in, cameras and everything."

Jason handed several gold foil badge stickers he kept in his wallet to the weary-looking mother, much to the delight of the children, whose faces were still smashed against the front door as they said goodbye.

"You know those are police stickers, right?" Allie teased as they crossed the street.

"Don't remind me. I'd kill for junior agent badges, but Marze won't bite."

"You need to be nice to me, or I'll tell people you're not as mean as you look."

"I'm a teddy bear," he sighed. "Everyone knows that."

"You, sir, owe me a burger."

Jason grinned for the first time all afternoon. "My pleasure."

Chapter Eleven

Residence of Jason and Victoria King
Tacoma, Washington

Jason reached up to loosen his tie as he came off the top step and reached the landing. He stopped in front of his apartment and stared numbly at the door, then released a heavy sigh. He placed a hand on the doorknob and felt a twinge of nerves in his stomach. Opening the door, a heavenly aroma reached out and embraced him, the scent of onions and tomatoes tickling his nose.

It had been hours since his burger with Allie and their fruitless search for Helen's daughter. It had been a long time since he had come home to the scent of food cooking in his kitchen. It never mattered if he could pronounce the name, but he recognized the flavor of Mediterranean comfort food his wife loved to serve.

It was a good sign that Victoria was cooking. But he had also been married long enough to know his wife's subtle signs of anger could be taken for comfort cooking to the untrained eye. He approached the kitchen slowly, his investigator's gaze on high alert. His wife loved to cook, but she only cooked her mother's recipes when he was in trouble. He dropped his keys in the bowl by the door and made his way into the kitchen.

"Someone's having a good day." He leaned over and kissed the top of her head, which was wrapped in a purple scarf. She curled an arm around him and hugged him. It didn't matter how many times he looked at her. He never got used to the sight of his gorgeous wife without the waist-length hair she had worn their entire marriage. Seeing her like this, it was hard to think of arguing with her.

"I feel much better today," she said, not taking her eyes off the oversized saute pan on the burner.

Another bad sign. Inwardly, Jason cursed. The size of the pot of food his wife was cooking was directly proportional to the amount of angst in the air. It was a law handed down through the generations of women in her family.

"How are you feeling about tomorrow?" he asked, knowing that she was scheduled for another round of chemo in the morning.

"I don't want to talk about tomorrow. Today, I have energy. I want to live in today."

"All right. Whatcha making?"

"Patatas bravas." She moved to toss the garlic skins into the trash. "I'm almost done with the aioli."

His beautiful, creative, musical wife was typically cool and calm in difficult situations, but she was also predictable. He didn't mind. It was comforting. In his job, uncertainty was the enemy. But patatas bravas, fried potatoes in a spicy tomato sauce, was the dish Victoria's mother made when she was upset with her father.

Stalling, he opened a cupboard for a glass and grabbed a beer from the fridge. He poured it and leaned against the counter. "You want to talk about it?"

"Talk about what?" she asked.

Jason lifted an eyebrow. "You have something on your mind. Are you ready to discuss it?"

"Yes...almost."

Her plain-spoken approach was one of the things that made her irresistible to him. He adored her passionate, fiery temper until there was friction between the two of them. Thankfully, she was also honest, even blunt, with him.

"Do you have time to eat?" She pulled a set of plates from the dishwasher.

"Yep. Marze sent me home for the night."

"That was kind of him. He reached out to me to see how I was doing and requested my chemo schedule last month. I didn't make the connection, but..." She turned and looked at him, letting the sauce bubble softly on the stove.

"Do you want me to finish making the aioli?"

"Yes, please. Anything on your missing person?"

"Nope." Jason tossed the last of the aioli ingredients into a bowl and began to whisk them. He held it out to his wife, who dipped a spoon in it and tasted it, bending her head in thought.

"More lemon," she said.

He always marveled at how the chaos of her cooking could explode onto the plate.

Victoria poured a bottle of mineral water into a wine glass and crossed her arms, cradling the glass. She took a deep breath and stepped into the conversation. "You're right, we need to talk, but I've been waiting for you to invite me in."

Jason set down the aioli and let the words hang in the heated kitchen.

"Something's going on, Jason," she said quietly. "I'm not the only one that's predictable when I'm upset. I guess the question is—do *you* want to talk about it?"

Jason picked up his beer and took another sip. The words were stuck somewhere underneath his breastbone. It had always been difficult for him to uncork his deepest emotions.

"It's Aimee, isn't it?" The silence in the air stiffened, the only confirmation Victoria needed. "I warned you about this."

Jason scratched his beard and stared at the floor.

"Lo que has hecho me molesta. Me molesta. Me fastidia. Me enfada." Victoria reached for her native language when her feelings became intense. She took a step toward him, forcing him to look at her. "I'm annoyed, bothered, and angered here, Jason. It should anger you."

"I am." He found his voice, finally. "I am angry. I can't stand it. When Aimee called me, it was like the ground opened up underneath me. It feels like I'm on a tightrope about to tumble into this...giant pit. But I can't walk away."

"I know you feel responsible for her, baby." Victoria walked across the room and took her husband's face in her hands. "But if you keep getting involved like this, you're going to get into trouble. That scares me." She made him look her in the eye.

"It scares me too," Jason admitted. "I just can't leave it alone. It doesn't feel right." He hated to see the look of disappointment cross her lovely face. "Is that weird?"

Victoria pushed backward in frustration. "Does Allie know what happened?"

"No."

She nodded in acknowledgment, the anger melting out of her voice. "She deserves the truth, and you need to give it to her before it causes problems between the two of you. She trusts you."

"She doesn't trust anyone," Jason argued. "I don't blame her. I don't either. Not after what happened before. I like Allie. She's a good agent, and soon she will be an excellent agent. But part of what makes us good at our jobs is that we don't trust anyone. I trusted a partner once. It didn't turn out well."

"I understand that," Victoria said. "It makes complete sense to me. Since I've gotten to know Allie, I can see that she's wounded. But I don't see any reason why she can't be trusted."

"I felt the same way about my last partner. What does that say about me? My entire career is built around being able to tell when people are hiding something, and I failed."

"You made a mistake."

Jason scoffed. "More like I was blind."

"You cannot let your past dictate your future. And with the FBI, you have other people's futures in your hands. Every time you storm into an empty house, you're putting your trust in her hands. And vice versa. You don't get to play chicken with each other's lives. You're responsible for each other whether you like it or not."

They stood in tense silence for a while, then Victoria leaned her head against his shoulder.

"You have every right to grieve, to feel betrayed and upset. What happened was wrong and evil. But Marze trusts you.

You're good at what you do. You and Allie are a good team. It's why I've been so intentional about getting to know her. I was just as hesitant at first, but then I came to a point where I had to decide. I don't have anything to hide, and neither do you. What happened was terrible, but you didn't do anything wrong. The agency cleared you. They put you back in charge of cases. *They* trust you."

He nodded, as if trying to believe it.

"The question is do you trust yourself?"

Jason slipped an arm around his wife, and they stood side by side.

"I have to make a choice tomorrow," she said. "I make a choice every day to fight. I need to know you're making the same choice. I can't face the future, no matter how bleak it is, without knowing that you are going to be okay."

"Please don't talk like that, babe."

"Facts first." She used his phrase against him. "I can't face death with the belief that you aren't able to trust or love people again. Please don't do that to me."

"Don't do that, V. Don't talk like that."

"This has always been about you and me, sucking the marrow out of life. We take the bad with the good. The bad is bad. There's no denying it. I'm not hiding from it. I just won't let it win. Life's too short. It's too painful. I won't live the rest of my days without hope."

"Please." He wrapped his arms around the fierce and fragile love of his life, tucking her into the spot below his chin, where she fit him perfectly. Jason inhaled the scent of her, soft and clean. This was home—*she* was home. The place that made him complete. Being her protector was one of the few parts of his life that always made sense. And yet tomorrow, she would fight another battle without him. Nothing made sense anymore. "Please don't give up on me," he said.

"I won't if you won't."

"I will never give up on you. On us."

Jason could feel his promise wash over her. She melted into him. He never lied to his wife. He meant every word. He would give his life for her, would try to be the man she wanted him to be. But he had to hold a place for doubt. He couldn't have another partner like his last one.

What if things turned out the same way? There were already too many questions. How could he know if anyone was who they said they were? Life was proving to be too brutal, too twisted, too broken.

He pushed down the anger trying to well up from within. "Come on," he said. "Let's eat."

Chapter Twelve

FBI Field Office
Tacoma, Washington

"One extra large watermelon green boba tea with tapioca!" Allie announced and placed the oversized drink on the desk.

"*Nope!*" The woman ripped off her headphones and grabbed the drink, standing up from a massive ergonomic gaming chair in a rush of fury.

"I'm sorry?" Allie said, confused. She had followed Jason's instructions to the letter, visiting an out-of-the-way boba shop on the University of Washington campus for the data analyst's drink of choice. This was not the reaction she expected.

Brandy Harroway tapped a manicured black nail on a neon sign that hung above her head. "No food or drink!"

"I thought it was art," Allie admitted. The entire cybersecurity section of the office was dark and decorated with a funky vibe.

"You thought it was a suggestion?" Brandy pointed, and Allie shuffled out of her office in shame and confusion. She backpedaled until they were standing at a small bar table in the hallway, where they came to a stop.

"Rules are rules, rookie." The petite security analyst smiled warmly and flicked her bright red hair out of her eyes. "No food or drink anywhere near my setup. I learned that lesson the hard way, and I will not repeat it. Doesn't matter who you are or what you've brought. Jason didn't tell you, did he?"

"Umm, no." Allie's face was scarlet, but she was trying to play it off. She wanted to remain calm in front of this confident and colorful co-worker.

"He's had a lot on his mind lately." Brandy shrugged. "But thank you for the treat." She took a sip, groaned in pleasure, then stepped up to the standing desk outside of her office space. "You guys must be desperate if he sent you for a boba bribe." Brandy pulled up the sleeve of her vintage leather Speedway jacket to check her watch. Ferrari red was the woman's signature color, but Allie marveled at the red plaid pants, white boots, and black shirt. What would look over-the-top on anyone else looked riveting on the energetic analyst.

"Boba bribe?"

"Jason knows how to motivate me. He hopes the extra attention and caffeine will buy him my full attention on your victim's phone."

"Yes, please," Allie admitted with a sigh. "She's been missing for over forty-eight hours, and I've got nothing."

"And?"

"And nothing." Allie sipped on a Snapple and placed her chin in her hand. "The neighbor saw a car at Stephanie's house the day she went missing. One she hadn't seen before. And that doesn't help me at all."

"I can tell you that this one is odd, just having looked at the phone," Brandy said.

"How so?"

"Your girl was paranoid about something. She's got some ninja-level encryption on her cell. I've been working on it nonstop since you brought it in."

Allie shrugged. "She was in tech. Was she just careful? Like you, with the food?"

"That's what I thought at first. I even reached out to a couple of guys I know in her company to see if this was standard protocol for intellectual properties up there, but they said it wasn't."

"Paranoid about what?"

Brandy sipped on her straw. "Hard to say. I don't get paid to infer motives—that's your job, *super noob*. But she took all kinds of precautions. She was pretty active in several online forums that catered to those who are more conspiratorial minded. From what I read, she wasn't too keen on the government tracking any of her activity."

"She designed video games, right?" Allie's brow furrowed. "Did she have something to hide?"

"Internet freedom is a fundamental freedom that should be protected. It's at the forefront of discussions within the cybersecurity communities. Anyone building online communities would most likely be highly tuned to this new battleground. Stephanie seems to understand that people's ability to exercise their rights to freedom of expression must also extend to actions and opinions online as well.

"Makes sense," Allie said.

"Our government supports internet access for all," the analyst continued. "That includes the development, governance, and use of tech that supports democratic values. Well, at least in theory, but don't get me started. I work for the feds, after all."

"So Stephanie was paranoid that someone was watching her online?"

"Basically, yes. She was also passionate about building tech that promoted freedom of movement and expression in online environments."

"So was someone watching her?"

"Hard to tell. I would need a warrant for her computer files. In order to get that, we would need to build an argument for probable cause."

Allie rubbed her temples. She had been grinding her teeth all morning, and by the afternoon, it was turning into a blinding headache. "She's been missing for two days. I've got a serial killer poisoning women and carving off their faces. But Stephanie doesn't fit their profile. She was young, blonde, and heavyset. All my other victims are trim, dark-haired women over fifty. But now I'm hearing that Stephanie was paranoid even before her mother was murdered. Do you think she was spooked by something in her personal life?"

"Could be. The very last text on her phone...I unlocked it just before you showed up. Emailed it to you and Jason." Brandy patiently enjoyed her boba while Allie grabbed her phone and pulled up the email.

Screw you. I'm sick of your bullshit. Don't contact me again or you'll regret it.

"The contact's name is Robert Hall," Brandy said. "It came in at 12:03 PM on Wednesday."

"Wednesday? I was with Stephanie on Tuesday at her mother's house." This is helpful for her timeline, at least. "Is that it?"

"Nope, your girl wouldn't take no for an answer. She called him and texted him back."

Robert, please. Talk to me.

"Did he call her?"

"Nope, nothing, nada," Brandy said into her straw. "Brutal, right?"

"So who is this Robert Hall?" Allie asked, still looking at her phone.

Brandy returned to her desk and came back with an iPad. She unlocked it and pointed out an attachment. "I included his license and place of employment. But there's more. He's an ex-con, so he's in our system." She tapped the file, and a Washington driver's license filled the screen. A handsome face with a strong mustache looked unblinkingly back at her from the photo. "Robert Hall, thirty-seven years old. He lives alone and works across the street at Jimmy Z's Arcade."

"An Arcade?"

"It's cute. Live music, food, and drinks. It's pretty family-friendly till ten p.m. Nice selection of pinball and vintage video games—*Galaxian, Tron, Pac-Man, Qbert, Donkey Kong,* even this perfectly restored *Zoltar* machine, just like in the movie."

"Which movie?"

"*Big.*"

Allie's expression was flat.

"Tom Hanks?" Brandy lifted an eyebrow. "Jason said you were a little sheltered. Homeschooled?"

A frown pulled at her lips. "He said that? No, I graduated from Kennedy Catholic in Gig Harbor."

"Huh, go figure."

"But can we get back to Robert Hall?" Allie asked.

"You're in charge, Special Agent Bishop." Brandy winked. "Hall served ten years for manslaughter. He got into a bar fight and killed a man when he was twenty-four. It's surprising because he gives me more Comic Con vibes than parolee on his limited socials."

"If he's on parole, can he work in a bar?"

"Technically, it's kind of a *barcade,* but yeah, he's been out for three years and is no longer considered a menace to society."

Allie texted the address to Jason and was about to leave. But then she paused. "Was there anything else in his social media that would be helpful?"

"You're learning." Brandy gave a half-cocked grin and blew a lock of hair off her forehead. "Looks like Stephanie and Robert played several local video game tournaments together. They even won one recently."

"Tacoma Con? She mentioned it, but not *him,*" Allie recalled.

"Well, they haven't declared anything publicly, not as far as

I can see. But I saw they do run in the same circles online and in person."

Allie was genuinely relieved to have a tangible lead. And she was glad to have had the time with Brandy, who was as cool and friendly as they came. "Thanks, Brandy."

"Don't mention it. But do me a favor?"

"Anything."

"Here's a dollar." She pulled the green paper out of her pocket. "When you go to the arcade, go visit my friend *Zoltar*. See if he has any interesting predictions about your future." She waved a quick goodbye and stepped back into her pristine office, leaving Allie to stare at the money and wonder exactly just what she had been asked to do.

Chapter Thirteen

FBI Field Office
Tacoma, Washington

"You mind if we walk?" Allie asked as they got to the elevator. "It's not that far, and I could use the fresh air."

"Sure thing."

They rode down to the lobby and set off through Tacoma's theater district. Allie loved her adopted city. There was a real charm here, with picturesque waterfront attractions, scenic views of Puget Sound, and summer temperatures rarely pushed over the mid-seventies.

Jason was unusually quiet, walking with his hands stuffed in his pocket. "You all right?" she asked as they crossed Ninth Street.

"Yep," he answered, but Allie couldn't help feeling that he was brushing her off. "Just tired."

Arriving at the arcade, they were instantly hit with the scent of pizza and adrenaline. A pair of college kids dressed in matching fraternity T-shirts were playing an intense game of air hockey. Jason went off to question the bartender, leaving Allie to take in the stimulating scene of buzzers, buttons, flashing lights, and electronic music pulsing at her from every corner. A little boy slipped past her elbow and plugged change into the Skee-Ball machine. In the corner, a couple egged each other on in front of an oversized *Guitar Hero* machine.

Jason returned and leaned close to her ear so he could be heard over the noise. "The man behind the bar says our guy is camped out on the *Street Fighter* machine."

Allie nodded and followed along, mesmerized by the cartoon images that beckoned from the screens.

Jason nodded to a round man balanced on a stool and pounding on the console of the classic game, a glass of beer perched precariously on the edge. He was heavyset, had thinning brown hair and a handlebar mustache, and wore a baggy T-shirt over khaki cargo shorts.

"*You win,*" the game declared, and the beefy man took a swig.

Jason stepped forward. "Robert Hall?"

"Who's asking?" he grunted, giving them a brief once-over.

"Agents King and Bishop with the FBI. We'd like to ask you a few questions."

"I paid my debt to the state," Robert bristled. "I don't have to talk to anyone."

"How about a game then?" Jason asked casually.

"What's the catch?" Robert sniffed and ran a meaty fist underneath his nose.

"No catch. Gentleman's agreement. You win, we leave you

alone. I win, we have a decent conversation about Stephanie Mercer."

His expression soured. "Stephanie?" He took another swig of his drink. "What the hell. You're on. No one beats me at this. Here, hold my beer, little lady." He tossed Allie a wink and waved Jason toward the console.

Both the demeaning name and the wink made her want to deck him right here and now. She had to bite down on her lip to keep back a scathing retort. She placed the man's drink on a nearby table and watched as Jason loosened his tie and Robert punched the two-player button.

A giant sumo character sauntered into the match as Player One while Jason toggled through the selection and came to play as an Asian princess, much to Allie's surprise.

"*Fight!*" the iconic game declared, and Allie watched in bemused horror as two grown men began manipulating the plastic joysticks in a simulated death match complete with low-budget sound effects.

She glanced around nervously and began chewing on a thumbnail when the first round went to Robert. Jason rolled up his sleeves and nodded to her. He looked confident enough. The machine declared round two, and Allie felt cold sweat form along the small of her back. *This is ridiculous,* she thought to herself but then pumped a fist as the second round went to her partner.

"*Final Round,*" the game declared, and the moments dragged as the cartoon characters grunted and chirped under the steely gaze of the agent and the ex-con.

"*Player Two Wins! Perfect.*"

Allie slapped her partner on the back.

Robert's shoulders slumped, and he retrieved his beer. "Well played," he conceded, but looked rather annoyed.

"I have to ask." Allie nodded to the game. "*Street Fighter?* Seriously, you went away for manslaughter...wouldn't *Pac-Man* or *1942* be a little more appropriate?" From the corner of her eye, she saw Jason shoot her a glance, and she instantly regretted the comment.

Robert didn't seem to mind. "I can appreciate the irony. You probably have your therapy...I have mine." He nodded to a quiet booth in the back. "We can talk over there."

He stopped off at the bar and got another drink, then smugly sprawled across the seat. The agents slid in across from him.

"We had a onesie pub crawl last night." He took a swig of his drink and dragged the back of his hand across his lips. "I was here until dawn running the *Guitar Hero* competition."

"Are you giving us an alibi for something or trying to justify your loss?" Jason asked.

"Both." Robert gave a low chuckle. "It's 'round up the usual suspects' time, right?"

"We're interested in your relationship with Stephanie Mercer," Allie asked.

"Yeah, you mentioned her earlier." Robert's expression didn't change. "This about her mom?"

"Had you met Helen?" Jason asked.

"Oh no," Robert smirked. "I'm not the kind of guy you take home to your mother."

"So you and Stephanie were in a relationship?" Allie asked.

"I'm not sure you could call it a relationship. More like online friends with in-person benefits."

"But you're the one who ended it."

"How do you know that?" His eyebrows drew together in a look of suspicion. "What did she tell you about me?"

Jason narrowed his gaze at the man. "Robert, are you aware that Stephanie is missing?

"Missing?" His expression finally faltered, and he looked scared. "What do you mean missing?"

"Two days ago, her house was broken into. Her wallet, phone, and car were found at her house, but there was no trace of Stephanie. The last text she received was a threat from you."

Robert swallowed hard. "I...can explain."

Allie spread her hands. "Please."

"Listen. It's not what it looks like. Stephanie is pretty intense. About her job, her video games. Whatever she's focused on, she zones in on. It's like an obsession. I like that about her. While we were together, as long as I was on her good side fighting alongside her, we were cool. If she was into something, she might disappear for a couple of weeks and then text me when she surfaced. I tried not to take it personally. It didn't make for much of a life or a relationship, but not many people see me as a catch, and we had similar interests."

"How did you meet?" Allie asked

"We would bump into each other here and there online. Last year, she needed to fill an online roster with local players for the Tacoma Con tournament, and I tried out and made the team. Like I said, she was driven and focused when she set her sights on something. So we practiced a lot together, and one thing turned into another. It was just a way for her to blow off steam."

"And yet you drop her like a bad habit two days ago?" Jason scoffed.

"Look, after her mom died, Stephanie called me. She wanted me to help her find her mom's killer. She was all hyped up on Adderall and Red Bull and wasn't making a lot of sense. I'd never seen her like that, and it freaked me out."

"Why?"

"She told me about your investigation and going back to her mother's place to look for evidence. She wanted my help."

"And?"

"And what?" Robert took another sip and wiped beer from his mustache. "I told her to find another sucker. I'm not an idiot. I might be an ex-con, but I went to college. I'm not following Stephanie down her rabbit hole, interfering with a federal investigation. Nope, thank you. I like my freedom. I have a place, a job I don't hate, and no girl is worth losing it over. Not worth it. Best case, she finds her mother's killer and gets arrested. Worst case, she finds her mother's killer and"—his eyes widened into saucers—"oh god, is that what you think happened?" He searched their faces.

"We don't know what to think, Robert," Allie told him. "We're just putting the pieces together. I don't like the idea that Stephanie went off half-cocked after a serial killer. I much prefer the theory that she picked a fight with her ex-con boyfriend. Where were you on Wednesday afternoon?"

"Les Davis Pier."

Allie squinted hard at the man. "That's where Stephanie met us the day before."

"It was her favorite spot. She and I went fishing there a

couple of times. On Wednesday, I finished up my shift here, then went for a long walk and ended up there."

"For how long?"

"It was a while. I was pretty upset. I knew Stephanie would call, so I left my phone here with Troy at the bar and made myself scarce. Mostly, I was freaked out about what she had asked me to do. I'm no gumshoe."

"Can anyone corroborate your story?" Allie asked.

He sighed through a curse. "No. I went home way after dark and didn't pick up my phone until my next shift. I didn't trust myself. I like Stephanie, and I knew if we talked about it then, I'd end up sucked into one of her ideas. It wouldn't be the first time. She was always persuasive and persistent. My only option was to go dark, with no contact with her."

Allie's phone rang. She stepped out of the booth to answer her supervisor's call.

"Bishop." Marze's voice was straight to business.

"Yes, sir?"

"Bad news. Pierce County Medical went out to investigate possible human remains discovered behind an abandoned strip mall on the north end of the city."

"Does the description match my missing person?" Allie's stomach dropped.

"It didn't last night when they processed the scene. The body is in pretty bad shape, and investigators on duty figured it was a drifter because of its location near the interstate."

"The scene? As in past tense?" Allie gripped the top of a chair in frustration. If the body had been misidentified and processed, there was little chance of turning up any evidence against their killer.

"The body is in the Pierce County Morgue. It is Stephanie Mercer, Allie. I'm sorry. Dr. Winters just confirmed it. He's waiting for you."

Allie punched an arcade game in aggravation. A turbaned head came to life, eyes flashing as he touched his crystal ball. *Zoltar Speaks*, the sign said. Allie glanced over her shoulder. Jason was chatting with the bartender, no doubt double-checking Robert's story with Troy. She grabbed the dollar that Brandy had given her out of her pocket and slipped it into the machine.

"Make a wish," the fortune teller commanded. Allie felt the hairs on the back of her neck stand up. She thought about Stephanie and Helen. The fierce bond between mother and daughter clamped an icy hand around Allie's heart.

In a sudden act of desperation, she closed her eyes and blurted out her wish. "I want to find my mother." She held her breath as the machine buzzed and a gold foil ticket was spat out.

Allie grabbed it and jammed it in her pocket, too unsettled by her own emotions to read its prediction. She strode back to the table and pointed a finger at Robert Hall. "The ME just identified Stephanie's body," she said flatly. "We'll be back with more questions. Don't leave town."

Chapter Fourteen

Pierce County Medical Examiner's Office
Tacoma, Washington

"Talk to me, Doc," Allie said as she strode through the double doors of the city morgue and slipped on a pair of gloves. Her mentor turned from the metal table, clipboard in hand, a mask over his mouth.

Allie generally enjoyed a chance to meet with Dr. Winters, but the hunch of her shoulders exposed her agitation and disappointment. This was exactly why civilians weren't fit to track down incredibly dangerous people. They could have good instincts, but their lack of training was a liability.

Now, standing over Stephanie's round form beneath the white sheet filled her with impotent rage. She had wanted to avoid this kind of violent conclusion.

Dr. Winters patiently surveyed her from behind his wire-rimmed spectacles. His wiry white hair looked distinguished next to his dark, unlined face. He shot a glance at Jason over Allie's shoulder and didn't bother with small talk.

"Breathe, Allie. I can see you're personally invested in this one. Let me warn you to prepare yourself. It isn't a pretty sight, I'm afraid, especially if you had an attachment to our victim."

"I don't have an attachment," Allie started to object but stopped to accept his advice. "I just met her—but I wanted to help her, to find the person who murdered her mother."

"An admirable attribute." He studied her for a moment.

Allie took a deep breath and collected herself. When she nodded at the medical examiner, he pulled back the sheet to reveal a gruesome sight. Jason winced. He pulled a handkerchief out of his pocket to cover his mouth. The scent of death and decay hit the agents with a sudden force that made Allie's eyes water.

"You can see why local law enforcement didn't consider this death in connection with your case," Winters continued with efficient eloquence. "At first glance, the advanced dismemberment from scavengers and decay make it look like our victim has been at the mercy of the elements for much longer."

"She's been strangled." Allie leaned over what was left of Stephanie Mercer, examining the ligature marks around the skin of the throat.

"How can you tell it's a she?" Jason asked, but shook his head. "Don't tell me. Please, continue."

"Any other signs of abuse?" Allie asked.

"No, we're running blood work now, but I suspect there was a different type of toxin involved than in your previous victims. There is a residue of some type on the victim's skin and clothing that may explain the strange attraction of the local wildlife to the body."

"How so?"

"It's possible our killer drenched the body in an accelerant, a pheromone that made the body irresistible to a whole host of nature's scavengers."

"A chemical?"

"It's possible, or it could be a natural substance. Gardeners spread the urine of wolves to detract deer from the property. At the same time, the blood of a coyote in heat could serve to stimulate a feeding frenzy capable of something to this level. But, I am going to need to run several tests to verify my hypothesis.

"We think the poison that killed Helen and our three victims may have been a natural substance." Jason relocated to the edge of the room. "What does that tell us about our unsub, Dr. Winters?"

"Excellent question. It's too soon to tell, but it may speak to a pathology of someone well-versed with natural substances. Homeopathic pharmacologist or a naturopath perhaps?"

"Do we have a time of death?"

"It's difficult to narrow down, but preliminary tests suggest between late Wednesday and early Thursday.

"That's in the window of Robert Hall's missing night," Allie suggested to her partner.

"Do you think he's capable of this?" Jason asked her, waving a hand toward the body. "He works at a video game arcade. And the good doctor here has identified highly informed medical knowledge as necessary to pull off at least four murders."

"He made sure we knew he had a college degree," she

answered. "He had ten years to study in a prison library and has no alibi. On top of that, Helen Mercer had a mystery person in her life that no one's been able to identify. Stephanie never introduced him to her mother. Did he make the introduction himself?"

"Possibly," Dr. Winters said. "Just make sure to do your due diligence."

Allie took one last look at the mangled form of Stephanie Mercer and turned away. Her partner looked a little green.

"Understood, Doc," Allie relented and motioned toward the door. "I won't rush it, and neither should you. We'll wait for your report."

"Patience is bitter, but the fruit is sweet." The seasoned ME smiled beneath his mask. "Heed the wisdom of Aristotle, my dear."

Allie placed a gloved hand on his shoulder in thanks and made her way toward the exit.

"You okay?" Jason checked in on his partner as they made their way down the silent hallway.

"I told you I had a bad feeling." Allie tossed her gloves in the trash and ran her fingers through her hair. "I hate being right. I'm never right when it counts—boyfriends, test answers, lottery tickets." She shook her head. "I think Stephanie found something that put her in the killer's crosshairs. If Robert is telling the truth about her tenacious, obsessive personality, she may have put herself in a dangerous situation."

"I wanted to hire her if you recall. We could use a few more people like her on our side."

Allie's cell phone chirped, and an unknown number

flashed across her screen. She answered as they exited the building.

"Agent Bishop."

"Allie?" A woman's warm voice reached out from the other end of the call. Allie blinked for a moment, thinking about her wish to Zoltar. Her heartbeat fluttered, and she stopped walking.

"I'm Sadie Talbot. I was a friend of your mother's a long time ago."

Allie suddenly felt foolish. "Thank you for calling," she stammered.

"I just got your message at my office and wanted to reach out. I'm sorry I took so long. I've been in Japan on extended business and am just getting caught up on all my messages."

"Completely understandable." Allie's mind scrambled to focus as the call filled with silence.

Jason raised his eyebrows in concern. She held up a hand and nodded.

"Would you like to have dinner?" The woman came to her rescue. "I would love to see you after all these years. We have so much to talk about, and it doesn't seem right to do it over the phone. It's the least I can do for Johanna."

The sound of her mother's name forced Allie out of her stupor. "That would be lovely."

"I'll send a car to your place. Just text me your address."

"But you're in Seattle, right? That's two hours away."

"Perfectly fine. My office will reach out to take care of everything. I'm taking you to Toula's tomorrow night. I've been living on sushi and ramen for two months. I need a steak."

"So, tomorrow?"

"If it's not interrupting anything important?"

"No, tomorrow will be fine. Thank you."

Allie said goodbye, and her hand brushed against something sticking out of the pocket of her pants. She pulled out the gold *Zoltar Speaks* ticket and stared at it between her fingers. Slowly, she lifted the edge to glance at the prediction. It was plain and simple.

Your Wish Has Been Granted.

Chapter Fifteen

FBI Field Office
Tacoma, Washington

"Preliminary lab report just came through from Dr. Winters." Jason dropped a document on Allie's lap, leaned against her cubicle, and crossed his bare ankles. Allie glanced up from the stack of photos taken at the scene and did a double-take. Her partner's professional attire was typically dramatic. He preferred well-cut suits in a variety of tasteful colors and patterns, Italian tailoring, and expensive shoes with or without socks. Today, however, Allie detected an extra level of care in his appearance.

He wore creased gray pants, and leather loafers that matched his watch. He had on a crisp white shirt with a masculine lavender and brown windowpane pattern underneath a chocolate jacket. His look was complete with a navy tie that wouldn't have worked as part of the ensemble except for the faint lavender and navy detail in his pocket square.

Allie rarely saw her partner wear a square. She studied him for a long moment and made a circular motion with her hand. "What's the occasion?"

"No occasion. Victoria asked me to accompany her to a doctor's appointment today." He shrugged and took a sip of his vitamin-infused water.

"So? You did that last week without preening. What's going on?" Allie squinted at him until the answer revealed itself. A smile pulled at her lips. "Is it Dr. Dreamboat?"

Jason glared at her.

"I'm right, aren't I? The medical whosiewhatsit." She couldn't hold back a laugh.

"We have an appointment with Victoria's medical oncologist, yes, if you must know. We're going to review some tests, and then I'm taking her to lunch."

"Well, I'm not sure who's keeping score, but I think you won. Congratulations," Allie teased, then thought better of it. "Hey, have you been to Toula's in Seattle?"

Jason whistled through his teeth. "Yes, on our first anniversary. It's swanky. Great view of Lake Union. Do you have a date, Bishop? No *Golden Girls* reruns for you tonight?"

"No. She was a friend of my mom's."

"Oh, so real-life *Golden Girls*." He considered it. "It's a start. She must have been a good friend if she's invited you to Toula's. My dad's friends invite me to happy hour at the VFW so they can impress me with their war stories."

At "swanky," Allie's level of discomfort rose. She could do sandwich shops and diners, but upscale? "Is there a dress code?"

"It's fancy. Wear your hair down, something simple but classic. You'll be fine."

Allie ran a hand down her ponytail. "Did you say something about the lab report?"

"Yes, Dr. Winters just sent these over. The preliminary report came back on Stephanie Mercer. No poison was found in her system. There was, however, an odd substance on the body as Winters had suggested. Stephanie was drenched in fresh chicken blood and store-bought predator scent."

"Ew." Allie scrunched up her nose. "Like a ritual? Voodoo or something?"

"No. More like a buffet. Dr. Winters confirmed his original claim. The unsub doused the body in an intoxicating substance for wildlife. The combination would arouse the natural scavenger's instincts into a literal feeding frenzy. The reaction is rare in nature, a perfect storm of certain factors. That's why he believes it was doused with these fluids, which would also explain the heightened decay and the mutilation of the body. If it wasn't for the local security guard being drawn to the noise and interrupting the animals, Stephanie's body would've been spread across three counties by dawn."

"It's like something from *National Geographic*," she sighed.

"I need to run, but I'll check in after lunch." Jason excused himself, leaving Allie to her thoughts as she read the rest of the report.

Stephanie Mercer was strangled and her body discarded. Her murder gnawed at Allie with the same ferocity with which her body had been devoured. It seemed particularly pointless. She studied the information in hopes that a pattern might emerge.

She didn't fit the unsub's criteria, so why was her body strangled and dumped behind a rural strip mall? Had she gotten too close to her mother's killer? The timing of Stephanie's own abduction and murder so close to Helen's would make Allie think that she had. Especially since she was clearly looking for her mother's killer.

But with Stephanie, nothing else was the same.

The younger woman did not fit their unsub's established disposal profile. Her face had been left intact, and her corpse had been purposely soaked in a fluid that would make wild animals go savage on it. On top of that, she was left in an urban environment, not tossed in a river. And if her mother's killer had come for her because she was getting too close, why did he leave all her investigatory evidence behind—phone, planner, and notebooks?

Allie switched gears and settled her attention on Robert Hall's violent past. His attachment to Stephanie and her rejection of him could have stirred strong, negative feelings in the man. He had openly admitted to not having an alibi.

Allie felt the nudge to dig deeper.

She poured herself a third cup of coffee and laid out information on the floor of her cubicle in a large circle so her mind's eye could take in information subconsciously. She turned in a slow circle and let her eyes rove over the information, photos from the victim's makeshift murder board, and additional images from Stephanie's home. Allie kept returning to the note tacked on the board referring to Helen Mercer's neighbor. *My new walking buddy.*

"Why didn't you tell us about your mom's new friend,

Stephanie?" Allie wondered aloud to no one in particular. "Did you know who it was?"

"Careful." A deep voice plucked Allie out of her concentration. "First you start talking to yourself, then you go bananas on a case file." Agent Dave Hagan stood in Allie's doorway, gesturing over his belly with a World's Best Dad mug. "You know what comes next, right?"

"What?"

"Streaking through the office naked, singing 'The Star Spangled Banner.'"

"That's not funny," she said with a sigh.

"It's a joke." He took a swig of his coffee. "Chill. Don't go calling HR on me. I just came to offer you help if you need some. Because you look like you need it."

Allie surveyed the whirlwind of her office and had to admit it didn't look very systematic.

"I promise you, I will ask if I need it. Thank you." Allie tried to hide her annoyance. Then she had a thought. "Dave, how are the girls?" she asked politely about his three daughters.

He eyed her. "Why? What do you want?"

"Nothing." Allie knew she looked suspicious, but she was in too deep to stop. "I'm just making conversation, trying to get to know people in the office."

"Well, you suck at it. Stop." Hagan added, "Please."

"Fine, but you've been working at the TFO for how many years?"

"Fifteen."

"Wow, congratulations." She tried to sound impressed. "I think you could help me. Did something happen within the TFO that I should know about? Maybe in the last year or so?"

Hagan's sneer faltered, and he glanced around. "Who told you?" he asked in a low growl.

Allie felt a thrill of affirmation. She was on the right track. "No one. I'm a trained investigator. I'm doing my job."

"Yeah, well, stop that too," he chided. "It's none of your business." He turned to leave and tossed back a final piece of information. "Marze wants to see you."

Allie broke into a cold sweat. She tiptoed around the mosaic of information strewn across her floor and stopped in the doorway. One glance over her shoulder, and she froze in her tracks. It looked like a disaster area. No one walking by would believe that she had been methodically sifting through information. Had Marze walked by and witnessed the mess? Allie scurried to scoop up the files and place them back in order as quickly as possible. By the time she finally knocked on the door of the Special Agent in Charge, she felt every bit the noob and the rookie that everyone around here kept calling her.

"Come in," Marze barked.

Allie stepped inside the office that was managed with military precision, which made her wince to think her new boss had observed her unruly process. It didn't help that her limited methods were yielding limited results.

"Bishop, did King brief you on the ME's latest report?" Marze asked.

"Yes, sir." She stood in front of his desk feeling like a soldier unprepared for inspection.

"Good. Have a seat. Anything new to add?" He walked around the desk, closed his door, and returned to his seat.

"Unfortunately, no." Allie chewed her lip and braced herself for a rebuke.

"This is a challenging case. But I wanted to take a minute and see how you're adjusting."

"Oh, um, thank you for asking." Her shoulders released some of the tension they were holding onto. She did better when she had clear direction and a tactical plan. "Right now, I'm spinning my wheels, and any advice you can offer is helpful."

"Unfortunately, wheel spinning is a part of the process. You need to be patient and occasionally bring in an extra set of eyes. I'm always available."

"Thank you, sir. That's good to know."

"Stephanie Mercer. Was she looking into her mother's case?"

"She was."

"Then that gives us a new angle and new data to sift through. Remember that being good at this job requires you to ask the right questions. What information did Stephanie access? Is it different from what you're currently looking at? Did she have previous information about her mother that drew her to a conclusion we're missing? I'm sure you're already asking yourself most of these, but I want to make sure I'm steering you right. Keep digging through the haystack."

"Absolutely. Thank you, sir." She sensed that he wanted to say something more.

"Bishop, I remember my days as a rookie at the LA field office. Feels like a lifetime ago now, but I had to wade through the reality of being on the lowest rung, having to prove to myself and everyone else that I was cut out for this. Just like you are, and just like every other agent in this building. I want you to know, on the record, I think you're capable of rising to the challenge. You did great work on the Gig Harbor High killings. And you have continued to do so since. Keep it up."

Allie walked back to her desk, thankful for the vote of confidence, and felt like she could walk a little bit taller. On her way out, she had been tempted to ask about Jason's previous partner but chickened out. Marze would read her into the situation if it was important enough to their work, right?

Back in her cubicle, she combed through a thin stack of paperwork. The geo data from Stephanie's phone had been turned off, probably with her advanced cybersecurity skills. So Allie was forced to rely on financial data from recent purchases to fill in a timeline of her last seventy-two hours on earth.

Anyone with Stephanie's advanced understanding of surveillance would be able to thwart Allie's makeshift tracking system. She had printed off a copy of a Tacoma map and was painstakingly recreating a dot-to-dot visual of the victim's final days. It was slim, but Allie hoped Stephanie had been so focused on tracking down her mother's killer that she inadvertently left them a clue.

Cradling the bust of Lincoln, Allie tossed it back and forth between her hands as she stepped back and looked at her pattern. It was data, but she wasn't sure if it was helpful data. A frustrated sigh escaped her. Sifting through everything had sent her down a mental corridor of her own making. Now, as the rest of her senses came back online, they alerted her to the quiet that had settled over the office. She glanced at her watch and realized it was time to head home. Staying late wasn't an option tonight. She needed to hurry home and get changed before Sadie's car arrived to pick her up.

The thought of dinner released a new level of nerves she

had managed to keep at bay while focusing on this puzzle. As she picked up her satchel, she mentally sifted through her closet, searching for something classic and simple. Did she own anything that fit the description?

She typically didn't care what people wore as long as they were comfortable and warm. But she had observed the confidence clothing gave when a person's attire matched the setting, as well as their status. It was interesting how often humans relied on clothing to convey messages about their subconscious values. As an observer of detail, she appreciated these universal patterns and the ways individuals manipulated them for their individual preferences.

Hurrying across the floor, she took the elevator down and glanced at her watch as she entered the parking garage. Jason hadn't stopped by her desk like he promised. She pulled up her phone, hoping that everything had gone well with Victoria's appointment.

It wasn't like Jason to blow her off. His texts were consistent, brief, and factual—something she appreciated, and one of the many reasons she felt comfortable with him and his wife. She sent them both a quick text checking in and closed her phone.

As she reached her car, a woman's panicked voice bounced off the cement walls.

"Jason, what do you expect me to do?"

Allie lifted her head with a start. Sensing the distress in the unfamiliar voice, Allie searched the parking garage until she located the source. Low voices were murmuring from a blue Camry parked on the level below Allie. Three steps took her to the edge, where she could observe the interaction through the gap in the levels without being witnessed.

Jason had his hands jammed in his pockets. His crisp suit now looked rumpled. If he lifted his head, he would see his partner, who stood directly above him. But his gaze was fixed on the woman in the driver's seat of the Camry. A hand came through the window and rested on his brown jacket. Allie couldn't make out many details from her perch, but she didn't see a wedding ring on her hand.

Allie's senses bristled with indignation and concern. Jason rubbed a knuckle across his beard in agitation.

"What am I supposed to do?" the woman asked. "It's your fault it's like this. I came to you for help."

Allie held her breath while silence filled the parking structure. The stress coming off the two was palpable, even from a distance.

Jason responded in a low, barely controlled voice. Allie couldn't make out the words.

She crept forward, trying to hear what he said next, but her foot came down too hard and echoed across the concrete. Jason lifted his head, and Allie dropped, flattening her body onto the cement. The woman said something that was lost in the revving of the engine, and the car sped away.

Allie scrambled back to her car and sat breathlessly in the front seat for a long moment. Did he see her? Should she lie and say she hadn't seen anything?

No, Allie hated obfuscation in herself and anyone else. It was the reason she felt gross about the scene she just witnessed. Why was a married man talking to another woman in a parking garage? It instinctively made her think the worst of her partner.

Allie hadn't been on the job very long, but she was not the trusting sort. She analyzed the data. Jason's absence this afternoon, Hagan's evasive response to her questions earlier, and Marze's concern about her transition—the evidence was leading in a disturbing direction. She shook her head and tried to find a solution that fit.

Was the woman in the Camry Jason's previous partner? The idea grabbed her full attention. She could get Brandy to access the security footage of the parking garage, and she could quickly search the Bureau's database to view agent history. It would be enough to quell her curiosity and move on.

Allie started her car, backed out of the spot, and accelerated toward home, which allowed enough time for rationality to creep back in. She couldn't pry into Jason's personal life behind his back. She knew exactly how she would react if someone treated her the same way. It wouldn't end well for any of them.

And besides, everything in her wanted to trust him.

Chapter Sixteen

Toula's Restaurant
Seattle, Washington

Sadie Talbot's driver texted at 5:59 on the dot. Allie stepped out of her apartment, smoothed her hair, and picked a piece of lint off her black silk dress.

The driver, a middle-aged man in a tailored suit, opened the rear door of a black Bentley in welcome.

"Thank you," she said, and between the dress and now the luxury car, complete with a chauffeur, she felt completely out of her depth.

"My pleasure." He gave her a professional smile, along with their estimated time of arrival.

Allie almost felt naked without her badge and gun and glanced at her apartment one last time. She leaned back against the plush material and watched the lights of the city glide past. It was hypnotic, and her mind returned to the problems of

Stephanie Mercer and Jason's mysterious meeting. Finally, she landed on the topic of Sadie Talbot.

For weeks, the woman had been a name scrawled in her mother's journal. When she had finally gotten up the nerve to track her down, it had been harder than she expected. She was disappointed to discover the dearth of information accessible to her. Without having an open investigation on Sadie Talbot, Allie was forced to limit her curiosity to Google. She turned up a thriving company with several listed numbers, a website, offices in downtown Seattle, and not much else. Sadie Talbot's company was also listed as a donor for several local causes. Allie wondered if that was the source of the woman's caution. A low profile meant low access, and maybe that was something a wealthy woman valued.

Lost in thought, the time slipped away easily. Before she knew it, the luxurious vehicle pulled into the gracious driveway of a stately restaurant. Toula's sat on the edge of the city in complete harmony with the natural, understated surroundings. The mid-century elegance sat above Lake Union and offered a stunning view through wide, rectangular windows.

Allie gripped her thrifted leather clutch and tried to swallow as the heavy glass doors were pulled back for her with ease. Stacked stone walls, lush fabric, and natural wood paneling had been modernized for the finest connoisseur. The hostess greeted her warmly, and Allie gave her name.

"Of course, Ms. Talbot is waiting for you at the bar." She led her up the stairs, past a grand piano, and into a lush lounge.

"May I freshen your glass for you, Ms. Talbot?" the hostess asked an elegantly coiffured blonde in an ivory Balenciaga pantsuit.

"Yes, please." The woman lifted a manicured hand toward Allie in greeting. It sparkled with diamonds.

"Allison?" Sadie Talbot asked, running a discerning set of blue eyes over Allie's lean form, assessing her simple dress and matching cardigan.

"Please, call me Allie."

She smiled at the woman, who sat straight back on a plush lounge chair. Sadie gestured to the chair across from her and took Allie's proffered hand in both of hers. "You look just like your mother," she said wistfully. "I'll admit I was looking for someone in a polyester suit and a badge, but look at you. You're gorgeous."

"Thank you for the invitation, Ms. Talbot."

"To you, it's Sadie. My employees call me Ms. Talbot," she said and leaned forward conspiratorially. "After all, you and I are practically family."

The hostess returned carrying a tray and a pristine martini. "May I escort you to your table?"

Sadie Talbot swept up her Hermes shoulder bag. Allie followed as she glided through the historic restaurant to a second-story dining room and a table for two, complete with a view of the magnificent sunset. Flames danced in a large stone fireplace in the center of the room. Seattle twinkled in the window, and sailboats bobbed gently on the water below them.

"Have you been to Toula's before?" Sadie asked as she took a sip of her drink.

"No, I haven't been back to Seattle much since college graduation."

"You were a Husky?" Sadie cried in delight.

"Were you?"

"Truth be told, I never went to college. In the end, I learned everything I needed to know from the school of hard knocks. Neither your mother nor I grew up comfortably, but I always wanted to be a Husky. All those good-looking men. Your father went to Gonzaga, didn't he?" Sadie asked politely. "You didn't want to follow in his footsteps? Well, I suppose not, after all."

Allie ordered an iced tea and tried to think of something the two had in common. She was desperate for a better grasp on her past. "How old were you when you met my mother?"

"Mrs. Mitchell's third grade class at Harbor Heights Elementary School. It was the wrong side of the tracks from Gig Harbor back then. I remember it was the first day of school. Wesley Caldwell yanked one of Johanna's braids on the playground, and I punched him in the nose."

Allie laughed despite her nerves.

"The rest, as they say, is history." Sadie smiled. "Your mother had a lovely foster mother that I adored. I spent every single moment over at their house. We were practically inseparable."

The waiter appeared discreetly as Sadie set down her glass.

"Good evening, Ms. Talbot, Chef Ibrahim sends her compliments. She's prepared a special tasting menu for you and your guest this evening." The young man nodded to Allie. "Any dietary restrictions?"

The pair looked at Allie, who blushed politely. "No. Thank you." Allie hadn't even been offered a menu, and she stammered. As one who felt most comfortable on her grandmother's farm, she was a fish out of water.

"We will be delighted with anything Aisha has prepared. She knows what I like." Sadie smiled happily and then noticed

Allie's discomfort. "This is my treat, Allie. They serve a three-course tasting menu that changes seasonally. I don't even open the menu anymore. You can completely trust them with whatever they set in front of you."

Allie smiled. "This is a far cry from the Thai takeout I would typically be eating tonight."

"I helped their new chef find a magnificent home near Gas Works Park last year when she took over." Sadie chatted easily. "I'm so glad they hired a woman as an executive chef. It's about time."

"Well, I'm sure you are an inspiration to many professional women in Seattle," Allie offered. "How did you get started in real estate?"

"Oh, you don't want to hear my story." Sadie laughed and placed her napkin in her lap. "It is filled with far too much compromise, pantyhose, and hair spray for anyone in your generation, I'm afraid. Not to mention, tears." She shook her head resolutely. "How is it to be a woman in the Federal Bureau of Investigation? Is it anything like what we see on TV?"

"No, I'm afraid not. Not nearly as much hairspray and twice the paperwork."

"But you have a windbreaker, right?" She leaned forward. "The ones with yellow letters on the back that say FBI?"

"Yes, I do, actually." Allie smiled as their first course was brought to the table. "And a badge and a gun."

Sadie's eyes grew wide with the unspoken question.

"I left it all at home. Today, I'm just Allie Bishop."

Sadie laughed out loud. "Speaking of strong women, how is Etta these days?"

"Grams? She's doing great. Still on the farm. I didn't know you knew my grandmother."

"That's because she wasn't my biggest fan. She thought I was trouble from the moment she saw me."

"I'm sorry?"

"She was right. I was trouble." Sadie winked. "But it served me well, and that was a long time ago."

Allie tried to enjoy the magnificent food.

"I was so glad to get your messages when I landed," Sadie continued. "I've wondered about you from time to time. But through the years, I wasn't sure if you would want to connect with anyone from your past. Your mother, she meant so much to me. But I want to know all about you."

Allie spent much of the course filling Sadie in on the most recent events of her life—her time at the ME's office in Tacoma; her training at Quantico, including the two weeks she spent in Albany under the guiding hand of Darcy Hunt; and these last two months working out of the Tacoma field office. "There doesn't seem to be much time for anything but work, to be honest."

Sadie gave a knowing nod. "The plain, hard reality of the working woman, I'm afraid. That is the one thing I hoped would change with time."

"Do you have any family?" Allie asked, wondering what the etiquette was for this type of situation.

"I don't. Over time, my work became my family. You?"

"Not yet. Right now, it's just me and Grams."

Allie enjoyed the second course even more than the first. She was glad she hadn't ordered wine with her meal, as she hated not being in control of her faculties. As it was, she was having a hard time managing all the delicious sensory details of the food and the restaurant—the impeccable service, the scent of the open-air fire and cooking meat, and gentle piano music—to say nothing of the nuanced conversation.

Throughout the dinner, Allie kept noticing the flickering glances of a man at another table. He was handsome, with dark hair, a full, well-trimmed beard, and wearing a blue blazer. But she started to wonder if she should be flattered or concerned. He was well-built, not much older than herself. But was this the type of place someone visited alone? She tried not to wonder about the tragic story that led him to a table for one.

Instead, Allie chose to focus on Sadie, desperate for details about her mother. "Have we met before? You seem familiar, but I don't remember meeting you as a child."

"The last time I was with you and your mother was on your third birthday," Sadie said.

"May I ask? The two of you had been best friends according to Mom's journal. What made you drift apart?"

"Life just took us in different directions. Johanna was focusing on her new family, and I had moved up here to start my business. We never meant the years to get the better of us. Time is funny that way. You look back one day and realize how much time has slipped on by."

"When was the last time you saw her?" Allie asked.

"Let's see...we met here in Seattle for lunch. You had just turned eight. She brought me one of your school pictures for my wallet. She was so proud of you. She just loved being your mother. But, did you say she kept a journal?"

"Yes, that's how I knew your name. Her last entry was a couple of weeks before she went missing. The writing suddenly turned cryptic, if not ominous, like she had an intuition that something wasn't right. Do you know what it might have been?"

"No, that's awful." Sadie paused for thought. "Your mother was kind and gentle, even if a bit naive at times. But I loved her because of it. She was a housewife, and it was her bliss. I never understood what she was doing in a bad part of Seattle the day she disappeared."

The older lady smiled wanly. "I remember when your mother got me to try out for the fifth grade play." Sadie looked off through the dark window as if lost in memory. "It was Mary Poppins. I tried to be brave—I'd never been on stage and I didn't have a dress to my name for the audition. Johanna made me spend the night at her house to prepare. She washed and combed my hair, lent me her best dress and shoes, and sat in the back the whole time I recited my lines."

"Did she try out too?"

"Oh, no. Your mother was shy. But she believed in me. It was magic."

"Did you get the part?"

"I did. And that got me into high school theater, which got me a job as the weather girl in Tacoma. It all started with Johanna."

"That's beautiful," Allie said. "Thank you. I never knew that part of my mother. There are so many pieces of her that suddenly feel important. Maybe it's becoming an adult or finding her journal after all these years. I'm investigating her disappearance as a cold case in my own time. Any information you have about that time in her life would be so helpful. Did you remain friends with my fath—with Beau?

"Ms. Talbot?" A petite Asian woman in a chef's coat strode toward their table as the dessert was being presented.

"Why hello, Chef." Sadie was sparkling again. "An exceptional meal, yet again."

"Thank you. I'm so glad you liked it. I took your advice. After your visit last month, I ordered a case of the heirloom vinegar you brought me."

"And?"

"You ate it tonight. It perfectly complements the pears and the citrus."

"Of course. It was exceptional. Aisha, this is Allison Bishop, an old friend. She's a special agent with the FBI."

"What an honor to have you at Toula's."

Allie shook hands with the accomplished woman but struggled to take in the interaction. Hadn't Sadie said she'd been in Japan for two months? Allie's investigative mind went into high gear. She struggled to assimilate the information and keep a smile on her face. The chef hugged Sadie before moving on to another table, and they resumed their meals.

"Do you remember the last thing you and my mother talked about?" Allie asked.

"Please. It's too painful to talk about any more of the past. May we just enjoy our final course and try to find a way forward?" Sadie asked.

"I'm sorry." Allie stared at her plate.

"So am I." She reached out and touched Allie's hand and then lifted her glass. "But let's toast your mother, her words, and her memory that brought us to today."

Allie didn't taste much of the expensive concoction on her plate, and the rest of their conversation was a little strained.

The man in the blue suit had disappeared before Sadie paid the check.

"Thank you for telling me about my mother," Allie said as the two walked outside. "I appreciated tonight in a way I can't express."

Sadie offered Allie an air kiss, a shimmer of tears in the woman's eyes. "We will do this again soon." She held Allie's hand with a vice-like grip and stepped away into her black Bentley. In moments, Allie was ushered into her luxury vehicle by the doorman.

On the drive home, Allie was lulled into a trance-like state by the heavy emotion, the meal, and the gentle motion of the car. Her eyes flitted shut for a moment, and then she sat up with a gasp. It came to her in a flash of memory. She didn't remember Sadie's face from her childhood, but she recognized her voice.

Chapter Seventeen

July 2005
Bishop Family Vacation Cabin
Bellingham, Washington

It *was all wrong,* eight-year-old Allie decided as she watched fireflies dance in the grass below her feet. This was *not* how summer was supposed to feel. Summer had healing properties, life-giving magic that soothed all your elementary woes.

But this year, the magic had left her, she decided. She stared up into the clear, starlit night and searched for answers. The palms of her hands bit into the asphalt shingles. Allie brought knobby knees up under her chin to escape the scratchy sensation of her bare skin on the roof.

From her earliest memories, the cabin had been their family's oasis, a magical castle in her imagination. Grams and Gramps had built it together over several summers when Daddy was a boy. They filled it with hand-me-down furniture,

Salvation Army plates, pots and pans, a rusted grill, and garage sale linens. Her mother's artwork lined the walls, and Grams's quilts and canned preserves filled the space with comfort alongside Gramps's hand-carved woodwork and her father's childhood games.

To Allie, it was a palace.

Every corner was packed with possibilities. When the three of them loaded up their Buick and moved in at the beginning of the summer, Allie knew she was the luckiest kid in the world. Her father was a math teacher at Gig Harbor High School. This afforded them six whole weeks of blissful morning fishing trips to Turtle Lake and lazy afternoons reading on the porch swing. Rainy days were for chess games with her father while her mother read poetry aloud. Then there were roasted marshmallows and camp songs around the fire, and starlit nights with nothing to interrupt their reverie but crickets and bullfrogs.

But everything was different now.

Mommy had been gone for an entire school year. Even though she and her father decided a trip to the cabin would be good, they both dreaded one more memory without her. The days were filled with the endless sound of Daddy chopping wood. His restless energy made Allie nervous, and she wandered farther and farther into the ravines and the woods.

She hiked for hours, fleeing the pangs of aching loss that washed over her at the sight of cast-off memories. She carved her mother's name in the tree, right on the spot where they had sat the year before for a picnic. Mommy had been delighted to paint the lone sailboat drifting across the water and promised to teach Allie to sail the little Sunfish next year.

Now it was next year, and the days stretched before the

young girl in endless misery. As long as she kept moving, she could outrun the loneliness that sat hard in her chest. She would get lost in the woods chasing a rabbit or wade knee-deep in a stream hunting for tadpoles. But the nights would betray her, the aching grief making it impossible to sleep.

Daddy had asked her not to leave her room on nights he went to work in town. He said the work gave him something else to do. He would kiss Allie goodnight and promise to bring her a treat, then send her to bed before the evening light had left the sky. Tires would crunch on the drive, the screen door would creak open, and low voices filled their home. Then the screen door would slam, and Daddy's car would drive away with another crunch of tires. The silence was stifling to Allie's frayed nerves. The stranger's presence felt like the final betrayal of her mother's absence. Finally, the tears would leak out of the corners of Allie's eyes onto her pillow.

Daddy never introduced her to the woman who kept vigil those long summer nights. Allie had no desire to meet her, nor did she care what the woman looked like. She wasn't her mother, and that was all that mattered.

His late-night trips to town grew more and more frequent. In the morning, there would be a pack of Twizzlers left for her on the table but not a single trace of the stranger's presence. Only the sound of bird song and the endless thud and thwack of chopping wood.

Allie observed the pattern of their new reality, began to notice when her father came to the table showered and dressed, smelling of Zest soap and aftershave. On those days, he served bologna sandwiches for supper instead of pork chops and fried potatoes. The subtle signs were all she needed to withdraw to read up in her room alone. She tried to get lost in *The Adventures of Tom Sawyer* and *Robinson Crusoe* or find solace in her beloved *Swiss Family Robinson*.

But the creak of the screen door was like nails on a chalkboard to her little soul. Tonight, in desperation, she opened her window, tossed a bare leg over the window sill, and climbed onto the shingled expanse. In the corner of the gabled roof, she was protected from the view of the driveway below and could stretch out under the stars. Up here, she was able to breathe, at last.

Wrapped in one of Grams's crocheted afghans, Allie listened to her father and the woman as they spoke on the porch below. The murmur of adult voices lilted into the silent night, and Allie wondered if it was the melody of growing up.

A falling star streaked across the sky, and she whispered her prayer into the night. Wherever the star was going, would it find her mother, guiding her back to their lonely cabin north of Turtle Lake?

Chapter Eighteen

Amalie Bakery
Tacoma, Washington

Allie quickened her step as she made her way through the morning commuters toward the vintage neon sign bearing Victoria's grandmother's name, Amalie. Her stomach roared at the delicious smells emanating from Victoria's family bakery. Red umbrellas perched atop cafe tables created an inviting tableau in front of the historic red brick building.

The bell above the door tinkled a warm greeting as Allie stepped inside the cozy corner bakery. Jason had texted her early this morning asking if she would meet him here instead of at the office.

The scene inside was just as pleasant. Allie paused to study a hand-painted chalkboard offering several Spanish delicacies, along with traditional fare and an assortment of coffees. Her eyes feasted on the impressive displays of macarons, ornate cakes, danish, muffins, bagels, and rustic loaves of bread. Allie ordered a large French press and a house donut from the young man behind the counter in a red apron.

"Buenos dias, Allie," Victoria called to her from the doorway behind the counter. She was radiant in a purple headscarf, with a dusting of flour over her apron and tank top. She settled a tray of muffins into the glass case and came around the corner to embrace Allie.

"V? You look amazing."

"I woke up at four a.m. with the most intense craving for my grandmother's *miguelitos* today." She laughed and tucked the corner of the vibrant purple back into its beautiful twist atop her head. "It's Wednesday, and I knew my nephew and Mama would be here in the kitchen. I couldn't stay away." She placed a hand on her thin hip and glistened with happiness. "I think I scared Jason. He wouldn't let me come alone. He's camped out in the back room waiting for you. Go ahead, I'll have Imanuel bring you your order."

Allie smiled to herself as she strode past the customers in the bustling cafe. She was relieved to see Victoria on a good day, and it helped loosen the knot of dread that pulled at her gut when she received Jason's summons this morning.

A red velvet curtain separated the two spaces, and Allie ducked inside. "This is an impressive setup," she said as she looked around the conference room.

Jason had spread his laptop and several papers across a large table in the center of the space and was connected to a screen that took up one wall. "Businesses rent this space regularly, and V's brother understands his audience." Jason stood and stretched. He looked a little less vibrant this morning than his wife, but from the stack of cups and pastries, it was obvious he had been here for a while.

"Don't take this wrong, but I thought you'd given up sugar?" Allie assessed the scene.

"This is one reason I *have* to," he laughed. "No one can resist Abuela's pastries. It would be rude. So I have to say no to *everyone* else to stay fit enough to chase down a suspect. But in here, it's like the Willy Wonka of fried dough. I don't even try to fight it."

When Allie's order arrived at the table, she took a bite of the handmade donut and rolled her eyes in appreciation.

"Exactly."

"You've been busy." Allie nodded to the papers spread across the table.

"Brandy made a discovery overnight. I was going to call, but I didn't want to interrupt your evening. How was the dinner?"

"Good." She nodded her head with hesitation. "I think? I'll tell you when I've had my coffee. I'm still processing." She pressed down on the plunger and poured the steaming goodness into an oversized white mug. "You?"

Seeing Victoria just now while wondering about his conversation with the woman in the blue Camry didn't sit well. She hadn't decided how to confront Jason about it, but she also wasn't opposed to a few leading questions.

"Quiet, thankfully." He took a sip of coffee. "We stayed at home. The new supplements V's doctor has her on have helped. They're taking the edge off the nausea and the fatigue. It's nice to see her able to eat again. I wasn't going to be the one to stop her, even if she does want carbs, cream, and sugar. She's always been an early riser. Growing up above a bakery will do that. But it gave me time to go over the newest files Brandy sent over." He tapped a key on his laptop, and the oversized screen was filled with the image of a file.

He explained while Allie ate. "Late last night, Brandy's search algorithm was sifting through Stephanie Mercer's personal emails. She discovered a disturbing conversation she had three weeks ago with a former co-worker." He highlighted several words on the screen, including *fear, violence, anger, warning signs,* and *threats* that popped out of the e-mail.

"On the first of this month, Stephanie reached out to Deborah Peters. Deborah is a retired software engineer. The two knew each other when Stephanie was just out of college."

"A mentor?"

"Possibly. But a quick search turned up something a little more ominous. Deborah's husband has a violent history. There are incident reports spanning over twelve years. The police were called on several occasions, until finally Deborah was hospitalized and moved into a shelter. She filed a restraining order against her husband, but it was pretty flimsy. He took his life suddenly two years ago, the day Deborah was supposed to be getting remarried."

"Ouch."

"Yeah." He shook his head. "This is why I don't watch TV much anymore. Sports, yes, but real life has plenty of drama for me."

"What does Deborah's past have to do with Stephanie's?"

"Remember how Robert told us that Stephanie had never introduced him to her mother?"

"Yep."

"According to the e-mails between Deborah and Stephanie, Helen was concerned about Hall's previous conviction for manslaughter."

Allie licked the sugar off her fingers. "Not a believer in rehabilitation?"

"Nope. Sounds like Stephanie's birth father was a tough guy too."

"So she turns to Deborah for what, advice?"

Jason skipped a few more pages forward. "Something like that. Stephanie and Robert had a late-night argument after they lost a gaming tournament. They'd been drinking, things got heated, and he smashed a vase against the wall."

Allie grimaced. She didn't like where this was going.

"It was a bit of a wake-up call for Stephanie, who poured her heart out to her old friend."

Allie stopped him. "But I thought Stephanie had begged Robert to call her. That is the opposite of what you're showing me."

"I had the same thought." Jason rubbed his beard and rolled up the sleeves of his Oxford shirt. "But he didn't tell us about the fight. So what else is he leaving out?"

Allie stared at Stephanie's heartfelt message up on the screen. "Good point. Robert told us she begged him to help her find her mom."

"He said she was intense." Jason wagged a finger in agreement. "Obsessive."

"Could be a bad combo for a man with a temper." Allie sighed. "Have you reached out to Deborah?"

Jason glanced at his watch. "She's meeting us here in half an hour. I thought it might be better than the office."

"If Stephanie and Robert had a violent fight, someone may have heard it?" Allie asked.

"I've got a call in to Robert requesting he meet us at the office, but I haven't heard anything yet."

"It's early. He's a night owl, but it may be good to canvass his building. See if anyone heard raised voices. It's an old building, thin walls." Allie said and poured a second cup of coffee. "What else?"

Jason pointed to the stack of papers on the table. "I've been reviewing the phone records you highlighted. Good work, by the way."

"Thank you." Allie picked up the thread of the conversation. "I put Helen and Stephanie's records through our system, looking for any obvious overlap. They were related, so it wasn't surprising that they used the same cleaners, florists, et cetera. But one number stood out. It's unlisted. It shows up on Helen's phone a handful of times. But that's not the most interesting part. It also shows up on Stephanie's phone once—hours before she disappeared."

"Coincidence?" Jason asked and dialed a number on his phone. "Morning, Brandy. I'm here with Allie and got you on speaker."

"Do either of you know what time it is?" a hoarse voice said over the line.

Allie chuckled. "Eight-thirty, girl. Not everyone keeps vampire hours. There's a box of bagels in it for you if you've got something for us."

"You two sound way too perky for anything before nine a.m. I am in the office, but that doesn't mean that I'm speaking yet," Brandy huffed and paused for a moment, possibly considering the offer. "Don't forget the schmear—honey *and* raspberry.

"Done."

"Good." Brandy sounded mollified. "I just completed the request Allie sent over yesterday. I've reanalyzed all the past four victims' phone records and found a surprisingly low level of overlap. Helen, Rhonda, and Tamara didn't know each other. They have very little in common except for one phone number."

"Is that odd?"

"Not necessarily. Whether it was a pet groomer, a yoga studio, or even a pharmacy. You would be surprised how often our lives intersect across a single point. But this one is odd because the number isn't registered at all. It's a burner. But... here's the kicker. Allie, you sent the same number to me yesterday."

Allie felt the hairs on her arm stand up. "The last number on Stephanie's phone?"

"Bingo. I've run a trace on the number to try to track its current location, but I haven't had any luck. It's either been dumped, out of battery, moved into an inaccessible area, or turned off. It isn't transmitting any locational data at the moment."

"Anything you can do?" Allie asked.

Brandy laughed low. "Is there anything I can do? Oh, rookie, you are so cute."

Allie felt her face flush. Across from her, Jason was grinning.

"I put an alert on my system that will go straight to you if the phone is turned on again," Brandy said. "It should immediately begin a trace, but to go any deeper, we're gonna need a warrant."

"On it," Allie said and opened up her laptop. "If we have a single number connecting all four victims, this may be the needle we've been looking for."

"I'll start sifting on my end. Don't you forget my bagels."

"Wait, Brandy." Jason tapped his computer. "Before you go, please pull up the vehicle registration for Robert Hall."

"You got it." Keys clicked in the background.

"Mr. Hall drives a 2011 Lincoln town car."

"What color?" Allie asked.

"Navy blue."

Allie looked at her partner. "You thinking what I'm thinking?"

"It depends, are you thinking—does Robert Hall's vehicle match the description of the car her neighbor saw in front of Stephanie's house the day she disappeared?"

"Yep."

"Thanks, Brandy." Jason clicked off the phone. "Well, how about that."

Victoria appeared at the door and spoke in a hushed tone, "Jason? A woman is asking for you. She looks upset, so I set her up with churros and chocolate. I'm brewing a fresh pot of tea for her. Are you expecting someone?"

"I am." He stood up and addressed his partner. "Deborah Peters."

The two agents followed Victoria back to a small table in front of the window, where a middle-aged woman sat staring at the food on the table. She pulled subconsciously on a Kleenex, tearing it to shreds.

"Mrs. Peters?" Jason asked.

The woman looked up with an anxious gaze. "Stephanie's dead, isn't she?"

Slowly, Jason nodded. "Yes. She's dead."

"He killed her," Deborah started to cry. "I knew it. I tried to warn her."

CHAPTER 18

Residence of Robert Hall
Tacoma, Washington

"Robert Hall?" Jason banged on the door of #10, 815 Pacific Avenue, a rundown apartment block across the street from Jimmy Z's Arcade. "This is the FBI. Robert, we have a warrant for your arrest," he said through the wooden door. The corridor smelled like wet dogs and fried potatoes.

Allie nudged the edge of a faded mat with her toe and watched a cockroach scurry out of sight. She placed a hand on her gun and ran a watchful gaze down the dingy hallway. No sound of movement came from inside the apartment. "Doesn't sound like anyone's at home."

Jason eyed the door. "His boss said he wasn't scheduled for work for the next several days, but Hall seemed like a serious couch potato to me."

The sound of a bolt clicking behind them got the agents' attention. Several more bolts scraped in succession, and finally, the door on the other side of the hallway creaked open.

"He's not here," a gruff voice said, and a slender man with a creased face stepped out, accompanied by a cloud of smoke. He wore an open button-down shirt and oversized spectacles.

Jason eyed the blunt hanging from his mouth. "Who are you?"

"Brian Temple. And I have a prescription," he explained as Jason waved away the haze. "For my glaucoma. Everyone says that now, but it's true for me. You can call my ophthalmologist." He pushed up his glasses.

"Do you know your neighbor, Robert Hall?"

"Hall? He's a smug prick. I'm not surprised if you're here to take him back to jail. He didn't like my habit and tried to report me to the landlord, acting all high and mighty."

"When was the last time you saw him, Mr. Temple?" Allie asked, trying not to cough.

"He stopped by a couple of days ago and asked me if I'd take care of his cat."

Jason frowned. "You don't like him, but you watch his cat?"

"So I have a soft spot for cats." Temple shrugged. "He's a late-night gamer, wears those headphones, and screams into the microphone. But he started bringing me leftover pizza after shifts. I asked him to feed my snake when I went to my mom's at Thanksgiving. Peggy seems to like him, even if I don't."

"Who's Peggy?" Allie asked, and Jason shook his head.

"My boa constrictor. She's on the couch. You wanna meet her?"

"No, that won't be necessary," Allie said with a hint of revulsion in her voice. "Where's the cat?" She couldn't imagine a worse combination than a jungle predator and an urban house cat.

"Right inside my door, sitting on a chair. They get along great."

The two agents exchanged a look. "Like, how?" Allie asked. "Do they cuddle?"

"All the time." Temple beamed.

Jason moved to redirect the conversation. "Mr. Temple, did Robert tell you where he was going when he dropped off the cat?"

"I told you, we're not friends. But I don't think he's coming back anytime soon. He made several trips to his car. A couple of suitcases, and a box or two. He brought me a huge bag of cat food. It wouldn't be a surprise if he skedaddled and doesn't expect to come back."

Allie felt a rock sink into the bottom of her gut, feeling that she had failed Stephanie for the second time. "Did you ever meet his girlfriend, Stephanie Mercer?" Allie asked.

"That loser didn't have a girlfriend," Temple sneered.

"You didn't see a blonde woman come in and out of his place?"

"This dump? I wouldn't bring a girl here if my life depended on it," he chortled, and started to cough. "I didn't see him bring a blonde over here, and despite my condition, I see a lot. You can tell a lot about a person if you pay attention. He may have had someone in the Metaverse or in those games he's always playing. Don't they all have alter egos in there?"

Allie looked at Jason, who shrugged.

Temple continued, "He may have had a hook-up with his gaming partner, but I can't believe he was in a relationship."

"Mr. Temple, where can I find the supervisor to get us a key?

"Super's out till after four. He has AA meetings every Wednesday over at the YMCA on Broad. Should be back after that."

"I'm guessing he didn't leave you his key when he gave you his cat?"

Temple shook his head.

Jason handed him a card. "Do us a favor and call me if the super shows up in the next couple of hours."

"You guys really FBI?" Temple stared at the paper in his hands.

"Yes, we are."

Allie's shoulders sagged as they headed back down the stairs. "What's the number for Tacoma Animal Control?"

"No idea, why?"

"Did you know it's a misdemeanor if an animal in your control harms a human, livestock, or domestic animal?"

"You're worried about the cat?" Jason asked.

"Someone needs to be. It's certainly not going to be Robert or his pot-loving neighbor."

"I gotta be honest," Jason said as they stood on the sidewalk, the breeze working the scent of weed out of their clothes. "I'm more worried about our case. I don't like Robert, but I'm having a hard time seeing him as a serial psychopath, charming his way into women's hearts, concocting poison cocktails, and then dismembering their bodies." His brow furrowed. "Still need to put out a BOLO on him."

"I agree." Allie rubbed the scar on the back of her hand, a souvenir from her father's final bout of violence that tingled when she was scared or frustrated. "Does that mean we have two separate killers? You think Robert may have killed Stephanie?" Allie asked. "But someone else killed her mom? What are the odds of that?" A headache was developing behind her eyes.

"Until we track down that mystery number, we don't have any way to prove Robert has a connection with any of our other victims."

"Only one way to find out. Let's track down Robert and get him to talk."

Chapter Nineteen

FBI Field Office
Tacoma, Washington

"Nothing?" Allie dropped her pen onto a yellow legal pad. "Thanks for the update. No, I understand. I appreciate the effort. I'll touch base tomorrow." She hung up the desk phone and plucked a pencil out of her hair, letting her curls slip around her shoulders. She ran her fingers through her hair, giving her scalp a stimulating rub. Sitting back up, she scratched off an item on her list with a quick jab of frustration.

So far, the BOLO they put out for Hall had turned up nothing of substance. The man skipped town two days ago, and Allie knew the chances of tracking him down in Tacoma were slim. She felt a bit like a rat in a maze, scurrying down one dead end after another in a fruitless pursuit of justice for Stephanie and her mother.

Most of the afternoon was spent on the phone with the state police. The warrant for Hall's residence was taking longer than expected. She glanced at her watch—4 p.m. Her legs were restless, so she stood from her chair and stretched.

"Anybody home?"

A knock came from the cubicle wall. Allie swiveled in her chair. "Brandy, hi." She motioned for the woman to join her.

The analyst placed a motorcycle helmet on the floor and settled into the empty chair alongside the case board and Allie's potted plant.

"And people think I'm edgy. You have a wicked sense of style," Brandy announced, nodding to the photos of the four faceless bodies on her timeline.

Allie shrugged. "Keeps me focused," she admitted. "I forget it unsettles people. After a couple of years at the morgue, it stops being disturbing. It's just a compelling puzzle."

"Jason told me I'd like you." Brandy gave her an appraising once-over. "I'll admit I thought you were a little *grandmacore* for me." She waved a hand at Allie's African violets sitting under a grow lamp and the small wooden bust of Lincoln.

In contrast to Brandy's ultra red bob, Ferrari leather jacket, black cargo pants, and matching nails, Allie's surroundings looked soft and cozy. Except for the gruesome pictures tacked to the whiteboard.

"I didn't know you had a motorcycle."

Brandy took a sip of her bright red boba and nodded, chewing on a bead of tapioca before answering, "I rebuilt my father's classic Ducati. He won it from a buddy in a poker game but never got it running. After he died, I got a little obsessed. Jason helped me source the tires. I even retrofitted a cup holder into the storage compartment."

Allie arched an eyebrow. "Impressive."

"Less fossil fuel, better parking, and I need the daily rush or I go a little nuts. Taking up high-risk hobbies, the Bureau claims, drives up their insurance." She winked.

"Like what?"

"Hang gliding, skydiving, white water rafting. Anything to get my heart rate up after a long day in my chair. But these days, I'm keeping my thrills to tracking down an SOB with a fetish for women's faces. I came up here for a status update and to stretch my legs. It gets a little dark in the tomb."

"Tomb?"

"It's what Eastman and King call my office, on the third floor. It's built around the elevator system for proper access to the main power, high-speed cable, and ventilation for the servers. But that limits my access to natural light. So I thought I'd wander over here for a change of scenery. Where is your intrepid partner, anyway?" Brandy stretched out a leg and crossed her ankles, making herself at home.

"That's a good question." Allie stood. "I'll see if he's in the office."

"Mind if I peruse your murder board?"

"Be my guest."

Brandy's confidence and skills were a little intimidating, so Allie stepped into the hall and took a breath as she went looking for her partner. Jason wasn't sitting at his desk, wasn't chatting with any of the analysts or bugging Hagan. She bumped into Eastman in the kitchen, warming up a cup of coffee. He hadn't seen her partner all day.

After hunting for him across the rest of the floor with no luck, she hesitated before checking in with Marze. She didn't want to put Jason in a position where he had to explain himself to his boss. But after her partner hadn't said anything about leaving the office this afternoon, so after double-checking her phone for any messages from him, she stopped Marze's office.

"Bishop," he said, holding a gym bag as he stood in his office in a Marine Corps shirt and shorts. "What's the latest on your unsub?"

"The neighbor said he left his place two days ago. We're running his credit cards and checking with anyone who may have insight into his location. I've questioned his mom and grandmother, but neither has any information on his whereabouts. Not very close, apparently."

"A prison stint can be tough on the family." Marze took a slug of his water, and the two looked at each other awkwardly for a moment.

"Um, have you seen Jason?" Allie asked.

"He stopped by around lunch and said he needed to take the rest of the day off for personal reasons."

"Did he say why?"

"Nope, he didn't offer, and I didn't ask. That's why they call them personal days."

Allie chewed her lip. She considered confiding in Marze. If she told him about the woman in the blue Camry, would that be a breach of trust? She didn't think it was her place, but the dilemma must have shown on her face.

"Believe me, Bishop. If something happened with Victoria, he would tell us. It's good of you to be concerned, but everyone needs space to handle the rest of their lives. This job will take every ounce of your attention if you let it."

Allie nodded. "Thanks, Chief."

"I'm headed out for a run, but call me if you need something," Marze added. "My knees won't mind if I cut it short today."

Allie grabbed a Snapple from the vending machine, giving herself time to sort through her feelings. It wasn't like Jason to vanish again. In their previous cases, he was transparent and reliable at all hours of the day. They hadn't been working together long, but it was atypical behavior for her partner. On the other hand, if Marze wasn't worried, she needed to let it go.

She stepped back inside her cubicle, still trying to squash the nagging feeling.

"Good news, bad news," Brandy announced, head down and tapping on her phone. "Which one do you want first?"

"My Grams always says good news can wait, and bad news is here to stay."

"Deep." Brandy nodded. "But that doesn't answer my question."

"Oh, then good, I guess."

"Good news—we were just granted an emergency warrant to track and tap the burner number that links our four victims."

"And the bad news?"

Brady kept tapping on her cell phone. "It hasn't been turned on since the day it received a call from Stephanie Mercer." She pointed to the timeline on the wall.

"The day Stephanie disappeared. You're right, that's not helpful."

"No signal, no tracking data."

"This psycho is in the wind," Allie said. "And after the failed attempt on Helen, he may escalate his timeline to kill again. Soon."

"He'll be looking for a new face?" Brandy pointed to the women on the board.

"Exactly." Allie wrapped her hair back up in a bun and speared it with a No. 2 pencil. "I don't want to sit around and wait for another faceless body to float up the Puyallup."

"There is something we could do while we wait."

"Until I get a warrant for Hall's place or a hit from my APB, I'm open to anything."

"Hall and Mercer, our potential suspect and the latest victim, were online friends. Right?" Brandy was spitballing. "They were relative loners IRL."

"What?" Allie asked.

"In real life?" Brandy gave her a quizzical look. "I bet you use proper punctuation when you text, don't you?"

Allie shrugged. "It's polite."

"Okay, so Hall and Mercer played games together online. It was all over their digital footprint. We haven't interrogated anyone in that space."

"You think Hall would be online?"

"Not with his established profiles. He's probably scrubbed or abandoned those. It's easy to set up different accounts. But he may have confided in someone who knew both of them. Word's probably spread about our victims by now. We can access Stephanie's IP address, go down the rabbit trail, and figure out where the two hung out and who they talked to.

"It's worth a shot. Mind if I tag along? Stephanie's life is like an iceberg, and there is only so much above the surface I can access IRL. I'd love to see what you turn up and how you work."

Brandy shot her a conspiratorial glance. "Let's go to my lair.

But I'll warn you, it can get a little tedious. Lots of sifting through chat rooms, a little questing, some cyber flirting. Do you speak nerd?"

"So, I'm wearing a Choose Your Own Adventure T-shirt." Allie pointed to the print underneath her blazer. "How nerdy can I get?"

"Very OG. Did you play Oregon Trail too?"

"What's that?"

"Never mind," Brandy sighed. "Jason said you were a Luddite, but I didn't believe him."

Allie wasn't sure how to feel about the fact that the two had been discussing her openly, but she shook it off as they headed toward Brandy's office. "Do you think anyone online will be willing to talk to us?"

"Maybe not you. You're a federal agent." Brandy gave a wicked grin. "But I'm not."

Chapter Twenty

Paradise Mobile Home Park
Kent, Washington

Jason ripped the corner of a plastic pouch of vitamins and electrolytes and poured the contents into his water bottle. He sealed the lid and shook the contents while the car slowed and he guided it off the 167 into the sleepy suburban community. He fished a protein bar out of the center console of his Charger with a grimace.

He had been looking forward to a swim after work at the Y near the office. Victoria's mother kept bringing oversized pots of home-cooked food for her daughter. Jason tried to freeze as much of it as possible and share the rest with his coworkers, but all the extra comfort food was starting to take a toll on his waistline. It didn't help that he wasn't sleeping well. He hoped a rigorous workout would help him get at least a few hours of sleep.

Jason clicked on his turn signal and made a left at a brightly painted sign. It featured a silhouette of two palm trees welcoming all to the Paradise Mobile Home Park. A glance around the premises left Jason questioning what part of paradise the owner was claiming. An asphalt drive formed the inner loop of the ramshackle community, which was clustered around a green swimming pool tucked inside a chain link fence.

Rusted RVs sat wedged alongside mobile home trailers and a handful of popular tiny homes. There was little room for privacy and hardly any green space among the concrete and asphalt. Jason wondered what the appeal would be besides cheap rent. But a handful of retirees lounged in the late afternoon sun. Kids pedaled bikes, and mothers chatted over wooden fences while laundry fluttered in the breeze, and he reminded himself that happiness is often a choice.

The simple, peaceful scene didn't match the one Jason had in his mind this afternoon when he got a frantic call from Colleen Yates just after lunch. Colleen explained that she had been on a cruise in Alaska with her sister and so out of cell reception for a week. When the boat had docked in Anchorage, she discovered her voicemail inbox was filled with desperate, slurred messages from her daughter, Aimee.

"She's using again, Jason," the older woman's smoky voice explained over the phone. "I can tell. She was doing so well. She's been sober for three months, going to meetings. Her sponsor was a better fit this time. She's the one who convinced me to take this trip. I never would've gone if she wasn't well."

"She's a grown woman, Colleen," Jason had said, scooping up his car keys and leaving the office without more than a mention to Marze. "You can only do so much."

"You're not a mother, Jason," Colleen retorted. "If your kids are hurting, you're hurting."

He softened. "No disrespect, Mrs. Yates." Jason was typically good with wounded people, but this situation always got the better of him no matter how much time had passed. "I saw Aimee early last night. She came to Tacoma to meet with me."

"She did?"

He didn't mention that she was agitated or that she asked him for a loan to help her move across the country. She wanted to start over in New York City. But he wasn't going to worry Colleen on one of the few vacations she was taking since she moved in with her daughter. What had concerned him most last night was how obvious it was that Aimee had returned to her substance abuse to console herself.

"You didn't give her any money, did you?" Colleen asked.

"No, not this time. I told her the only money I would loan her was for rehab and offered to take her straight over. I know a place that would accept her. I've been calling around since we spoke last week."

Even though Victoria's cancer treatment was eating up everything extra he had in savings, he was willing to find a way to get Aimee the help she needed.

"She called you last week?" The worry sharpened Colleen's voice. She knew her daughter's destructive patterns only too well. They all did. Jason had been juggling calls from a worried Colleen and a heartbroken Aimee for a long time now.

Jason and Victoria had been part of Aimee's life for years, but the pattern of late had become disturbingly regular. Months would go by without a word from Aimee. That was when she was on an upswing. Then a late-night phone call would announce the tumble into a tailspin of self-sabotage and regret, and they would all try to support her without enabling the downward spiral.

Whenever she showed up on their doorstep, Victoria would invite Aimee in to try to offer nourishment to her gaunt body and comfort for her raw and wounded spirit. Until this year, Victoria would bake huge batches of cookies to send with her or freshly baked bread and homemade soup. But her cancer had slowed her ability to care for Aimee in food. But it didn't stop Victoria from sending Aimee home with her new down parka this spring.

Jason knew Victoria did it to keep Aimee from calling and interrupting him at work. Victoria disapproved of the woman's decisions, but the guilt-ridden destruction she left in her wake was far more unsettling for Jason. Victoria insisted this was dangerous for him. She didn't want a distracted husband inadvertently making a mistake on a case or charging into the line of fire.

Aimee could be a lot, especially after everything she had been through. It was hard to remember the pretty, self-sufficient woman she had once been, her thriving real estate business, and a lovely home in the suburbs. And not too long ago. But pain had fueled a turn to alcohol and drugs, claiming the remnants of her old life.

On his way here, Jason thought about turning the car around, letting Aimee hit rock bottom on her own. Let the whole rotten situation just implode in on itself. He had been powerless to stop it before. Why would this be any different?

But it wasn't in his nature to just let things go. His conscience wouldn't let him. No matter how crazy Aimee was,

Jason would always feel responsible for her. That much would never change.

He parked his car behind the blue Camry and sent Victoria a quick text. He thought about sending a note to Allie explaining his absence, but he didn't know where to start. There were too many holes in the story to explain. So, preferring silence to dishonesty, he said nothing.

Climbing out of his car, he moved slowly down the street. Aimee's mother had moved in with her so she could keep a close eye on her. Colleen was the one who kept it nice and tidy, unlike some of the junkier houses of her neighbors.

Jason found it hard to believe that Aimee had sunk so low. Taking the edge off the pain with boxed wine had been how it started. But at the funeral, a friend slipped her over-the-counter pain pills. That day, she discovered how easy it was to move through her days in a fog of disconnection. Unfortunately, she couldn't escape the daily realities of her shattered life. Instead, she chose to numb the screaming pain one, two, or four pills at a time, with a chaser of vodka just for good measure.

The only real hardship was waking up to find nothing had changed except for her supply of medication. Her role as a real estate agent gave her access to strangers' medicine cabinets until she was fired and resorted to selling personal items—whatever would ease the ache.

Now, she was just a shell of the level-headed woman she used to be. No job, and no home, and her only friends were people she leaned on for food or drug money. Jason wasn't sure she would ever recover.

Walking up to the old mobile home, he surveyed the scene. The place was quiet. A light was on inside. He paused on the cinder block step and knocked on the door. Someone peered through the blinds in the window of a neighboring RV. He gave a nod in greeting.

Finding Aimee's home silent, he waited a little longer and tried the door. Locked. He knocked again and waited. Still, silence. He punched in the code Colleen had provided for the lock. It chimed and gave him access with a simple click.

A cold feeling of dread swept over him as he stepped inside. The place had a dated appeal—nothing like her previous home—yet another sign that Aimee had ceased to care about anything besides dulling the pain.

His footsteps echoed dully across the linoleum floor.

"Aimee?" Jason called out, and slowly took in the scene. A box of cereal spilled across the counter, and a stack of grimy dishes sat in the sink. He stepped slowly toward the back of the trailer, noticing the discarded laundry and empty food wrappers that littered the place. A thin mattress sat on the floor of the main room.

Maybe she had gone for a walk? He wondered if he should order a pizza and wait for her to return. He would feed her and bring her to his house until Colleen got back the next night. Victoria was feeling better. She might go for it.

Jason heard a sound and stopped to listen. The gentle *plink-plink-plink* of a dripping faucet was coming from the bathroom.

He knocked on the flimsy door. "Aimee?" The door swung wide, and the sight of a tennis shoe sticking out behind the shower curtain alerted his brain.

Sweeping into the bathroom, he tore back the shower curtain.

The Face of Evil

Aimee's sightless eyes stared past him. Fully clothed, her body was slumped in the beige tiled tub. Pink water hovered on the edge and dripped steadily onto the floor as the tub threatened to overflow.

"Oh, god. Aimee! No!" Jason made a desperate lunge for the body. Water sloshed onto the floor as he reached for her pulse. Even in the panicked movement, the gesture was in vain. Blood bloomed into the disturbed water. A razor blade lay on the floor by his feet.

His hand brushed her neck, but her body was cold and clammy to his touch. He sank onto the toilet with trembling legs and buried his face in his hands.

He sat there and let some of the heaving and the guilt and the sorrow subside before he dialed 911. His stomach churned violently. As imbalanced as she was, Jason never expected this.

Images of Aimee's husband and little boy flashed across his mind. Their deaths had led to this. But it wasn't their fault that Aimee did this.

All that guilt belonged to someone else entirely.

He leaned against the bathroom doorway as he waited for the ambulance, staring vacantly at the body before him. He then whispered, in a voice laced with anger, "This is on you, Paul. Every damn bit of it."

Chapter Twenty-One

FBI Field Office
Tacoma, Washington

"Oh, I almost got it...*yes*. Victory!" Brandy speared a tamarind prawn from the paper container and bit into it with glee.

"I can't believe you can rebuild your own Ducati and chase criminals across cyberspace, but you don't know how to use chopsticks?" Allie laughed.

"I grew up on all-American fare. If you mixed your ketchup with mayo, you had radical leanings in my house."

"Seriously?"

"Truth. We all grew up with the same St. Matthew's Parish cookbook. It's all jello molds, Hamburger Helper, and meatloaf. They gift it to you on your wedding day, along with cholesterol medication and thirty-seven casserole dishes. If you deviate from the rules, no one lets you date their son. It's very strict.

How about you? You grew up on a farm, right? Where did you develop a taste for Asian cuisine?

"My biology professor in college was from Thailand. She was an incredible teacher and an even better cook. She would invite us over to her place for dinner, and I eventually became her teaching assistant. Also, chopsticks aren't actually Thai. But her husband was from Vietnam, and they had a bit of a food rivalry. I never had anything like it growing up, so she taught me how to cook.

"Can you make golden duck?" Brandy asked.

"Oh no. That would be expert level. But I can do Mediterranean meatballs and a decent pad thai."

"If the food I ate growing up tasted this wonderful, I'd have spent more time in the kitchen instead of the garage growing up." Brandy stabbed a noodle with her chopsticks and slurped it down. After five hours of non-stop work in her online universe, Allie had ordered them dinner from her favorite spot, Thai Pepper.

She had been amazed to watch the vivacious data analyst shrink back at the site of the simple wooden utensils. Allie quickly put together a makeshift chopstick assist. Folding the paper wrapper into a tight square, she tucked it between the two sticks and wrapped it in a rubber band.

"Ta-da." Allie handed over the tightly shaped contraption.

"That may be the nicest thing anyone has ever done for me, Bishop."

"I'm not a super noob anymore?" Allie teased.

"Not today." She raised her coconut water and toasted Allie's Snapple. They had been camped out in the "tomb" all evening. Brandy had taken over the space outside her office as a casual lounge away from the high-tech gear. There was a camaraderie that developed out of persistence and laughter.

A chime trilled on Brandy's computer back inside her office. "Oh, that's a good sound," she sing-songed.

"Yeah?"

"I had Rosie—"

"Who?"

"Rosie. She's what I call my slice of the FBI mainframe I get to play in. I've augmented her with my special proprietary setup for a localized supercomputer. It pings off several servers here in the city not typically in use at night. The public library is a wonderful resource, and so is the Y and the UofW School of Dentistry. Go figure. They have a surprising amount of computing power and bandwidth after about four in the afternoon. Anyway, I had Rosie sift through the lives of our four victims, looking for any overlap, but it didn't turn anything up. Now that you've got a suspect, I ran the program again, looking to see if Robert Hall is our missing link."

Brandy was back at her desk now, tapping away at the keys. Soon enough, the familiar face of Robert Hall appeared on the screen. "It appears we got a hit. I've located a link between your victim, Rhonda McTavish, and your suspect."

"Really? How?" Brandy was a machine of efficiency and technical knowledge which made Allie feel way out of her depth.

"Hall was employed by a temp agency shortly after his release from prison. It looks like they were a clearinghouse for those in the state penal system returning to the workforce. Rhonda McTavish was a supervisor while Robert was going through training. Before they sent him out to jobs."

"So they may have had contact?" Allie grabbed the printout as soon as it came off the printer.

"At least on paper. Data analytics is a bit more of an art than a science."

"You're like a colorful Lara Croft."

"Thank you. But without the guns. I'm a pacifist. It's the reason I'm an analyst and not an agent."

"Interesting."

"I'll tell you the story on our next online stakeout. But I'm ready for some more *Hidden Tavern*. What do you think so far?"

"I think I get the gist of it. Basically, players come to chat about games, ask questions, and swap gear?" Allie was new to any kind of gaming, so the last hour had been a crash course on what was possible in certain online environments.

"Bingo. Think of *Hidden Tavern* as an online watering hole. Over the past few nights, I've been on here creating a profile and getting to know the local fantasy players. Did you have a chance to look over those user chats yet?"

"Yeah, I didn't turn up anything of consequence. Do we think this is where Robert Hall and Stephanie connected?"

"Based on their previous internet activity, this was a central hub of their communication. Looks like more players are getting on. We'll be able to engage someone in a little bit. Until then, you and I are going on a quest!" She handed Allie a video game controller and pressed X, sending her into a vivid online world of orcs, elves, dwarves, and dragons.

Brandy chatted easily while she kept her eyes on multiple screens and sauntered through piles of code the gaming platform was built on. "Stephanie seemed to have covered her tracks on multiple levels," she said as she scanned the chat in several different rooms. Brandy pointed to the screen. "Your boy Robert was on here too, less than a week ago."

In the online world, Allie had trouble walking in a straight line and regularly found herself turning in circles and walking into walls.

"Bingo, mother lover!" Brandy clicked on a file that revealed Robert Hall was the identity behind the name Galavant. "He left a wide trail of personal information that suddenly dried up forty-eight hours ago."

As the night wore on, Brandy had more and more conversations with online players, but still no information on Stephanie or her username.

Allie struggled in the matches as Brandy assisted. The game controller in her hand was clunky and cumbersome.

"Come on, Allie! Take off his head!" Brandy shouted as Allie struggled to swing a heavy sword and decapitate an Orc that was threatening her hoard of life jewels.

"Holy crap," Allie said when she finally defeated her foe. "I honestly think I would have been better at this if we were fighting in person."

"You think you could defeat a three-hundred-pound warrior with a battle axe in hand-to-hand combat?" She popped a piece of gum in her mouth.

"I don't know how your hands are so fast at this thing." Allie tossed the controller on the desk and glanced at her watch. "I'm not sure how much closer this is getting us to Stephanie's killer."

"Be patient. While we've been playing, Rosie's been engaging hundreds of players in AI-generated conversations. If anyone makes it past the first half dozen prompts, my system alerts me, and I take over."

"Really?"

"Think of it like supremely efficient online canvassing."

"Wow."

"You didn't think we were just playing video games the whole time, did you?"

Allie shrugged and looked at the floor.

"Playing the games builds credibility for our online profile," Brandy explained.

"I don't know how you do all this." Allie yawned. "I should probably call it a night."

One of Brandy's bait chats popped up on the screen.

"We got a nibble!" Brandy rolled her chair up close to the desk and took over for the AI.

"Who is Starcatcher365?" Allie squinted at the dialogue unfolding on screen.

"Not sure yet." The highlighted text appeared on Brandy's oversized screen on the wall above their heads. "Let's see what they're talking about."

Erham_8: I know we aren't supposed to talk about it, but has anyone heard from Galavant?

Starcatcher365: We're still not talking about it, lol.

Erham_8: Yeah, but I'm kinda worried now. It's been three days.

Starcatcher365: I told you he was always a live wire. That one day he was gonna blow.

Erham_8: For real. Do you think he hurt Charlemagne? Charlemagne's been offline too.

Starcatcher365: Like I said, we're still not talking about it.

Erham_8: Yeah, yeah. I'm starting a game, wanna join?

Starcatcher365: Time to discover Ketheric's secret.

"Who's Ketheric?" Allie wanted to know.

"That's the bad guy in the game," Brandy pointed out.

"So now they're talking about the video game. What about their friend Charlemagne?" Allie was bewildered. None of this made any sense to her.

"This is their safe space," Brandy tried to explain. "It's their reality where fake things feel real and real things—like death—feel fake. It's a coping mechanism."

"I still don't get it." Allie slumped into her chair.

"To each his own. But you don't have to, that's what you have me for. And Rosie. But are you ready for this? Charlemagne purchased titanium battle armor and a Hawthorne potion with a personal credit card last May, and the name on the invoice was—*Stephanie Mercer*.

"Whoa."

Brandy took a screenshot of the invoice and printed it for their files.

"So if Charlemagne is Stephanie, and Galavant is Robert Hall, can you find out the name behind Erham_8?"

"Of course, just give me a little time. Check back in the morning, and I'll see what I got."

"Thank you, and you too, Rosie." Allie gently tapped the server. "I'd like to pay them a visit *in real life* and see if they know where Robert Hall is hiding out."

Chapter Twenty-Two

Residence of Eric Hamilton
Tacoma, Washington

"Morning, Eastman," Allie croaked in a hoarse whisper as she climbed into his vehicle.

"Dang, you don't look so good." Agent Ryan Eastman gave Allie a head-to-toe inspection in a glance, then pulled out of the parking garage. "Here." He handed her a brown bag with an energy drink wrapped inside. "Heard you were slaying Orcs with Brandy Harroway last night. Figured you could use something a little stronger than a Snapple this morning."

"God bless you." Allie cracked open the energy drink. "I swear she's a robot. Does she sleep or does she simply respawn in the tomb?"

"Why do you think we call her a vampire?" Eastman chuckled. "Hagan had a chemical analysis run on that red tea she drinks all the time."

"Let me guess, it's the blood of her conquests mixed with

boba and unicorn sweat." Allie took a sip of the drink and immediately felt better.

"So where is your partner this morning?" he asked, and unwrapped a breakfast sandwich. It filled the small space with the scent of bacon and egg.

I wish I knew.

"Marze didn't tell me." Allie fished a pack of almonds out of her bag and dropped them in her hand. "Only cleared my request for someone to accompany me on this interview."

Eastman shook his head.

"Do you have something you'd like to say on the subject?"

"Not me. That's a conversation you need to have with Jason."

Allie didn't enjoy talking behind her partner's back, but she was tired of all the secrecy. "I'm the last person to gossip, but I gotta say, the whole office is avoiding something, and it's making me nervous."

"You have good instincts." He turned at a red light and started away from downtown. "Look, all I can say is, I was assigned to Jason after everything that went down. Let's just say I'm surprised he's still here. He's a good guy. He's got a big heart, maybe too big. You know? Clouds his judgment. Something dramatic is always happening in his life, first his partner, now his wife."

She didn't like Victoria's cancer being held against her partner. It wasn't his fault.

"Thanks for your input, Eastman. But unless you're going to share more than your opinions and baseless claims, it doesn't help me."

"I'm just saying you have reasons to ask questions. I'm just trying to help."

"Really? This is you helping?" The Red Bull was ripping through her veins now, and she was ready for a fight. She was sleep-deprived and edgy with caffeine, but most of all, she was tired of ignoring the giant secret surrounding her partner.

"Rawr, tiger." Eastman gave her an approving once-over. "I like this side of you. Look at you defending your partner. Careful, or people might think you have a heart."

"Well, we wouldn't want that now, would we?" Allie gave the faintest smile over her drink.

"So this guy we're going to have a chat with...what do I need to know about him?"

Allie cracked her knuckles and tried to get back on track. Eastman was simply trying to help, and she could appreciate his position. It didn't look good for Jason lately. But something inside of her told her to go against her instincts and trust her partner. She just prayed she wasn't making a massive mistake.

Eastman pulled into the neighborhood and parked down from the house in question. Allie flipped open her phone and read the note from Brandy that had rolled in around three in the morning. "Eric Hamilton. According to Brandy, he's a friend of my missing person of interest, Robert Hall. They went to college together. Looks like he's a content creator."

Allie examined the driver's license info they had for Erham_8, aka Eric Hamilton.

Eastman frowned. "A content creator? What the hell is that?"

"YouTube, TikTok, Twitch. It means he makes videos of himself online and gets paid for it."

"You mean he can afford a place in this neighborhood by making TikTok videos? You gotta be kidding me."

"Well, the place is listed in his mom's name."

He switched the car off and unbuckled. "All right, let's go shake this tree."

They approached the Hamilton family's sprawling mid-century home, and Allie knocked on the door.

It was opened by a tiny woman in tennis whites. "Mrs. Hamilton?"

"Yes? What can I do for you?"

"I'm Agent Bishop. This is Agent Eastman of the FBI. We need to have a word with your son, Eric. Is he available?

"Eric? Is something wrong, officer?"

Eastman took over. "It's agent, ma'am, and please, it would be helpful if we could speak with Eric." Something about his age and stature melted the opposition of the middle-aged woman, who blithely swept open the door and invited the strangers into her living room.

"Hey Mom, we're outta 2 percent—" A stocky man with thinning hair and a bad case of bed head stepped out of the kitchen wearing slippers and Green Lantern pajamas. Allie decided not to judge, not after a night spent with Brandy fighting for the empire of Enon.

"Eric, this man and his partner are with the FBI."

He blanched as his mother invited everyone to have a seat at the dining room table off the main foyer.

"What is this about?" Eric said.

"We need to ask you some questions about Robert Hall," Allie said.

A frown line appeared between his eyes. "Robert? Why?"

She ignored the question. "When was the last you spoke with him?"

"About a week ago."

"Over the phone?"

"Yeah—what is this? Has he done something?"

"How long have you known him?" Eastman jumped in.

Eric shifted in his chair. "We had a couple of classes together back at Green River Community College. We reconnected online a couple of years ago after he..."

"Was released from prison." Allie filled in the blanks. "We're aware of his history. What else can you tell us?"

"Uh, I helped him get the job at Jimmy Z's."

Allie glanced at his mother, who looked a shade of green and had yet to say anything beyond her initial greeting. "Is Robert's past why you were concerned about his behavior toward Stephanie Mercer?"

"How do you know about that?" Eric gruffed.

"You expressed concern about your friend Charlemagne, aka Stephanie Mercer, recently."

Eric's chair scraped against the floor as he stood up. "That was a private conversation. Who told you that?"

Eastman waved a hand at his chair. "Have a seat, Mr. Hamilton. We have more questions."

He stood there glaring at them.

"In that conversation, you were specifically concerned about Robert's interaction with Stephanie," Allie continued. "Why is that?"

Eric ran a hand through his greasy hair. "Look, I've never talked with the FBI before. And you guys being here in my house makes me a little nervous. I don't want to say something that's going to get me in trouble."

Allie could understand his discomfort at them being here. It was a fairly normal reaction. But his reluctance to say something that might get him in trouble was concerning. "What exactly might get you in trouble?" she asked. "Is there something you're hiding?"

"No—I'm not hiding anything. I just don't want to say anything that might get Robert in trouble."

"Did he do something to hurt Stephanie?"

He looked away. "I don't know. But I'm not saying anything," he repeated.

"Stephanie is dead, Eric."

Eric's mother uttered a sharp cry as a hand flew over her mouth. "Eric?"

He went pale and slowly slumped into his chair. "She's what?"

"Her body was discovered on Monday. The medical examiner confirmed she was strangled. Her body was left exposed to be devoured by animals." Allie studied his reaction.

He cursed, and his mother placed a hand on his arm.

"If you know something, now would be the time to tell us," Allie said.

He pinched the bridge of his nose and cursed again. "Look, Charlemagne, Galavant, and I were a regular squad. I make videos of advanced players succeeding in video games. They're kind of like training videos for others who want to learn. Reactions to graphics, bugs, Easter eggs, and the like. I had an eighty-twenty split with Steph and Robert, ten percent each on all income we brought in from the videos to compensate them for their time. Steph didn't need the money. It was research for her, a way to blow off steam, and to build credibility as a gamer. When she transferred her cut to Robert last year, that's when I knew they were more than friends. I'm not sure what their relationship was officially, but there was something there."

"We have a chat where you expressed concern that Robert might have hurt Stephanie," Allie said. "When did you get concerned for her safety?"

"After Steph's mom died last week, she offered to do another training video, but her heart wasn't in it. She couldn't focus, couldn't hold it together. I told her we'd take a break and give her some time off. Robert and I could do them on our own until she was ready." He ran a meaty hand across his chin. "But she had something else in mind. She said that the feds thought her mother was murdered by a serial killer, and she wanted us to help her track him down. She was always a big fan of true crime. I think she thought it was like some kind of real-life quest. But Robert freaked. He didn't want any part of it. They screamed at each other. I bailed. I really don't like conflict." He ran his hands through his hair. "God, she's dead?"

"You said that Robert freaked, that they were screaming at each other," Allie said. "Do you think he could have killed her?"

The younger man looked dazed. Then he shrugged. "Maybe? He's practically the rage monster of the online world. I've seen him smash stuff when he's pissed. His eyes literally turn red—it's creepy. I swear, if he killed her, I'm going to..." He let the sentence drag.

"As you may know, Robert has vanished. It's imperative that we find him."

Eric nodded. "Robert has an old RV. It's registered in his grandfather's name. We partied in it a couple of times, but I have no idea where he might have taken it."

"Do you remember the location?"

"I left my AirPods there once and had to go back the next day. I can probably look it up on my location history." He fished his phone out of his pajama pocket, and Allie handed him a card.

By the time the two agents were buckling their seat belts inside Eastman's vehicle, Allie's phone pinged with the location. "Looks like a campground on the edge of Wapato State Park." She punched in the coordinates.

"Inform Marze and alert the local police," Eastman advised as he drove. "Ask them to post a person at the entrance, and we'll coordinate at the rendezvous. Make sure they know not to engage Hall without us unless he attempts to leave the premises."

* * *

"ROBERT HALL, THIS IS THE FBI!" Allie called out after knocking on the door. "We have a warrant for your arrest. Come out with your hands up." Flashing blues and reds danced across her face as they stepped back from the ancient Jayco RV.

On their route here, the state police had informed them the subject was on-site. Allie's nerves were on edge, but she was also enjoying an adrenaline rush that put every sense on high alert. Now, they waited, and she knew that her best tool, outside of her sidearm, was common sense and patience.

She banged on the door a second time, repeating her

demand, and stepped away from the RV. Sweat trickled down her back despite the cool evening air. Behind her, she could hear the rustle of uniforms.

The door to the RV flew outward, and Robert Hall emerged on unsteady feet, his hands above his head.

"Don't shoot," he slurred, and stumbled down the steps and into the dirt on his knees. Allie felt the thunder of footsteps behind her as she clicked a pair of handcuffs on him, her nose curling at the acrid scent of sweat and cheap rum.

"Robert Hall, you're under arrest for suspicion of murder."

Chapter Twenty-Three

TFO Holding Facility
Tacoma, Washington

"Allie. We've got your guy in interrogation room six," Marze greeted her as she emerged from the elevator doors and onto her floor. "Nice job."

"Thank you, sir."

"Scale of one to ten, how drunk is your suspect?" he asked as they headed for her office.

"With ten being the worst?" Allie asked, stowing her windbreaker and flack jacket back into her go bag. "Eleven. I nearly got a buzz standing next to him."

"Well, the arrest sobered him up a bit," Jason said from her doorway. "And the uniform that brought him in claims he spewed chunks all over the floor of the black and white."

Marze pinned Jason with a straight face. "King? You ready for this?"

"No," Jason admitted. "But Allie's got this. I'm here to support her."

"Works for me," Marze said. "Keep me posted, you two." And he headed off.

Allie glanced at her partner. His face was haggard, his eyes sunken. He wore a denim jacket, a white T-shirt, gray jeans, and trainers. She had never seen him out of a suit on a weekday. One more sign that something was deeply upsetting his world.

"You okay?" she asked. "You need any of your green juice or anything?"

"It's going to take a lot more than juice for me today." He shrugged and glanced over the case board. "Look, I'll explain when I can. Right now, bring me up to speed. You can take point with Hall. I'll just observe."

She nodded. "I've spoken with a mutual friend of Stephanie and Hall. He confirmed they were in a relationship, but after the death of Helen Mercer, things went south fast. Stephanie tried to enlist the help of Hall and another friend to track down her mother's killer."

"Really?"

"The friend witnessed a fight between her and Hall and bailed. Brandy uncovered an online chat where the friend expressed concern that Hall may have hurt her. Speaking with him in person, he said it wasn't beyond the realm of possibility that Hall could have killed her."

"Okay, but do you think Hall carves off women's faces for fun?" Jason asked. "Video games to serial killers may be a bit of a stretch."

"There's still a lot that doesn't add up," she admitted. "Cutting off faces and dousing Stephanie's body so it's mangled by animals speaks of an entirely different psychological profile. There has to be more going on here than we can see right now. But I have enough evidence to question Hall for her murder at the very least."

"Then press away. Let's see where it leads."

"Allie." Brandy burst in and handed over a thin manila file folder. "Jason, good. I'm glad I caught you. Take a look at this."

Allie flipped it open, and Jason looked over her shoulder. He grunted in approval. Allie finally took a deep breath. She felt a rush of confidence. "Let's do this."

"Mr. Hall, what part of don't leave town didn't you understand?" Allie asked as she pulled out a chair in the interrogation room. Robert Hall wore a ratty Oakland A's jersey, cut-off cargo shorts, and flip-flops.

"I'm an ex-con," he moaned without lifting his head. "I went away for manslaughter. I know how the system works. You cops always go after the easiest patsy you can find. Me, in this case."

"I'm not a cop," Allie reminded him, and scooted her chair in. Jason took the one beside her.

"You think that fancy badge makes you any smarter? No matter what I say or do, just because I've been convicted, I'm automatically your prime suspect. Be serious. Did you even investigate anyone else?"

"I didn't get a chance. You skipped town."

"You know I don't have an alibi for the night Steph disappeared. This is not my first rodeo. I ran because *this* scenario was practically inevitable."

"So you admit you were responsible for the death of Stephanie Mercer and her mother."

"Absolutely not." He groaned and set a hand over his stomach.

"If you puke in my interrogation room, I will drag a mop and bucket here myself and make you clean it up." He burped, and Allie nearly fainted from the stench. "Does the name Rhonda McTavish mean anything to you?"

"Should it?"

"She was a supervisor at Green Apple Staffing," Allie explained.

"So?"

"You were employed by Green Apple Staffing for twelve months."

"Worst twelve months of my life, even worse than being inside."

Allie set a picture of Rhonda down on the table.

He shrugged. "Doesn't ring a bell. What does this have to do with Stephanie?" he asked.

Allie placed a new photo of Rhonda on the table, this one without her face.

"Oh god." Robert recoiled. "Is that..." His stomach visibly lurched, but he managed to keep everything down. "Is that what happened to those women, the ones that look like Helen?"

"That's Rhonda McTavish, this is Tamara Heathers, and this is Helen Mercer." Allie laid out all the photos in front of him. She studied his reaction carefully, but no dilation of the pupils, no flush of the cheeks, nothing to indicate pleasure or pride. Instead, he pushed the pictures away and placed his head in his hands.

"Please, no. I didn't kill anyone."

"Stephanie called you, didn't she, right before disappeared?"

"Robert, we have a call from a burner phone to each of these four women," Jason added. "If we find the burner in your things or a receipt to the same gas station where it was purchased, you're going away for a long time."

"I don't have a burner phone." He sat up finally and looked desperately at the two agents. "I didn't kill anyone."

"But you admit you texted Stephanie threatening her?"

"She was obsessed. She thought she was a friggin' private investigator, and she wouldn't let it go. I wasn't going to mess with a federal investigation. I told her to leave me alone."

"Is that what happened, Robert?" Jason asked. "She wouldn't take no for an answer?"

"Hey, I cared for Stephanie. Enough to stay away from her when I was upset."

"That's not what Eric Hamilton said," Allie told him. "He witnessed a fight you had with Stephanie and expressed concern over her safety."

Robert blinked. "You talked with Eric? He said that?" He smashed the table with his hand. "You have to believe me."

"You know what I believe, Robert? I believe in numbers. I believe in facts." Allie laid out several receipts for large amounts from an off-track betting site.

Robert slumped in his chair.

"The numbers don't lie, Robert," Allie said. "You owed a

significant amount of cash, the way I see it. The cut from Eric's gaming videos wasn't cutting it. Stephanie even offered you her take. But it still wasn't enough, so you found another side hustle." This time, Allie set down a corresponding spreadsheet with hefty deposits over the past several months from a convicted drug dealer.

"I have to hand it to you, Robert," Jason said. "You are a busy man. Did Stephanie find out about your side hustle?"

Robert stared at the evidence that was mounting on the table.

"She wanted a gun."

Allie frowned. "A gun? For what?"

"She called me all hyped up about something her mother had said, something about her new walking friend or something like that. She was planning to confront him, I think."

"She said that?"

"Yeah. Stephanie and I had an encrypted chatroom, and we'd check in once a day at an agreed time. That's where she asked me."

"Why did she want a gun?"

"I didn't ask," Robert said. "But I refused to help her."

Allie struggled to find the truth between her suspect and the evidence.

"I didn't kill Stephanie," he continued. "And I didn't kill her mother. I wasn't going to help her hunt down her mother's killer, no matter how badly Stephanie wanted revenge. She kept asking me how it felt to kill someone with my bare hands. It was sick. I told her I hoped she never had to find out. I may have questionable morals, but I'm not a killer. Not anymore. That's a line I won't ever cross again."

They were at a stalemate.

Robert sighed. "I can give you my alibi for the night Stephanie was killed."

"An alibi?" Jason said. "I thought you went for a walk?"

"I have a standing date with someone," he explained. "I leave my phone at the bar and tell them to cover for me in case anyone comes asking."

"Who?"

Robert squirmed. "I'm not scared of you. There are worse things than prison."

"Is she worth it?" Jason asked.

Allie glanced at her partner, confused.

"Robert here has an alibi that puts him in a compromising situation," Jason explained. "So compromising, he would prefer to go back to prison than share where he was. Or should I say who he was with?"

They stared at the man in cuffs sitting before them.

"Jamie Hickson," he finally blurted.

Jason shook his head. "Good lord. You've got some balls."

"Someone want to clue me in?" Allie's head swiveled between the two in confusion.

"Jamie Hickson is the wife of David Hickson," Jason said. "You might know him by his alias 'Big Daddy High.' He's one of the largest importers of marijuana in the Pacific Northwest."

"When I was in prison, I shared a cell with David. Jamie and I met when I got out. She came to check on me and brought me a home-cooked meal." He shrugged. "One thing led to another. She got me the connection for the side hustle. I dispense pot to my neighbors. That's all."

"That's all?" Allie asked.

"Jamie and I are consenting adults." He smirked, but then got serious. "Yes, Jamie's my alibi. We were together weekly, and my boss would cover for me so David's guys didn't catch on. You can ask either of them. I know I don't have a future with Jamie—she has kids with him. I don't know what she sees in me. Maybe she feels some freedom doing something outside of David's purview. He's not just a person. He's a corporation, a way of life, and you can't walk away. That's why I didn't tell Stephanie. It's hard to meet women at my age, with my background." He sighed and shook his head. "I don't know if she knew about Jamie, but it was obvious Stephanie and I weren't meant to be a while ago."

"Why didn't you just tell us you had an alibi?" Allie asked.

"I don't want word to get out that I'm taking care of Jamie on the side. I promised I'd keep it to myself."

"You're more afraid of Big Daddy than the FBI?" Allie asked.

"I know how my bread is buttered. The Hicksons take good care of me."

"Until word gets out that you're sleeping with the boss's wife," Jason retorted. "What will she say if we show up on her doorstep?"

"Good luck. She's got the best lawyers in town," he sneered, but then softened. "Look, you don't need to show up on her doorstep, for god's sake. If David finds out about us, we're both dead. Just call her. Call her and ask." Robert shook his head, clearly irritated by the whole scenario. "And now"—he leaned back in his chair and folded his hands over his stomach—"I think I want to speak to my lawyer."

The conversation was over.

Chapter Twenty-Four

FBI Field Office
Tacoma, Washington

"Whoa, you're bleeding."

Allie looked down at her clenched fist. A faint trickle of blood slipped off and plopped onto the floor. She forced herself to open her hand. The broken shaft of a No. 2 pencil was embedded into the flesh of her palm, but she felt nothing.

"Geez, Allie. Come on. Let's get that cleaned up." She followed Jason into the break room, where he guided her to the sink. "Listen, this is frustrating. But it's not a mistake. You had to look into that scumbag. He's a convicted felon with a violent history who made threats against our victim.

She rinsed cold water over her hand and gently rubbed soap into the tiny wound. "I knew something wasn't lining up. I just couldn't put my finger on it."

"It's not as dire as you think. When we catch the man who

killed Stephanie and when we go to trial, the defense is going to trot out Robert Hall first thing. They're going to use him to create reasonable doubt in our case. It's a no-brainer. Arresting Robert Hall was the best thing you could have done for Stephanie. It proves we looked under every rock and in every hole, that we left no stone unturned. He's not our guy. It hurts. This moment feels like a setback, but it's not a waste of time. I promise."

He was right. In her focus on finding and interrogating Robert, she hadn't considered any of that. She turned the water off and blotted her hand with a paper towel.

"Are you with me?" he asked.

Allie nodded.

"Good." He motioned to her hand. "You're lucky they don't put lead in those things anymore."

"The clock is ticking," she said on their way back to her desk. " If Robert Hall isn't carving off women's faces, that means someone else is still out there, probably befriending another beautiful woman. Someone's mom, grandmother, or wife, and she'll get dumped in the Puyallup."

"You were one person doing a two-person job," he said quietly. "This is on me."

That got Allie's attention. She quickly ran her fingers over her eyes, wiping away a frustrated tear. She dropped into her chair and swiveled to look at her partner as he hovered in the doorway.

"I owe you an apology," he said. "I'm not one of those people who are very good at keeping my personal and private lives separate. So I don't even try that hard. That's why it's been nice to have you get to know Victoria. I am an agent because I care about people. That doesn't end when the case is over. It doesn't start when I walk into the office. I worry about my wife in the middle of the day and my cases in the middle of the night. I'm human. I don't apologize for it."

"You shouldn't have to. I—"

"I'm not done." He crossed his arms and leaned into the door frame. "When I first started with the Bureau, I naively thought there would be a clear distinction between the good guys and bad guys in this job. I thought it would be simple—black and white, us versus them." He shook his head and stared at the ceiling. "Turns out I was wrong."

A heavy silence settled over the two, but Allie didn't say a word. She didn't want to break the bridge of trust that Jason was attempting to build between them.

"There you are." Marze stepped into the kitchen, breaking the spell. "I got your message about Hall. Has his alibi checked out?"

Allie nodded. "I spoke with his fling a few minutes ago."

"He called in a high-priced attorney from Bickner and Pitt. The guy just showed up and walked out with his client," Jason added.

Marze huffed. "So you're back to square one?"

"Not exactly," Allie said. "We still have the burner phone connection between our victims."

"It's a long shot, but we've done more with less," Marze reminded her. "It's Friday night. Go home, get some rest. Let the dust settle and come back strong." Marze disappeared around the corner.

"Stephanie asked Hall for a gun," Jason reminded her.

"First thing Monday, we need to revisit the findings on her mother's case."

"I've already been over every inch of it," she sighed.

"We'll do it together."

She thought she might have detected an apology in that statement.

Drained from the day's events, they seemed unable to find the thread of their previous conversation. Jason returned to his desk, leaving Allie to pack up her things while trying not to brood about her failure. She was disappointed that he didn't share more of his story. Whatever he had to say, she just needed to be patient.

Shouldering her satchel, she started for the elevator. By the looks of it, she was one of the first people to call it a day. Most of her fellow agents were still at their desks, bantering or finishing up paperwork before they checked out for the weekend. As it was, Allie was beat, and she planned on taking Marze's advice to rest up.

Getting into her car, she fired up the stereo and rolled down the windows. As was typical for a Friday afternoon, traffic was congested, but she soon made her way through it and started for home. Her thoughts bounced between the various details of the case. It took sheer willpower and finding a song on the radio she liked to steer her mind away from work.

Finally, she neared home. But as she reached her block, she kept driving, passing it up and continuing into a modest suburb. Sitting in an empty apartment wasn't going to help anything.

So she took a left at the intersection toward Gig Harbor and joined the line of commuters escaping the city over the Tacoma Narrows Bridge. The scent of salt water tugged at her senses, unraveling something that had knotted up inside her through the course of today's events.

Allie stared at the horizon and slipped into the restorative meditation of the ocean. Only when the band-aid on her hand brushed against the steering wheel did Allie consider the question tugging at the back of her mind. She delicately touched the bruised flesh on her palm. After interrogating Robert Hall, she had been alarmed to find the broken pencil sticking out of her hand. Even more alarmed to see Jason's horror at her self-impalement.

It was moments like this when the single, perennial question of her life came crashing down on her, making it impossible to ignore.

Am I anything like my father?

The stark thought broke out of its mental box and drifted undesired through her mind. Typically, she could keep the darker corners of her soul at bay beneath the consuming concentration of a case. But this one in particular, with a serial killer preying on women, was driving a needle of pain into her subconscious.

Allie had been frustrated by their setback, which she could admit, but the pencil incident spoke to something she wasn't sure she wanted to understand. She had been so furious about her failure that she didn't even notice the pain of a gaping wound, the trickle of blood on the floor, the splintered writing tool. Then there was the troubling stack of broken pencils stashed in the drawer in her desk. Like a growing pile of shame.

Why do I even keep them?

Allie loved the feeling of scratching a No. 2 pencil across a yellow legal pad. It was grace to her perfectionism, a balm to the edge of criticism she heaped on herself when she made a mistake. She never questioned her perfectionism before, but the growing impulse toward even the mildest form of sadism, like the shattered pencils that she tucked quietly away, demanded attention when your father was a serial killer.

She let her mind drift backward in time, seeking out the source of her perfectionism. Was it just her natural personality or a trait she learned trying to seek her father's approval? She remembered him as meticulous, exacting, and even critical, though not always. Could the seed he planted grow into something darker, make her capable of hurting others without remorse?

Jason said that being human made him a good agent, and Allie had to agree. He was excellent at the core of his job, getting assets to share information with the FBI. Allie had sat next to Jason as he interviewed victims. He had a tender touch with hurting people. They confided in him, poured out their stories, and filled in missing details, suspicions, and gut feelings. She had always been envious of this skill, but for the first time, she wondered if it was more of a burden than she ever realized.

Either way, Allie was thankful to have her partner back. The fact that he had started to confide his story gave her solace. She could wait. It helped her realize that she was beginning to trust Marze and Jason. Victoria, too. If she wanted to serve her team, she needed to be a whole person on Monday morning, which meant she needed to get dirt under her fingers. She needed the press of hard work and sunshine to help her sweat out today's adrenaline and defeat.

She needed the farm. And she needed Grams.

Chapter Twenty-Five

Residence of Etta Bishop
Gig Harbor, Washington

"You wanna talk about it?" Grams slowly lowered herself onto the porch step alongside her granddaughter.

The crickets chirped their summer song, and the smell of freshly cut grass filled Allie with a sense of accomplishment she hadn't felt in weeks. Arriving at her childhood home unannounced, she had searched for a task she could throw herself into. Something to absorb her body and mind and throw off the heavy weight of the workweek.

In the barn, Allie had stripped out of her professional persona and changed into her grandfather's coveralls. She tied the navy sleeves around her waist like a belt and fired up the mower. In her tank top, she enjoyed the heat of the summer sun on her skin, allowing the mindless roar of the engine to drown out the noise in her head. She found solace in the straight lines that grew across the sprawling backyard of Grams's small farm.

"I just got off the phone with Bill Tubbins. His grandson was supposed to come out tomorrow and mow. He told me to tell you hello."

"Will? How old is he now?"

"Fifteen," Grams replied.

Allie vaguely remembered a little blond boy in striped OshKosh overalls. "Fifteen? Time flies."

"It does. I remember when your feet barely touched the pedals on that John Deere. I was sure you would tip it into the pond, but your grandfather knew you could handle it."

"I was eleven, I think."

"But you didn't look it," Grams recalled with a wistful grin. "You were a tiny slip of a thing, all elbows and knees."

"Everyone always thought I was eight."

"Till you opened your mouth and started using all your two-dollar words."

Allie smiled. She stared into the fading evening light, the bright blue of the mid-summer sky turning pink and then dark blue as the first stars began to wink overhead.

"I just needed to do something with my hands," Allie admitted. "I spent all week inside making such little progress that it's embarrassing. I needed to see something get accomplished. I was getting twitchy."

"Nothing feels better than good clean work," Grams agreed. "If I'd known you were coming, I would have picked up something at the market. I don't keep much here at the house when it's just me."

They had feasted on tomato sandwiches with freshly baked bread, cucumber salad with dill, and homemade peach cobbler, all right from the farm. Grams had offered to bring up a ham from the cellar, but Allie had objected. They enjoyed the life-giving nourishment and the simplicity of it all.

"It was the best meal I've had in a long time. And anything you can get at the market isn't comparable to what you grow here."

"Ha!" Grams resettled herself on the stoop. "So you went to Toula's up in Seattle this week?"

"That was something else, Grams. You should have seen it. It's such a beautiful space. Only problem is that it comes at a ridiculous price tag. It would make your eyes water."

Grams harrumphed accordingly.

"Did you ever meet Sadie Talbot?" Allie asked.

"I remember her. She was a friend of your mother's."

"You know that after we caught up to Mick Shepherd last month, the FBI searched our vacation cabin?" Allie said. "By all appearances, Shepherd had spent some time squatting in there."

"Yes, they called me and asked permission so they wouldn't have to get a warrant."

"During their search, they found a journal."

"A journal? Whose?"

"It was Mom's. She had started it for me."

Grams said nothing but waited for Allie to unpack her burden.

"Sadie Talbot's name was inside, so I reached out to her. That's who treated me to Toula's."

"And here I was thinking that the FBI was starting to pay their agents far too many of my tax dollars."

Allie laughed. "Trust me, they're definitely not."

"So you wanted to speak to an old friend of your mother's, hoping that would bring you closer to her."

Allie loved this woman. "Yes. I was hoping she might know something about where she went, why she disappeared. After all this time, I hoped the pieces would come together. I feel this sudden urgency to know more about Mom and her final days. But, I don't know, maybe it was just reading her thoughts to me? I haven't had anything like closure. Not ever. And as I get closer to the age she was when she disappeared, I just want to know what really happened to her."

The pair sat in silence for a long time, staring into the serene sunset.

"I never understood it," Grams said finally. "But I've never believed your mother left. I know that in my heart. I love her like my own daughter. And oh, how she loved you. So the only other option is that something terrible happened to her—but that was just as difficult to think about—it hurts right here whenever I do." Grams tapped a bony finger to her chest.

Allie let the words sink in deep.

"Johanna was born to be a mother," Grams continued. "It was in her DNA. She nurtured stray cats around here, stray people like Sadie Talbot—even your father. When they got married, I was so hopeful and relieved. I wasn't a natural nurturer. Your father was sensitive, and we were a mismatched set from the beginning. I didn't know that until you came along. For years after his arrest, I thought I messed your father up, that how he was was my fault, me and Gramps—I was democratic in my defeated parenting theories. But then we got a second chance with you."

Allie swatted away a moth and waited for her to continue.

"With you, it was easy. We were older and a little wiser, humbled by what happened with your dad. I think we were both just grateful we got to keep you. That the state would allow another young person in our home after the way your father turned out. It seemed like a miracle, and I wouldn't question it. Course, I knew it came at a cost to you. The price you paid to live with us was that Johanna was gone."

Allie hadn't ever heard this side of her grandmother's story. They always lived in the present, with beans to plant, apples to harvest, wood to chop, and dishes to wash. It had been a simple dance of survival that eased Allie through its steps with a tender grace.

"I never believed Johanna would run off," Grams said finally. "Not for a minute. She loved you too much to leave you without a word. And when they found her car… We all knew it meant something terrible, but who had the heart to say it out loud? Not me. But I was always thankful that Beau was coming around more and asking us for help with you. It felt good to be needed in your lives." She shrugged. "By the time you came to our house for good, I didn't know what to say to you on the subject of either of your parents."

"We didn't talk much back then," Allie agreed.

"We were so stunned when it all came out. Those years after your father's arrest and trial were so miserable. For all of us. No canvas is immune to grief."

"Grams, do you think he did it? Do you think he killed her?"

"Get me that shawl on the rocking chair, will you?"

Allie stood up and grabbed the pink blanket Etta had

crocheted. She lovingly draped it over her shoulders and found her spot beside her again.

"Your father stopped talking to us much after Johanna disappeared. I don't know the answer to your question, Allie. Your father had a second life in which he killed people. Did he kill your mother? I spent many a night lying awake asking myself that. The truth is, I don't know. Her car being found in a bad part of Seattle didn't fit your father's methods though."

Maybe she would never know the answer. Maybe no one would. But now, after reading and re-reading the journal, that wasn't so satisfactory anymore.

"But how was your time with Sadie?" Grams asked.

"I was hoping I would remember her, but it was vague. I remember her out at the cabin. She would come out when Dad claimed he had a night job in town he had committed to. But now that I think about it, he never introduced me to her, and we never met officially. I'd go to bed, and someone would come to the house. By the time I woke up, she would be gone, not unlike a dream. That's odd, right?"

"Everything about your childhood was odd, except maybe Johanna," Grams sighed. "And we all thought she was kookie back then. She was so playful, touchy-feely, and free with her emotions. Turns out we were the sick ones."

"Grams, I don't think I ever heard you say that. I loved it here. You and Gramps were good to me."

"Did you feel loved?"

"I did." Allie leaned against her wiry, independent grandmother. Touch was never one of their strong suits, but it never bothered Allie. "I felt safe. That was the best thing you gave me. I felt safe, and that was better than love. The rest came in time. You kept my world together. You and Gramps taught me to survive and thrive in a cruel, broken world. It was the best kind of love, the kind I needed most."

Allie felt Grams release a silent sob, eyes trained on the last vestiges of light hovering above the treetops. She felt the woman's tiny but powerful hand grab her arm and squeeze it. "After everything you went through, I was so scared we would hurt you," Grams said through her tears. "I'll never forget the first time you hugged me, after everything. It was nine months and two weeks after you came to stay with us. I think I'd been holding my breath since the day the social worker brought you here with that musty old duffle bag. I was so desperate to scoop you up and cradle you in my arms. But I didn't want to scare you. You had these giant, sad eyes, like you'd been to hell and back." Grams patted Allie's arm. "One night, you got sick, spiked a fever. I brought you a cold rag for your head. Poor little thing. I think it was the first time you let your guard down. You reached out and hugged me. I melted inside. For the first time, I felt a tiny ray of hope, and I knew we were gonna be okay."

It was good to talk like this. It was as if all the years had conspired to gift them memories of the best of what had been.

"I need to ask you something. While we're being honest." Allie rubbed the gash the pencil had left inside her palm. "Am I...am I like my dad? Do you think I have some of him in me?" She braced herself for the answer.

The reply was swift, if not harsh. "You're nothing like my boy."

The declaration made Allie's head swim with relief.

"I can look back now and see something cold and cruel that your father carried in him. No one ever measured up to his standards, even as a little boy. Maybe I didn't want to acknowledge it. I didn't have any other children after all, and I wasn't sure what was normal. But the difference was so stark between your childhood and your father's. You have so much of your mother in you. All her gentleness and curiosity live on in you.

They sat on the porch and watched the stars fill the sky as the day released its hold on the world. The two women shared the space without saying anything else. A bullfrog serenaded them from the pond, and the wind chimes sang in harmony in the evening breeze.

Grams rubbed her thin shoulders and stood. "Welp, I'm off to bed." She looked at her granddaughter and gave her a sad smile. "I want you to know I'm glad you reached out to Sadie Talbot."

Allie's face brightened. "Really? I was nervous telling you."

"I know this is delicate for both of us, but you have a right to your questions. You have a right to know what happened. I see that now. I see the peace you bring to others. In horrible circumstances, it doesn't change the reality, but it helps. No matter what you dig up, we'll survive. We've gotten this far."

"Yes, we have."

"Night, sweet girl."

"Night, Grams."

Allie listened to the screen door slap shut and her grandmother's steps as she made her way to her bedroom. The steady sounds of life always brought her comfort. Not ready to turn in herself, Allie lifted herself off the porch. She pulled up the sleeves of her grandfather's coveralls against the cool night air and inhaled the scent of life trapped in its folds.

She missed Gramps. The pair had been bookends to her

world. Without him, everything leaned precariously, and after he died, Allie wondered when her world would topple.

She walked out to Gramps's workshop, carefully examining the faded woodwork, the rusted hinges, and the ancient equipment. The farm, the orchard, and the giant vegetable garden keeping it all going was Grams's mission in life after Gramps died. But she was seventy-nine this spring. She had a small army of neighbors chipping in to keep her afloat, but how long could she last alone?

Allie flipped on the lamp above Gramps's workbench and perused his shop. She picked up several blocks of wood, feeling their weight, inspecting the knots and shapes, and holding them to the light until she found the one that felt right. Lifting the knife off its peg, she laid it on the stone hearth of the fireplace, the sole source of heat in the shop on long nights.

She found some kindling in the corner, dusty from neglect. Then, lighting a match, she touched it to the bundle of sticks. Allie watched the fire spring to life. She wondered how many cold winter nights Grams visited Gramps's memory here, keeping the place clean and a fire ready in the grate.

She turned the piece of wood in her hand slowly and found the easy rhythm of cut, curve, scrape, turn, and repeat. Allie carved away the extra wood, revealing a rook's small but distinctive form. She whittled away the bulk of the weight around the slender chess piece, leaving its distinctive notched crown. Blowing away the final pieces of dust, she studied it.

She had watched her father for hours over the top of a chessboard. He would study every move on the board before advancing his players across the battlefield. Chess was a language she and her father had shared.

Until it all shattered into a million pieces. Allie rubbed at the scar on the back of her hand—a souvenir from the ravine where her father had killed his final victim. Ten-year-old Allie had screamed at the sight and fled, slicing her hand as her father scrambled up the ravine toward her.

They tried to tell her the nightmare that followed his arrest wasn't her fault. She had helped to stop a killer from hurting anyone else. But in quiet moments, Allie felt guilty for wanting her life back, even living in ignorance with a serial killer.

She turned the wooden chess piece in her hand and wondered what Sadie had left out of their conversation. They both lost when Johanna disappeared. How had she processed her friend's disappearance? Or had she just moved on, burying the grief to cover the pain?

It was why Allie avoided therapy. She didn't believe talking about her broken past would help soothe her wounded heart. Digging around in the past was dangerous. Allie feared the gaze of a professional, no matter how empathetic. Would they uncover familial secrets that she worried had been carved into her DNA? Would they tell her that yes, there was indeed something of her father inside her?

She drove her knife into the edge of the wood.

There were too many unanswered questions. In fact, Grams's answer to her question about being like her father had been quick. Too quick? Had she rehearsed it? Had she been watching Allie all these years, secretly watching for similar traits to her father? The initial relief of her grandmother's words faded in the flickering firelight. Allie felt a twinge of remorse for her skepticism. If she couldn't trust Grams, she would never be able to trust anyone.

Grams's affection had never replaced her mother's tenderness. Grams's care was a different kind, but it was still good, what she needed. There was kindness, but there was also strength and wisdom. Johanna had poured love into Allie. The generous, unfiltered affection children crave. Grams loved Allie with every ounce of her being. Allie never questioned her heart. She had taught her granddaughter to survive and thrive when all around her was crumbling.

Allie looked at the chess piece for a long time. Then, in an act of defiance against her father, she tossed it onto the log and watched it disappear into the flame. She stared at the fire, letting her weary mind wander through the doubts of the past and the unknowns of the present. She didn't dare look into the dark abyss of the future.

Finally, when her chin dipped on her chest and she nodded off in her chair, she bobbed awake. Allie looked up to see that cooling embers had replaced the fire. She closed the iron grill and switched off the lamp, leaving her memories smoldering in the grate.

Chapter Twenty-Six

Residence of Etta Bishop
Gig Harbor, Washington

Allie bounded up the porch steps and touched the wrist of her sports watch, checking the pace of her laps around the pond. She had risen early with a clear head, eager to be outside on the farm on a perfect summer morning. Daylilies danced along the footpath, and bluebirds flitted through the apple trees in the orchard.

During her workout, Allie had made a decision, enjoying the clarity that came with physical exertion. Now back on the porch, she twisted off the top of her dented water bottle and pulled her phone out of her shorts. She took a drink and dialed the number for the archives department of the Seattle Police Department. A recorded message gave her the procedure to request the case file. This was the part where Allie had chickened out in the past.

But not today.

This time, she stayed on the line until someone picked up. Allie recited the information she had been compiling for weeks—her mother's full name, date of birth, last known residence, criminal case report, and incident report number. She waited with bated breath while the person on the other line clicked the information into their computer.

"All right. Hold on." Minutes went by, and when Allie thought she might have been forgotten, the voice returned. "I found the box of files back in the archives. We haven't digested that section yet. I can run copies off and send them to you, but I'll need you to email me a copy of your license, fill out a request form, and pay a small fee."

"That's fine."

"Would you like me to send it to your home address or an insurance company?"

She wasn't quite sure why she didn't give the caller her home address, but something in her gut told her to be careful, poking around the past.

"You know, I'm happy to pick them up."

"All right. Give us twenty-four hours. Been pretty slow around here. You can pick it up at the Archives reception desk on the third floor. Make sure to bring your license and forty-five dollars."

"Thank you."

Allie ended the call feeling like she had just scored a small victory. As a teenager, she had asked Gramps to take her to the place where they recovered her mother's vehicle. It was just an alley in downtown Seattle, off Third Street, behind a rundown Ross and a Walgreens. It was completely uninteresting in every respect except that it made no sense in Johanna Bishop's story.

Gramps died not long after their stoic field trip, and Allie had never returned.

Now, she went inside, started up the coffee pot, and plucked fresh eggs from a basket on the counter. She sliced two pieces of Grams's bread, popped them into the toaster, and opened a jar of Grams's prized blackberry preserves. It was only a matter of time before her grandmother padded into the kitchen. Neither of them ever slept much once the sun made an appearance. Years of tending to chickens had made them both early risers.

"It's nice to wake up to coffee brewing," Grams said, buttoning up a plaid work shirt that had worn thin and soft over the years. Allie placed toast and fried eggs on two Fiesta plates, while Grams filled the coffee mugs.

Grams made the sign of the cross and led them in a simple blessing. They said "Amen" together, and Allie tossed salt and pepper on her eggs.

"It's good to see you eating," Grams said after a moment. "You're so thin, girl."

"That might be the pot calling the kettle black." Allie relished her food. "I forget how much better a farm-raised egg tastes until I'm out here. I think that's why I eat Thai takeout or Vietnamese. So much flavor."

"Store-bought eggs might be from the devil," Grams smiled.

"Let me cook for you tonight. I'll run into town and get some rice, coconut milk, and curry paste."

"You cooked for me just now." Grams pointed to her plate.

"I'm capable of real meals, Grams, not just breakfast."

"I never doubted you."

Allie's phone chirped as she stepped to the coffee pot for a second cup. She picked it up and glanced at the number.

"Hey, Brandy. What's up?"

"Sorry to bother you on a Saturday, girl, but I figured you'd want to know."

"No problem." She stirred in a little cream.

"We got a hit on that cell phone this morning."

"The burner?"

"Yep. It was turned on and transmitted data for less than a minute, then switched off. I can't trace where it went next, but I got the name of the person on the other end. I just sent it your way. I thought you'd want to know."

Allie placed her laptop on the table and connected to the Wi-Fi. Grams collected the dishes and took them to the sink.

"Okay..." Allie said as she opened her inbox. "Am I seeing this right?"

"That's the other reason I called," Brandy explained. "The person he called is Vanessa Martin, a Tacoma local, fifty-four years old."

Allie understood the implications immediately. "She's the right age, with dark hair and green eyes. And she looks pretty in her DMV photo. No one looks pretty in those things."

"I know, right? She's on Facebook, and it looks like she's been on a lot of dating sites too. Belongs to a golf club in Lakewood. I can't believe you have to be on Bumble if you look like her and like to golf. Why aren't men running after her in droves?"

"Getting dates may not be her problem."

"True. But she's got someone's attention. I sent you a side-by-side comparison with our other victims as a reference."

"Oye," Allie said as she opened the file. "These women could be sisters."

"Exactly. This guy has a type, and she fits."

"Brandy, I'm going to call Ms. Martin. Would you mind reaching out to Jason and Marze with the update? Tell them I'll follow up after I've made contact."

"On it. Let me know what you need."

Ending the call, Allie pulled a legal pad from her bag and jotted down the number Brandy sent over.

She dialed, and it went to voicemail, which wasn't surprising. A charming voice politely asked her to leave a message after the beep.

"Ms. Martin, this is Special Agent Allie Bishop from the Federal Bureau of Investigation. I'm calling you about an ongoing investigation in your area, and it is vital that you return my call immediately. Thank you for your time." Allie gave her phone number. Even though the phone would keep the information for her, it was good etiquette.

She took a sip of her coffee and pressed the button to call a second time. Then, a third. On the fourth attempt, a woman answered with a flustered greeting.

"Hello?"

"Vanessa Martin?"

"Speaking."

"Ms. Martin, this is Special Agent Bishop."

"Yes, I just listened to your message. What is this about?"

"I'm sorry for my persistence, but we are currently conducting an investigation in your neighborhood, and I need to ask you a few questions. Can I get a moment to talk?"

"Of course."

"This is going to seem like an odd question, but the implications are serious. Have you been in contact with any new neighbors or acquaintances lately?"

"Well, no, I've been in the garden all morning."

"By lately, I mean over the past few weeks or months."

"Oh," Ms. Martin said, "I guess I spoke to the man who just moved in a few weeks ago. I haven't met his family. They stayed behind for a while to tend to a sick relative. So sweet."

"And was that the person who called you just a few minutes ago?"

"I'm sorry." Vanessa's voice grew strained. "What?"

"You received a phone call less than thirty minutes ago. Was it from him?"

"Are you recording my phone calls?"

"No, ma'am. Not at all. But a federal warrant has been granted for the number that called you. It is the subject of my current investigation."

"Oh, my goodness."

"What can you tell me about the caller? And please, it's very important."

"Well, his name is Mark. I can't remember his last name. But he's always very polite. I can't imagine anything untoward..."

"And how did you meet?" Allie pressed.

"I was weeding my azaleas. He jogs down the street sometimes early in the morning. I like to garden before it gets too hot. He stopped to ask me if I make my own compost. I do, actually, and we started talking about landscaping. Like I said, he just moved into the neighborhood. Truth be told, I thought he was lonely. Probably misses his wife."

Allie felt her adrenaline start to overwhelm the caffeine. "What makes you think he's lonely?"

"Well, he was very chatty and offered to help me move my gardenia. No one offers to help a neighbor anymore. But that's why he called this morning. He was at the hardware store, and they had a sale on potting soil. I've been wanting to replant my begonias. I've got these little black bugs that I can't get rid of. Terrible little pests got into the soil."

"I understand. Can you give me a description of Mark?"

"Well, let's see, blue eyes, dark hair, medium height, early thirties? A bit scruffy, you might say, but quite good looking."

"Did he say anything else this morning?" Allie asked. "Besides the potting soil?"

"Oh. That's right. He promised to bring me some heirloom seeds, a wonderful tomato his wife had sent him in the mail. And peonies. I love peonies.

"May I ask if you live alone?"

"Why? Am I in danger?"

Allie didn't want to scare her, but she needed to be honest. "Possibly. I'm not trying to frighten you, but this is a very serious matter. Do you live alone?"

"No, I do not. I live with my sister, but she's in Vancouver this weekend with her new boyfriend."

"Ms. Martin, you've been very helpful. Thank you for your cooperation. You have valuable information about a situation we've been tracking for a while. In fact, this troubling case is progressing rapidly. Would you be comfortable meeting my partner and me at the Tacoma Field Office?"

"Well, I don't know if that's necessary," she balked. "I don't want to get involved, and I certainly don't want to get anyone in trouble."

Allie tried to think fast. She didn't want to lose this lead. She needed to make her understand the gravity of the situation and find out what else she knew about their unsub.

She shifted her voice. "I don't want to alarm you, Ms. Martin, but this situation is part of a disturbing pattern, one that is highly dangerous, and I believe it would be wise if we met in person, away from your home. It's imperative we meet immediately."

"But it's such a beautiful day. I have a tee time at one. Can we meet after that?"

"No, ma'am. You have information that could be pivotal to our investigation, and your safety may be compromised. I'm quite concerned." Allie offered a change of venue to make her more comfortable. "Would you be able to meet me in one hour at the Amalie Bakery off Fawcett Avenue?"

"Downtown? You want me to meet you downtown in an hour?"

"Unfortunately, we have reason to believe your neighbor Mark is not who you think he is. For your own safety, I'm afraid this is urgent. Lives may be at stake."

Your life. But she didn't say it.

"Is this a prank? Am I on TV?" she asked, a tremor in her voice.

"I wish you were. This is very difficult to take in, I understand."

"How do I know you're who you say you are?"

"If you have a pen, I can give you my badge number. Then please call the FBI's Tacoma Field Office. The general directory will be able to verify my status. Feel free to request my Special Agent in Charge, Finnigan Marze. I've apprised him of your name, and he'll be willing to verify my identity and that of my partner, Special Agent Jason King."

"Well. Okay, thank you. I have a pen."

Allie completed the call and sent her the address to Amalie's bakery. It was the closest location between Gig Harbor and Vanessa Martin. Allie slammed down her laptop and hurried for the shower. This was not the way she had expected her day to go. But with the dead end that Robert Hall was, she would take it.

"No curry?" Grams called from the garden as Allie hurtled back down the steps fifteen minutes later.

"Sorry, Grams." Allie blew her a kiss. "Gotta catch a killer."

"So what else is new?" Grams muttered to her strawberry patch.

Chapter Twenty-Seven

Amalie Bakery
Tacoma, Washington

"Come on!" Allie pounded the palm of her hand on the steering wheel and signaled to change lanes on the Tacoma Narrows Bridge. She was trying to get around a U-Haul that was taking its sweet time. Glancing at the clock on the dash, she stepped on the gas. A traffic accident two miles back had slowed her down, and she didn't want to be late.

Her cell phone buzzed with a call from her SAC.

"Bishop."

"Yes, sir."

"I just got off the phone with a fairly agitated woman who wanted to know if we were bugging her phone. Wanted to know if you were really in the FBI, and should she meet you at Amalie's?"

Allie chuckled. "I gave her good enough reason to be frightened."

"I agreed that you sounded too young to be an agent but assured her you're one of the best we have. Asked her to cooperate with our investigation for her safety and the safety of our community."

"Great. Thank you."

"So what's your plan?"

Allie heard a beep on the line. "One second. Jason's calling in—I'm gonna connect him."

"Jason? I have Marze on the line."

"Okay," Jason said, "I'm at the coordinates Brandy gave for the call from the burner phone."

"What did you find?"

"Nothing. It's on the side of the road in the middle of the country. Nowhere land, actually. I got out and looked around. There's a footpath. I think this might be a popular fishing spot off the Puyallup River. But other than that, it's just the side of the road."

"All right," Marze took over. "Allie, head on to the bakery and reassure Vanessa Martin. We need to secure her cooperation. She fits our unsub's profile. Right age and appearance. She even identified a new acquaintance she met recently. He's a jogger who claims he moved in last month and has been very helpful and overly friendly."

"Does he match our description of the unsub?" Jason asked.

"To a tee," Allie said. "He phoned Vanessa today because he wants to come over tonight and drop off some seeds for her garden. Chief, I think he's our guy, and this is our move. I want to move forward on a sting if we can get Vanessa to cooperate. We can do it with just the two of us. We can get Vanessa to a safe location, and I can stay at her house. If this 'Mark' is watching the place from the outside, I could pass for her. If he knocks on the door, I'll engage him and can be Ms. Martin's niece or something. He's cute. I'll flirt. But we'll get eyes on him and can arrest him."

"You're going to flirt?" Jason said across the line. "I'm not sure that's a good idea."

She rolled her eyes and switched lanes. "Fine. I'm not flirting. I'm just going to Ms. Martin's home so we can engage him without putting her at risk."

"I'm with Jason," Marze interrupted. "We'll do a sting, but nothing so shoestring as the two of you and a cell phone camera. This guy has killed four women, Bishop. I'm not sending you in without full backup."

"But—" Allie argued.

"I will authorize a sting, but only one that's fully coordinated."

"Seriously, sir?" Allie asked. Something like this would take longer to pull together, and felt like overkill.

"Jason will work out the details. I'll set up a safe site for Martin. Bishop, your job is to get her to agree to a night in the Tacoma Holiday Inn. Make her comfortable. Be convincing. Call me back when she's on board. I'll have an agent meet her at the hotel."

They ended the call, and Allie circled the block in front of the bakery, finally locating a parking spot. She hurried into the charming bakery. It was the perfect setting to put anyone at ease, complete with the scent of freshly baked pastries, families with strollers, and a cute retired couple reading the paper. The setting helped Allie release some of her frustration toward her team. Marze had far more experience than she did at this job, but she felt like a full sting operation was a little much. The last thing they needed to do was scare their guy off. It wouldn't take much in a quiet suburban neighborhood to do that.

Vanessa Martin hadn't arrived yet, so Allie went outside and selected a table on the sidewalk. She welcomed the wide angle of shade from a red umbrella. Five minutes later, a woman wearing a lilac golf skirt and white top crossed the street. Allie observed her similarity to the previous victims, noticing her athletic build.

"Ms. Martin?" Allie stood and offered a hand.

The woman paused and surveyed her with a skeptical eye. "Yes. And your name?"

She was being wisely cautious.

Allie presented her creds. "I'm Special Agent Allie Bishop. We spoke on the phone.

Vanessa visibly relaxed. "Thank you. I spoke with your supervisor. Forgive me. A single woman can't be too careful, and your call rattled me."

"That's totally understandable." She motioned to a chair. "Please, have a seat. Can I get you anything?"

"No." She gave a tight smile. "Just answers, please."

"Of course. So I'll be as direct as I can. We have a rapidly developing situation and believe that making contact with you was in your best interest."

"Agent Bishop, am I really in danger?"

"Yes, ma'am, we believe that to be the case."

"But I don't understand. Why me?"

Allie nodded. "Over the past several months, law enforcement has been tracking a person who has been killing women in Tacoma. Women that fit your general description."

"Mine?"

"Fit, attractive women over fifty with dark hair and green eyes. Strong cheekbones."

"But that could be a very large group," Vanessa stammered.

Allie opened a file on her phone and pulled up the photos of the previous victims prior to their murders. She turned it so Vanessa could see. "The phone number that called you today also contacted each of these women."

"Oh, dear god." Vanessa placed a hand over her chest, her eyes fixed on the likenesses. "What happened to them? Please."

Allie recalled Marze's directive for her to get Vanessa on board with the sting operation. Sitting here now, she figured the best way to secure that was through fear. "Unfortunately, they were poisoned. Their faces were removed, and their bodies were dumped in the Puyallup River."

Vanessa touched her cheek and let out a cry of alarm. "Took their faces? What does that mean?"

"It means that he took a scalpel and cut the skin away."

The older woman whimpered. "Wh—why would someone do that?"

"I wish I knew. Unfortunately, we can only follow the trail up to this point. But this is why it is so vital that we secure your safety. We've been tracking the phone number that called you this morning, looking for any link between our previous victims. Honestly, this is the first time we've been able to get ahead of this individual."

Vanessa's eyes narrowed at Allie. "Are you saying the man I know as Mark has killed those women—and done *that* to their faces?"

"We believe so, yes. Up until recently, the suspect had been tracking women down every few months. But he's escalated. Maybe because something went wrong with his last victim. We aren't certain. We do believe that he will continue this cycle until someone stops him. That's why we need your help."

"Me?"

Allie nodded. "Honestly, the only thing it would require of you is to allow us to keep you at a safe location. The FBI has authorized us to prepare a sting. We'll place an undercover team on surveillance outside your home."

Vanessa closed her eyes briefly and took a deep breath. "Do you think he's watching my house? But Mark seems so kind."

"We don't know if he's watching your house, but he does have plans to return. And I understand the confusion over hearing that someone you trust and like is not a good person. It's perfectly normal for that to be disconcerting. But I am asking you to trust me. For your own safety."

"So what do I need to do?"

"We will need you to monitor your phone and answer any phone calls or texts from Mark as if you were still going about your day. With your permission, the FBI will tap into your phone so we can hear what's going on, even coach you along if necessary. The only risk would be the phone calls. But an agent will be with you to assist you through the communication as long as you feel comfortable and believe you'll be able to stay calm and speak as you normally would."

"Is that all?" Vanessa drew a napkin from her purse and dabbed sweat off her brow.

"No, actually, before that, we'll need to take your statement. Then an agent will escort you to a safe house."

"That sounds dubious."

"It's a local hotel."

"Well, why didn't you say so?"

Allie placed a hand on Vanessa's in solidarity. She liked this elegant woman, and she admired her strength. But the touch was electric, and Allie couldn't help but feel responsible for the person sitting across the table from her.

Chapter Twenty-Eight

Residence of Vanessa Martin
Tacoma, Washington

"What's that smell?" Eastman barked as the door of the surveillance van slammed behind him.

"Pollo al ajillo, my friend." Jason stood over an aromatic casserole dish of rice and chicken, filling the tiny space with the mouthwatering scent of traditional Spanish food.

"Garlic chicken?" Eastman slumped into the seat. "You brought that to a stakeout? It's bad enough I have to breathe your recycled air. Now you have to stink it up with garlic."

"You won't feel that way after you try it." Jason spooned the rice and chicken concoction into paper bowls and handed them around to his teammates. They were parked in front of Vanessa Martin's house and had time to kill.

"Did Victoria's mom cook for you again?" Allie asked, accepting a bowl.

"Yep. V went in for chemo yesterday, and her mother

wanted to make us something hearty and filling. V called me this afternoon, begging me to keep it out of the house. She can't keep anything down, and she doesn't want to ruin another of her favorite comfort foods."

"Oh, I miss home cooking." Allie's stomach roared in appreciation. She hadn't had a chance to eat since breakfast with Grams this morning. Since Marze had approved the sting operation, they'd been scrambling non-stop to plan the op and install surveillance cameras around Vanessa Martin's house.

Jason took another bite and pointed at her with his fork. "I thought you went home yesterday."

"I did. But Grams doesn't cook for herself, and she didn't know I was coming. But everything is out of her garden—fresh tomato sandwiches on baked bread. I can't complain."

"You're killing me. Next time you go, bring me back the tomatoes. I make a mean ziti. Or I'll give them to V's mom. That woman is a magician with tomatoes."

"Of course. Grams's produce with your mother-in-law's cooking? That's gotta be a win."

Allie glanced over her checklist. Brandy and her team had initiated a sweep of cell phone transmissions in the area, looking for any signal emitted from the burner phone. The team had assembled just before dusk and piled into a van embossed with the name "Northern Lights Painting Services." They parked down the street from Vanessa's quaint yellow bungalow and prepared to spring their trap.

"Marze?" Jason handed the Special Agent in Charge a plastic fork and napkin.

"Holy hell," Marze said after he took a bite of Jason's homemade food.

"See?" Jason grinned and kicked up his feet on the seat next to him. "Aren't you glad I shared?"

"My compliments to your mother-in-law, Jason. Can your wife cook like this?"

"On our third date, she made me her mother's paella recipe. The next day, I bought her a set of knives and a cutting board for my place."

"A true romantic," Eastman huffed.

"I try," Jason said. "But seriously, I was a first-generation latchkey kid. My brother and I grew up on homemade PB&J. On Sundays, we'd make Kraft mac and cheese if it was on hand. The pizza man was at my house so much I thought we were related."

"You're a lucky SOB with this food," Marze said around a bite. "My mother-in-law has been on a diet since 1981. I keep threatening to tie her to a chair and force-feed her a cannoli. I think she'd be nicer if she just ate something."

"Allie, you want some more?" Jason offered her seconds.

"Maybe afterward."

"Nervous?" Her partner dished himself a second helping.

"That's a good way of saying it." She glanced at her phone for the twelfth time.

"All the prep work is over, but now comes the hard part," Marze told her.

"Waiting?" Allie asked.

"I remember my first stakeout in the van." Eastman was chatty with a full stomach. "We got a tip on this warehouse selling counterfeit goods. It was a big operation, straight from Hong Kong. Cell phones, cameras, laptops, plasma TVs, luxury bags—you name it. We set up and watched the place all night.

Six of us cramped in this thing for twelve hours, waiting for the owners to come so we could make the arrest."

"And?" Allie asked.

"Nothing."

Allie's eyebrows shot up. "What happened?"

"Apparently, the counterfeiters paid more for information than we did. They cleaned out the place from the back while we watched from the front."

"No way."

"Yep. Quarter of a million dollars' worth of gear walked out the door right under our nose."

"Gentlemen," Brandy said, and she slipped into the van. "Guys, I don't mean to get personal, but it smells like a tin of anchovies in here."

"Hey, it could be Bishop?" Eastman raised both hands.

"Ummm, I don't think so. Bishop's fastidious. She's got houseplants in her office."

Allie gave her a quizzical look.

"It's true, you're neat. It's a compliment," Jason said. "V's mom sent food."

"Yummy, hand it over." Brandy looked excited and extended her hand. "Vanessa Martin's all set up. We mirrored her phone to our location. If she gets a text, we'll know about it here." She fired up her laptop. "Wilson is with her and will guide her so she can respond properly if he contacts her."

"Dean and Boatwright are in the garage waiting for our signal," Marze said.

"King, you better save me some of that chicken," an agent said through the speaker.

"I gotcha, buddy."

Brandy accepted a bowl of food and asked, "You're not worried our guy might get spooked with all these people hanging around?"

"Right?" Allie said. "That's what I wanted to know."

"This one is all hands on deck," Marze said. "The higher-ups start paying attention when we have a serial killer carving off women's faces. The plan is to arrest the unsub when he rings the doorbell. Nice and easy—no surprises.

The crew huddled together for the next half hour, watching the screens as they bantered. When Brandy's laptop chirped, everyone fell silent. "We got chatter." Brandy clicked on her screen. "A text just came into Vanessa's phone. It's him."

Allie chewed on her thumbnail. She thought about Vanessa Martin, forced out of her home by a psychopath who enjoyed carving off women's faces. She felt the urgency that tonight needed to go right.

"He's on his way. ETA ten minutes," Brandy announced.

"It's showtime," someone said through the radio.

Chapter Twenty-Nine

Residence of Vanessa Martin
Tacoma, Washington

"We have movement in quadrant two," Brandy said as she clicked a key. The footage from her surveillance camera flicked onto the main screen in the surveillance van.

Allie's breath caught in her throat. The lean figure of a man in a light gray hoodie, blue jeans, and tennis shoes entered the screen. His casual gait conveyed confidence and ease.

"Brandy, can you get anything on facial recognition?" Marze asked.

"Not...yet. The hat and the hoodie are impeding the software." She clicked several stills of the man as he walked up the street.

"Eastman, do we have any clue what direction he came from?" Jason asked.

Allie studied several angles from the cameras they had positioned down the street. "I don't see a car. Did he park somewhere and walk?"

"Vanessa told us he claimed he'd moved nearby," Jason commented.

Allie scoffed, "But he probably told that to every one of his targets."

"Before they died a slow, painful death in his arms," Brandy added.

"What's he holding?" Eastman asked and peered at the gray screen in the fading light.

Brandy zoomed in on the man's hand. "A plate or something?"

"Looks like cookies," Eastman said.

"Allie, didn't we suspect that some kind of baked goods poisoned Helen Mercer?" Jason asked.

She nodded. Her stomach clenched. She hated watching their unsub through the screen when he was so close to their physical location. Every fiber of her being wanted to end this nightmare tonight.

"Subject is within twenty feet of the van," Brandy said. The agents fell into a hush while their unsub sauntered down the sidewalk across from them. The streetlights clicked on in synchrony as the evening light faded from the sky.

Marze radioed the team. "All agents, be advised. Unsub is approaching the premises. Wait for my mark to engage."

Allie held her breath. Her body buzzed with nervous energy.

The unsub cleared the camera hidden on the back of the mailbox and stepped onto the property. He strode onto the sidewalk and moved toward the door. Then he paused.

"Why is he stopping?" Allie asked.

"Guys?" Jason said suddenly. "We have a problem."

"Is he tying his shoe?" Allie stood in the van.

"Why isn't he ringing the doorbell?" Jason asked.

"Do not engage," Marze interrupted. "Wait until he rings the bell."

"He noticed something," Brandy said suddenly.

"Something in the bushes." Jason sat up straighter.

"Can't see what he's looking at," Eastman said. "He's standing in front of it."

Allie instinctively ran her thumb across the scar on her wrist and held her breath.

"He's moving." Allie felt her chest clamp down in a vice-like grip. "Wait, I see it. It's a red flashing light."

"Dammit," Brandy said. "Yeah, he's moving. The *wrong* direction. It's a camera, our surveillance camera." She groaned and pressed her fists into her skull.

"How?" Jason demanded.

"Why is any of our equipment blinking, Brandy?" Marze demanded.

Jason looked concerned. "Sir, we need to move."

"Wait," he said. "Dean, Boatwright, wait for my signal."

Allie swore under her breath.

"It's the battery," Brandy said. "It's alerting us that it's about to lose signal and is running out of charge."

"It's gonna ruin my op." Allie put a hand on the door as she watched her unsub shoot away from the house and dart down the sidewalk.

"He's made us," Eastman barked.

"Go!" Marze yelled.

Allie led the way out of the van, everyone bursting into the night air.

"Stop!" Allie locked eyes with him for half a second, and then he burst away into the dark at lightning speed. The two agents inside the house rallied from their hiding spot.

Marze grabbed his radio. "All units, pursue our suspect. White male, six feet, dressed in a gray hoodie and baseball cap. Be advised that the suspect is violent. Approach with caution and apprehend by any means necessary." A block away, sirens roared to life.

Allie pounded down the street with Jason running at her heels. Half a block later, she struggled to keep the unsub in her sights. He sprinted between houses, dodging between cars and over hedges, expertly evading his pursuers. Jason and Allie ran at a full clip but watched him slip into a dimly lit wooded area on the outskirts of a park. Allie felt her heart sink even as she closed the distance.

Allie finally stopped as she reached the bank of trees. She didn't have a clear line of site. The terrain was unknown, the visibility was gone, and the suspect had a good fifty-yard head start. She updated the team on their location, and both agents drew their side arms and flashlights. Winded and breathless, they explored the dense patch of woods together. Soon, the rest of the unit had joined them.

"There's a path here," Jason's voice carried in the darkness. "Looks like it leads to a dry riverbed."

"What are the odds it also leads to the location where he used the phone today?"

"I'd put money on it."

"You think he's using the river system to navigate the city?"

"Right under our noses."

Allie slammed her open palm against an oak tree, accepting the sting as a painful rebuke.

"What am I supposed to say to Vanessa Martin?"

"You can tell her she was just awarded a staycation, courtesy of the Federal Bureau of Investigation. You want me to pick out her pajamas, or would you?"

"It's not funny, Jason."

"I'm not laughing, Allie."

They emerged from the woods and headed back to the Martin residence. Flashing lights lit up the porch from the police cruisers parked in front of the bungalow. Marze stood on the front steps, hands on hips, deep in conversation with a uniformed officer.

"This is Officer White," he told them. "He'll be coordinating the K-9 search with Officer Corrigan and the Puyallup police."

Allie nodded her introduction. "Please tell me Brandy got a hit on facial recognition?"

"Not yet."

She bit her tongue to keep back a retort. Her boss didn't deserve her anger. She should have insisted on being outside the van. Insisted on a smaller sting, fewer people, less technology. Fewer variables that could go wrong in the heat of the moment.

"We did pick up the plate he had with him," Brandy said as she walked up, but it wasn't any consolation. "We're hoping to get a print off of it, but I don't think this guy is in our system. If he had a DMV photo or a passport, I'd have found him on facial recognition by now. He's a ghost. It's weird."

"What about the cookies?" Jason asked.

"Eastman bagged them. He's already en route to the lab."

Cookies won't catch our killer.

"Not sure that's going to be very reassuring to Vanessa Martin," Jason said, expressing Allie's sentiments.

Marze stood on the small porch with his jaw clenched. "Look, the sting was my responsibility. This is on me."

"No, sir," Brandy said. "That diode in need of a battery was my responsibility. Should have never happened."

For the first time, Allie saw her hardened, ex-Marine of a boss look beat. In a way, this was personal for all of them. "The buck stops with me." He turned to Allie. "Ms. Martin is safe. We'll regroup. And we're going to get this guy."

Allie wanted to believe him. They had come so close. The problem was that their unsub knew that. He would go completely dark now and change his tactics, if not decide to lie low for a long time.

"Yes, sir. We'll get him."

But she wasn't sure that she believed that anymore.

Chapter Thirty

Historic Woolworth Building
Seattle, Washington

"Can you spare some change, ma'am?" A filthy hand reached out towards Allie's knee.

She stood on the corner of Third Avenue and Pike Street in Seattle. The neighborhood was called 3P by local dispatch, named for the block between Pine St and Pike, otherwise titled "the bad part of town" in articles that covered her mother's disappearance. Newspapers had well documented the history of the location, including some of the darkest moments of Seattle's battles with crime and the latest fad of drugs plaguing the city.

"I'm sorry, I don't carry cash, but here. Best bagel in the city. Has salmon and schmear." She handed over the white paper bag and enjoyed the toothless smile she received in exchange. She wasn't hungry anyway. The food from Pike Place Market had only been to settle her nerves.

Allie moved down the street, stepping over singed tin foil and detritus in the area that was home to the city's fentanyl epidemic. Addicts crushed the blue pills and burned them on aluminum, inhaling the vapors with a straw. The tin foil scraps replaced the heroin needles that had littered these streets when her mother had disappeared. The city had done a lot to clean up in the area in the last decade, but remnants of the old ways remained.

Allie moved down the crowded sidewalk just off the beaten path from Seattle's notable tourist stops. Allie navigated the neighborhood by memory. The address from her visit with Gramps years ago was fuzzy, but she would never forget the location where Mom's car had been found, on blocks in the alley behind the historic Woolworth's building, now a budget clothing store on Third Avenue.

Allie's eyes noted the brick wall, the oversized trash bins, and the occasional makeshift campsite. She was looking for the telltale graffiti. Her eyes landed on the spray-painted rose that grew two stories above the alley, the last memorial of her mother.

The story of a young suburban mother who disappeared without a trace in Seattle's slum had gripped locals with a vengeance. The site where her Honda Accord was found had been littered with candles and roses for weeks. Allie recalled the images she found in the archives, touched by the kindness of strangers she would never meet. Someone from the local art scene had created the black and red symbol that towered in the back of the building.

Allie reached out and touched the landmark—a rose with a teardrop slipping off its petal. She remembered being moved by its presence years ago on her trip with Gramps and was intrigued to see it still there, despite all the changes the city had experienced in the intervening years. Now, Allie leaned against the faded image.

"Hey, Mom," she said quietly. "I met Sadie. I'm not sure what you wanted me to find, honestly, but I promise you. I'm looking. I will find the truth." She didn't care who was watching. The alley was a grimy place between the buildings where merchandise was loaded into the retail store. But, unlike Gramps, she didn't have a headstone in a quiet cemetery to visit.

On the difficult days in law enforcement, Allie realized bringing other people closure only made her ache for her own. "I miss you." Allie pressed her head into the gritty brick wall for a long moment and then stepped back to survey the scene.

She brought out her phone and took a few shots of the rose in the summer sunshine. The department store was on a list of proposed historic preservation sites. But Seattle was desperate for condo space, and several proposals to rezone the entire area had come to Allie's attention recently.

Finding her mother's journal had rekindled Allie's desire to connect with her memory. It also fueled the desire to find tangible reminders of her mother's life and loss. This graffiti memorial presented a tangible memorial to that. The thought that it could be demolished by a stranger who was only interested in gentrifying downtown made her stomach twist in anguish. But, like so much of her relationship with her mother, it was beyond her control.

She thought of looking up the artist who painted it. Maybe

she would commission a piece of artwork for her bare apartment? Or maybe a tattoo.

Allie touched the wall again, said a final goodbye, and moved back down the street. The text from the Seattle Archives had come through early this morning, and driving up the coast gave her a chance to process.

After yesterday's frustrating setback, she planned to regroup, deciding to use the lull to focus on her personal life and knock a couple of things off the to-do list in the process. She would head north to the archives, pick up a copy of her mother's files, then head back to her apartment to catch up on laundry.

She wandered back down Pike Street and ordered another salmon bagel with schmear. She found a picnic table by the pier and enjoyed watching a father and son pitch fries at demanding seagulls. Their laughter made her miss the normalcy of a parent and brought her mind back to the questions the journal had stirred up.

Tossing her trash into a receptacle, she returned to her car and pulled into traffic. The SPD repository was in the north part of the city, and the detour to the port meant she would have to backtrack a bit.

Allie checked her rearview mirror and changed lanes. Exiting the highway, she followed the instructions from her phone, which routed her around the inevitable summer construction. Then she turned onto a two-lane road toward Lakewood. A glimmer in her rearview caught her attention, and a gold Mercedes took up her mirror.

"Hello?" Allie remembered the car from the freeway, but now it was close. Too close. "Well, pass me already."

The Mercedes crept closer until it was riding her bumper through the winding curves. Allie sped up around the next curve but didn't like the way the car was keeping pace with her. At Quantico, she had studied defensive driving and knew how to handle her machine, but an erratic driver was dangerous and unpredictable. The afternoon sun glinted off the windshield and obscured her view of the driver behind the wheel, but the car's behavior wasn't natural.

She eased off the gas and watched the double yellow line, waiting for a place where it was safe to exit to the left or the right. Before she had a chance to get off the road, the vehicle accelerated. Then, as if it was out to get her, she watched helplessly as it slammed into her car's rear end, jolting her forward against her seatbelt.

Slamming on the brakes, the car swerved violently, and Mercedes continued to accelerate, pushing her down the road at a dangerous pace. Allie's fingers gripped the steering wheel like a vise, and she struggled to maintain control. She attempted to switch lanes, but the Mercedes moved right behind her. Now, they were hurtling down the two-lane road straight toward oncoming traffic. Ahead of her, an oncoming truck laid on its horn.

"What are you doing?" she screamed as she jerked the wheel back into her lane. The gold car accelerated again, this time clipping her from the side. Allie swerved, overcompensated, and held on for dear life as her car left the road and careened into a ditch. The car came to a swift and sudden stop as it slammed into a short wall of dirt. The airbags deployed, slamming into Allie's nose, cracking her sunglasses, and busting out the side window.

Allie's vehicle ticked quietly as she groaned and gently prodded her nose. She sat there, stunned for a long moment before reaching out a hand to grope for her phone. Thankfully, it was still secure in the cup holder by her seat. Drawing it out from a spray of broken window glass, she swiped the screen and dialed 911.

"Seattle Emergency," said a voice from the other end.

"This is Agent Allie Bishop with the FBI. I've been run off the road north of Seattle." She gave her location.

"Agent Bishop, I have your location. You said run off the road? Has the driver of the other vehicle pulled off?"

"No," she huffed. "They're long gone."

"Are you injured?"

"Just my pride." Allie did a quick scan of her body but didn't think anything was broken.

"Glad to hear it. Are you in danger?" the dispatcher asked.

Allie listened to the stillness of her surroundings. All she could hear was the settling of her busted car.

"I don't believe so." She answered a few more questions before her mind started to feel fuzzy.

"I've dispatched a cruiser to your locale. Sit tight. We'll be with you soon."

"Thank you. Please note that I have a weapon."

"Understood. I will alert the Bureau's Seattle office."

"And I was deliberately run off the road by a gold Mercedes, Washington plates, with potential body damage to the front and right side, heading north toward Lakewood.

"Ten-four. I'll circulate a description. Would you like to stay on the line with me until help arrives?"

"No, I'm okay."

Allie felt herself start to go into shock. Her hands were trembling. Groping in the shattered glass, she grabbed her bag. Her door opened with a loud, resistant creak. Climbing out of the ditch, she swore wildly. The front of her car looked like a crushed can. She stepped away to a safe distance and dialed Jason.

"Guess we're about to find out just how close of friends we are," she muttered while the phone rang in her ear.

She sighed. Her mother's files would have to wait.

Chapter Thirty-One

Mile Marker 65
Seattle, Washington

Allie watched the winch of the tow truck grow taut and ease the mangled shell of her vehicle onto the back of the flatbed. Cars slowed on the windy asphalt, and curious passengers gawked at Allie. She already missed her sunglasses.

"Officer Rodriguez with the SPD just checked in," Jason said as he strode up to stand beside her. "Nothing yet on your gold Mercedes."

"I'm not surprised. I didn't get a look at the plate number." They stood shoulder to shoulder while her car was being loaded onto the truck. Finally, the tow operator stepped back to verify the garage's address and promised to deliver what was left of her personal vehicle within the next few hours.

"What were you doing in Seattle anyway?" Jason asked as they walked the road's shoulder to his car.

"I—" She didn't want to lie. "I was picking something up

for my family." It was almost the truth, she decided. "Thanks for coming."

"What are partners for?" he said as they climbed into his Charger.

Allie flipped the mirror down and glanced at her face. Purple rings were rapidly forming around her eyes. "Yep, that's gonna leave a mark. Wonderful."

"You have a lot to be thankful for," Jason said, and pulled onto the road, quickly accelerating into the flow of traffic. "Your tire tracks had you headed straight for that concrete piling beneath the lamp pole. If you hadn't been able to swerve at the last minute, I wouldn't be taking you home right now."

"Believe me, I know. I was there. This wasn't an accident, Jason."

He cocked an eyebrow. "You sure?"

"Of course I am," she snapped. "He was on me for half a mile. I couldn't get away. You saw my back bumper. He hit me at least twice."

"You don't think he was drunk?"

She rolled her eyes. "*No*, I don't think he was drunk. It was malicious. Intentional. I'm not a moron."

He nodded. "Okay...no need to go on the defensive. I believe you. Do you have any other open cases at the moment?"

"Nothing of note. I'm still a rookie, remember?"

"So, would our unsub deliberately try to follow you and run you off the road?"

"I have no idea. I mean, why me? Why now?" Allie fought hard to find a pattern, to put the varied pieces into a cohesive fashion. But her brain wasn't exactly working at optimal speed right now. "I didn't get a look at him last night outside Vanessa

Martin's place. He had the streetlight behind him. But I'm sure he looked right at me. But why would he come after me? And besides, Stephanie Mercer's neighbor gave us a description of a dark sedan the afternoon she was taken, not a gold Mercedes."

"True. It's not a subtle choice for an assault."

The two drove on in silence. Allie's adrenaline began to wane, and heavy fatigue began to settle into her bones. Her eyes fluttered with exhaustion.

"Here." Jason handed her a water bottle. "You need to hydrate. Helps with the shock."

"Thanks. Got any of those vitamin packets? I could use a pick-me-up."

"Glove compartment." Jason pointed with his chin. "Your body did what it was supposed to do today. It will demand rest to recharge and refuel. It's natural."

"If you could explain that to our rogue serial killer, I'd appreciate it."

Jason turned the car onto Interstate Five as Allie nursed her vitamin water. "If you need to take a day and rest up, see a chiropractor, get a massage or something, please do."

"Thanks, Jason. I appreciate you coming all this way. I didn't want to deal with an Uber driver. Would have probably just hitched a ride with the tow truck driver."

He winced. "He was pretty ripe. Not sure they have showers this far north. But seriously, Allie, I wanted to apologize for being MIA much of this past week. It was unprofessional."

Allie said nothing, wanting to give him space to talk.

"Victoria has been on my case all week," he began.

She pulled out her ponytail and ran a hand through her hair, unsure where this conversation was going.

"She thought it was about time I told you about my partner."

"Only if you're comfortable. If you trust me, that is. I get it. You don't need to tell me just to satisfy any curiosity on my part." She waited.

"I trust you. It's just...I didn't just lose a partner, Allie. Paul Yates was my best friend." Jason drove on for several minutes. He seemed to be searching the horizon for the courage to open that part of his soul.

"He was the best man at my wedding. Paul introduced me to Victoria. He was my family. Growing up, my dad wasn't in the picture, and my older brother and I weren't all that close. That was for reasons I can explain at another time. But I didn't know anything about life. Paul's brothers were always out in the backyard working on some kind of car, playing streetball, and riding bikes. We were the youngest, same grade. We got chosen last for everything, and when we played with his older brothers, we were fierce rivals. But it also forged us in the fire. We competed at everything. Grades, girls, sports, you name it."

Jason passed a slow-moving RV and switched back to the right lane. "Anyway, Paul was a natural athlete, but I didn't have to work as hard at school. We pushed each other. We made all-conference in football. Paul was the quarterback, and I was his wide receiver. We could read a play without speaking a word. We'd been playing against his brothers since day one, which made us fast and fearless."

Allie continued to listen intently as he continued.

"In fifth grade, we decided we'd be professional football

players. I chose the Forty-niners. He wanted to be a Dallas Cowboy. Pretty sure it had something to do with the cheerleaders. We finally settled for the LA Rams if we could play together. It sounds dumb saying it out loud now. But with Paul, you believed him. He had that kind of charisma. He carried it into everything he did—student government, the debate team, and even a summer job. He got us hired on as runners for the biggest music venue in Seattle, and we'd drive these major musicians, Macklemore, Phil Collins, and Questlove. It was insane, but he made it look easy, a piece of cake. Junior year, Paul was sacked coming up the middle. He didn't get up. They took him off the field on a stretcher, unconscious. The game resumed, and the coach tried to put me back in the game. But there was no game without Paul. I finished out the season, but my heart wasn't in it. His season was over due to concussion, mine due to loyalty. No brainer. But his injury did something to him. After that, he never could throw a pass the same again. It effectively ended any chance of a career."

Allie tried to envision Jason in high school as she was swept into the story. Jason continued as the motion of the car lubricated his memory.

"Paul was the idea man. I was his ride or die. After football, Paul set his sights on the police department. I think he enjoyed the rush of an emergency. He was a natural-born leader. I liked the camaraderie, and I enjoyed the physical demands. Plus, I looked great in the uniform too," he smirked. "I think I liked how it felt to help little kids and families. Restore order to people's worst days. I was proud of who I'd become. I would probably still be on the force if Paul hadn't set his sights on the FBI."

"This was his idea?"

"Totally, and that might seem like a cop-out, but my identity was being Paul's wingman. I was very good at it. We were like Iceman and Slider."

"Who?"

"From *Top Gun*? Come on, Allie."

"I thought that was Maverick and Goose."

"That's the underdog story. Iceman and Slider were the pair that went straight to the top and blew away the competition. But doing Quantico with him made it easy."

"How did you get the same post after training?" Allie asked.

"The TFO is a smaller office, as you know, but it was expanding the year we graduated, and someone retired. Everything came easy for Paul. We just got lucky." Jason ran a hand over his jaw as he thought.

"One day, Paul and I were investigating a trafficking scheme. We were casing a building outside of Tacoma when a Bureau task force from a DC field office swarmed the location."

"Wait," Allie said. "A Bureau task force swarmed your stakeout? Why?"

"It was Internal Affairs. In all the action, I got separated from my team, and I just figured we stirred up a hornet's nest. I wasn't worried until I saw them lead Paul away in handcuffs. They were there to arrest him, and the op was so secret that even Marze hadn't been briefed."

"Ouch."

"So long story short, I spent the next forty-eight hours trying to prove my innocence in all kinds of underhanded dealings that Paul was running on the side. We had an informant on this underground mafia organization. She was giving us all kinds of great information until she began to suspect that Paul was playing both sides of the card. She confronted Paul, and he denied it. The very next day, before she could ask me about it, her Ford Expedition exploded in her driveway."

"Oh, Jason."

"Aimee came home from getting pizza to find what was left of her husband and seven-year-old son smoldering in her driveway."

The pieces finally clicked together in Allie's mind. Aimee was the woman in the blue Camry. She had to be. "What happened to her?"

"Nothing good. She gave Paul up immediately and was scheduled to testify at his trial. But after the death of her family, she was never the same. She could barely hold it together through the deposition. And the case never went to trial. Paul skipped out on his bail. Left his parents on the hook for a hundred thousand dollar bond. That was one of the worst days of my life."

"You felt guilty," she said. "For not seeing it."

He nodded. "How could I not know? We were inseparable. I kept asking myself if I had been willfully blind, but with all this distance from it, I don't think I was. When the dust settled, I had no credibility in the office. Internal affairs held me up for months. The worst part was watching all our cases unravel because of Paul's actions. People that had trusted us to get them out of harm's way. Dozens of terrible people got off without even a slap on the wrist because our cases were compromised."

Allie couldn't imagine watching months, or even years, of casework turn to dust. "That's painful."

"The only people who believed me were Victoria and Aimee. Aimee had witnessed Paul's dark side. She got her hands on some compelling evidence that eventually cleared my name. She's the only reason I still have a job. So I felt responsible for Aimee after that. But she didn't hold up well, and I don't blame her. She slipped deeper and deeper into substance abuse. She'd tried treatment once already. I thought she was doing well." He paused, and Allie thought he might be trying to hold back tears. "But last week, her mom called and asked me to check on her. I found her fully clothed in her bathtub. She'd slit her wrists."

"Oh, Jason. I'm so sorry. I can't imagine. What a nightmare." Allie stared out the windshield and was quiet for a few moments. "And Paul? Did they catch up to him?"

"No idea. Interpol issued a warrant for his arrest. But he disappeared. I still look for him in a crowd."

Allie was grateful for his trust, that he had finally opened up. She could feel the weight of his pain sitting on her own chest. "Thank you for telling me," she said. "That's devastating, and I know a thing or two about betrayal."

"You were a kid when you found out about your dad. Do you..." He paused hesitantly and then pressed forward. "Do you question every single interaction you had with him a thousand times in your head?"

Allie nodded. "Of course. Betrayal makes you go back over everything."

"I just wonder how much of it was real. How much of our relationship was one long con."

Allie felt an old ache in the pit of her stomach. "It does

make you second-guess others' motivations," she sighed. "Being skeptical is easier than feeling like a fool again."

"Yeah." They drove on in silence, enjoying the comfortable atmosphere of their shared understanding.

"Thank you for sharing. I know what it feels like to have people question you, whisper behind your back, and doubt you." She knew Jason didn't want to be pitied, but she couldn't help but feel crushed for him. "It's hard to trust people. I get it. Seriously. Whatever you need. No explanation."

He smiled. "Victoria said you would say that."

Chapter Thirty-Two

Location: Unknown

How could I be so stupid?

He clawed at his neck while pacing the dingy basement. There was no excuse for his incompetence. He chastened himself, digging his nails into his arms and his chest.

Stupid, stupid.

He ran his fingers through his hair and tried to stifle a scream. He clamped his hand over his mouth. He felt the pain of his nails digging into his face. He paused. Not the face. He needed his face. People loved his handsome face. They trusted it.

He scratched at his chest and paced in the dark, damp room. He could move through the space with his eyes closed—twelve steps and turn, nine steps and turn. He paced in agony. Scratch, step, scratch, step. Twelve steps and repeat.

The Face of Evil

The police had almost caught him this time, nearly stopped him from his work.

Stupid, stupid, stupid.

The words pounded in his head in time with his footsteps on the bare floor. He paced and groaned at the pain that radiated off his shoulders. Thin streaks of blood saturated his shirt.

Something rustled in the corner. He turned his head with primal alertness at the sound of feet scuttling across the floor. He stalked his prey, watching the mouse dart between the shelves as it looked for morsels in his pristine workspace.

Slowly, he lifted a scalpel off his workbench and waited for the creature to move in his direction. He stepped up on the stool and watched the gray body travel in a haphazard line toward the edge of his perch. He pounced with lightning speed across the floor.

The tiny scream lasted only a moment. Then he appeared behind his workbench with a grin of fascination, a spray of blood speckling his face.

"Well, hello." He studied the pocket-sized mouse skewered on the scalpel. "What should we do with you?" He glanced around the workshop at yellowed jars of floating specimens ranging in size and shape. They stared back at him in silent witness.

"You'll be good practice." He gently laid the dead mouse on the edge of his workspace.

"Mother always says practice makes perfect. And I need the practice so that I don't make any more mistakes."

Stupid, Stupid.

He writhed and slammed a hand against his head.

"No, not the face." He spoke to the dead animal. "Faces are

precious. Pretty faces, pretty people." He gazed around at his prized possessions. His collection of faces stretched onto wooden displays. They kept him company, a chorus of beauty frozen in time, preserved against decay and death.

"See my faces, little one." He spoke to the tiny animal as he began to pry off its fur with tweezers. "Faces are the hardest. Father always said so. It is so difficult to make them look natural and lifelike. It's all in the eyes." He took a breath of formaldehyde-soaked air. "I just need practice. I keep my mistakes to learn the best formula to preserve the color and the texture." He looked across the beakers, Bunsen burners, thermometers, jars of solutions and powders, and the pipettes crowding his workbench.

"See, most of them look just like they did when I took them, but that doesn't mean they fit right. I learned that the hard way. It's not the same as tanning leather, the only skill Father left me. This is a greater art form."

He peeled open the insides of the animal and removed its organs. He enjoyed keeping his hands busy.

"No, that's not true," he said to what was left of the mouse. "Father taught me to be strong and bear the pain. Mother wasn't strong. I had to protect her. It was my job. Take the pain, but not the face. Don't leave a mark on the face."

Scooping the chemicals up from a jar on his workbench, he added his unique recipe of preservatives to the animal carcass with a practiced hand.

"Mother always said I'd be a scientist one day. She loved my experiments. She was proud of me. Unlike Father." At the thought of his father, he stepped away and screamed again. He jabbed the scalpel into a battered chair cushion over and over until the frenzy slowed.

"Excuse me." He returned to his work and drew a thread and needle from his bench. "Father made Mother sick. It's his fault she is the way she is today. I don't like to think of Father, to remember the bad things he used to do to her. It makes me angry, and when I'm angry, I make mistakes."

Stupid, Stupid.

He grimaced, trying to control his emotions. If he hadn't been so stupid, they wouldn't have tracked her down and gotten to her house before he did. If he hadn't seen that light in the bush and the van across the street, he wouldn't have been able to help Mother.

He stitched up the belly of the mouse. "She needs the faces. The faces will make Mother better." He dropped the perfectly skinned corpse into a jar of floating mice and nodded in satisfaction.

"I just need practice, more practice." He turned off the light and exited his lair, stepping into the sparse kitchen.

"Hello, Mother." He leaned over a woman in a wheelchair. "You look sad today. Are you tired? I won't make a peep. You need to rest." He took her hand in his. "I'll make dinner for us as soon as I finish all my work. How does fish sound this evening?"

He set to work, taking a case of his favorite local fish from the freezer. He'd collected them during the fall. But his supply was starting to run low. He began the process of purifying the toxic fish oils. He created a series of acid precipitations until it crystallized into a toxin. The process was tedious, but he didn't mind.

"Practice makes perfect." He had a good feeling about this one.

Chapter Thirty-Three

Puyallup Skate Park
Puyallup, Washington

Allie shut the door to her rental car and started across the grass. She saw Jason exiting his Charger, so she stopped and waited for him to catch up.

He gave his partner the once-over. "How are you feeling?"

"How do I look?" Allie asked, a little self-conscious, and tenderly touched the bruises that had sprouted beneath her eyes overnight.

"Honestly?" He grimaced.

"Always."

"Little rough, but you're lucky to be alive."

"Everything hurts this morning. By the way, I got a call from the lab as I was pulling in. First, the prints we pulled off the scalpel are not in the system. Second, they sent us a report on the analysis of cookies left on Vanessa Martin's lawn."

"Finally, something we can use. What did it say?"

"They were oatmeal raisin."

"Don't toy with me, Bishop."

"Okay," she grinned. "The report lists a substantial amount of a toxin that was baked into each one. It's a conclusive match to the toxin found in Helen Mercer's stomach and the other two victims."

"Thank you." Jason pumped a fist. "We're getting closer. Do we know what kind of toxin?"

"No. I think that's odd. Is it possible our unsub works in a lab?"

"Anything's possible. What are we looking for again?"

"Our dignity?"

"Allison Bishop, was that another joke?" He smiled. "It was. Painkillers must be kicking in."

Allie rolled her eyes. She zipped up her official windbreaker despite the midday sun. The thin material satisfied her desire for another layer of protection as they approached another decomposing body.

"Bishop, King," Officer Corrigan greeted them as they dipped below the caution tape.

"You don't look happy to see us," Jason offered, sliding his hands into a set of gloves.

"I'm not. The body was found by three ten-year-olds hunting frogs on summer vacation. They came to the skate park with an older sister and stumbled on this one in broad daylight. My captain is fielding calls from the entire Puyallup PTA this morning."

"Brutal," Jason sympathized.

"Which way is the body?" Allie asked, and Corrigan led them through the municipal park's terraced cement steps.

"This bend in the river had always been prone to flooding," the officer said. "Someone on the city council came up with the brilliant idea of turning the unused land into a park."

"Except flood plains are notorious catch-alls for waterways. The perfect spot for anything larger than a beach ball to wash up on shore," Jason said.

"Exactly." Corrigan ran a hand across his sweaty brow. "Thank you both for coming so quickly. You beat the medical examiner and forensics."

Jason nodded. "Any identifying marks?"

"Besides the missing face? We're miles from where the previous bodies washed up."

Jason surveyed the narrow waterway. "Did the kids see her face?"

"Oh yeah. It's full Friday the 13th up in here. These bodies give me the heebeejeebees. Makes *me* want to sleep with the light on. Poor kids. They're going to need some therapy, for sure."

Allie silently wondered if their unsub dumped this body in a different spot after their recent run-in. The three stepped onto the grassy embankment and made their way down the slope. The pale form of a woman had been caught in the sawgrass and muck. Two gloved officers were standing over the body. Another officer, masked and dressed in waders, had drawn the body closer to the edge of the bank.

"Any idea how long she's been in the water?" Allie asked as she pulled on a pair of gloves.

"No," Corrigan said, "but there is a distinct order of decay. This body is a lot different than the others. Still without a face."

She scanned the body. "That's odd. Typically, submerged

bodies don't look human when they float to the surface. They look less human as the cells break down and take on water. It makes them difficult to identify. This one has actually been preserved."

Allie had crouched on the edge of the bank to view the body, but the slight motion of the body bumping against the embankment released the vapor of decay right at her face. Her eyes watered, and she stepped back from the body into the open air. She couldn't breathe.

"Wow. That's...powerful." Allie had always been a little critical of Jason's weak stomach when it came to the dead they investigated. But this aroma was particularly pungent. She placed a fist over her mouth for a moment and waited for her stomach to settle.

After begging an extra mask from Corrigan, she squatted down again. "Looks like she was wearing some kind of clothing when she went into the water, but not much is left. Safe to say she's over the age of fifty. There's a C-section scar here, so she's given birth at least once. Dark hair, like our previous victims." Reaching out, she gently tapped the skin. "You want to know what's odd?"

"Besides the fact that her face has been removed?" Jason quipped.

"The clothes are rotting off the body, barely hanging on the skin. That would typically signify that she's been in the water for months, based on the state of the material."

"But she's not even bloated."

"Bloated? She's hardly even pruny. Which isn't normal for a waterlogged corpse."

"Does that explain the odor?" Corrigan asked.

"The smell alone would immediately indicate that this wasn't a fresh kill. But like I said, this body has been preserved." She took several pictures with her phone.

"How do you mean?" Jason asked.

Allie removed a small folding knife from her pocket.

"What are you doing?" Corrigan asked.

"It's okay. I'll own it to Dr. Winters when he gets here. I've documented the exact condition of the body, but I want to do a little impromptu experiment." Allie's morbid curiosity had taken over, and she needed answers. She bent over the body, and the two men leaned around her to see. She made a two-inch incision along the woman's upper arm. Without prompting, maggots burst from the flesh in a slime of green putrid liquid and gas.

Officer Corrigan immediately vomited his breakfast into the water.

"Allie! Come on. You gotta warn a man before you do that." Jason coughed, hands on his knees, bent double with the force of the smell.

"That's impressive." Allie wiped the knife on the grass.

"You're impressed? With maggots now?" Jason held his handkerchief over his nose and mouth. "I worry about you sometimes."

"Obviously, what happened to this woman is a tragedy. But our unsub preserved the outside of the body artificially for who knows how long, while the inside rotted."

"Any idea how?"

"None at all. I'll be interested in Dr. Winters's spectro-chemical analysis of the flesh. Jason, do you know what this means?"

"It means I took the wrong shift today," Corrigan quipped as he wiped his mouth.

"It means our unsub began killing women earlier than we thought," Jason answered.

"Yes," Allie raised a finger in the air, "and that he's skilled in preservation. He's gone to great lengths to experiment on these women. But it also means we have a serial killer with a very advanced knowledge of chemistry and anatomy. He's preserving human flesh, *and* he's found a poison that works quickly on its victims, paralyzing them so that he can remove the face while they're still alive. Then he dumps them when he has what he wants."

"Which would be their faces." Jason shook his head.

She took a step back and continued to study the body. "I wonder why he held onto this one for so long."

"So we've got a much larger timeline than we first thought?"

"Looks that way," she nodded.

"You're telling me we've got a mad scientist monster who can run a four-minute mile, and our crime scene could be anywhere along the Puyallup Causeway?"

"Who looks like Bobby Kennedy and has a fixation with older women," Allie added.

He sighed. "Corrigan, you're right. I'm not going to sleep well tonight."

Allie pulled her gloves off. "Unfortunately, neither is Vanessa Martin."

Chapter Thirty-Four

Residence of Jason and Victoria King
Tacoma, Washington

"Hello, beautiful," Allie said as she opened the door to the Kings' apartment. "Music or movie tonight? I've got *The Best of Ella Fitzgerald* and *Casablanca*. And I managed to pick up that adaptogen non-alcoholic wine that Jason keeps raving about. It will go perfectly with our pho."

"Did Jason ask you to babysit me?" A raspy voice came from the living room while Allie unpacked the containers of food in the kitchen.

Allie followed the voice, wandering into the living room where Victoria lay in her recliner underneath a handmade quilt and an IV solution of saline and vitamins.

"No," she fibbed. "He was heading out on a case with Eastman and asked me if I knew a good pho place because your oncologist said bone broth would be good for you."

"But you didn't have to bring me food. He could have had it delivered."

"Right. But have you met me? Takeout and classic movies are about as exciting as I get. If I find someone to share my passions, you're stuck with me for life."

"I haven't seen *Casablanca*." Victoria looked up. "Oh, Allie. Your eyes. How are you feeling?"

"Fine if I don't look in the mirror. The car took the biggest beating." She smiled and sank onto the couch. "Anyway, *Casablanca* has the best one-liners in movie history. I thought it was cliché, but then I realized it's the OG of movies."

"I can't wait. I might fall asleep, though, so don't be offended."

This was the weakest she had seen her friend. It worried her, but she said nothing. "Sleep is a good thing. Jason said you haven't been getting much?"

Victoria mustered the energy to be exasperated. "Nope. Apparently, it's not enough that I'm cold all the time, my hair is falling out, and I don't have the energy to do anything outside of this chair. No, I have neuropathy in my hands and feet."

"So the acupuncture isn't helping?" Allie asked.

"A bit. My mom has been taking me, and it's hard to know if the pain would be worse without it. But it gets me out of the house. They gave me this disgusting tea, though I can't handle it. Jason objects to the whole thing, but he brews it for me every morning."

"Right, because humans aren't supposed to be porcupines," Allie quoted her partner. "Are you up for some food?"

"I'd love to try, and I'd love to talk about anything other than my health. Please, tell me anything." She slowly pushed herself into a sitting position. "Tell me about the case. Jason said you found another body?"

"We did." Allie helped her adjust her chair. "The autopsy report came in this afternoon."

"That seems fast?" Victoria asked.

"Right?" Allie walked back toward the kitchen. "That's what I said. Through the marvels of medical science, the last couple of victims have been identified by their replaced joints or specialized dental work."

"I guess that's only natural if the killer is targeting 'older women.'" Victoria made air quotes.

Allie returned with a glass of hyper-healthy, non-alcoholic wine and set it on the table beside Victoria's chair. "The body belonged to Sandra Monticello, a bus driver from Puyallup who had a complicated set of dentures made a few years back. She was reported missing over eight months ago."

"That predates your other victims, right?"

"It does." She returned to the kitchen and came back with two piping-hot bowls of pho. "And this newest body opens up the possibility of countless more victims. I was just starting to rework our timeline when Marze told me to take a break."

"Good for him." Victoria moaned with pleasure as she took a bite of her food. "So good. Now, tell me about this accident. Jason said someone tried to run you off the road."

"I'm still processing it myself, honestly. I woke up this morning, and I'd forgotten it happened. Then I tried to get out of bed, and my body remembered."

"I know how that feels," Victoria huffed. "Have the police found the car that ran you off the road?"

"Not according to Marze. And they take a special interest

in every case involving law enforcement, in case it's some kind of retribution. But I told him I haven't been an agent long enough to have made enemies, I don't think. It was the one point he and I agreed on. Honestly, I don't know what to think about it all."

Allie had confided in Marze that she had been traveling to Seattle to pick up the case report for her mother. It felt important, after the incident on the road, to have someone who knew the full picture. He encouraged her to focus on one case at a time but didn't fault her for asking questions. He understood it came with the territory.

"My African violets are doing well," Allie said, hoping to change the subject. "You were right. They love the grow light."

"I knew you'd like them. You're such an old soul." Victoria gave her a tired smile. "My grandmother Amalie loved her violets. Are you watering them according to the schedule I gave you? You can easily overwater those, and it takes weeks to recover."

Allie nodded and glanced around the apartment. Every open surface held a soothing green plant. But as she studied each of them, it looked like even Victoria's plants were a little wilted. She couldn't help but wonder if they sensed her pain.

Allie finished her pho and sipped her drink. "Not bad."

"Leave it to Jason to find a way to make alcohol healthy," Victoria laughed, but then sobered. "Did he tell you about Aimee Duff?"

Allie nodded again.

"Good, I'm glad he finally decided to tell you. It was all such a tragedy." Victoria set her soup spoon aside as if exhausted from the action. "Sometimes I can't help but wonder what it would be like if I had married a football coach."

"What do you mean?" Allie asked.

"The hours would probably be the same, at least in season. The same goes for the pay. But at least he'd be pouring into kids or something. I know what you do is noble, but it's a painful career, let's be honest. It's hard on families too."

"I wouldn't know," Allie said softly.

"Oh, that was insensitive of me, Allie. Forgive me. Cancer has made me brash and a little callous. It's also made me question everything."

"Everything?"

"I know it's not a competition. Jason has a dangerous job, but I have cancer. I'm a music teacher, and I may die well before Jason. I guess I've had time to process the weird justice of the whole thing. But I've been thinking about Aimee and Paul a lot."

Allie sipped her drink and let her friend process.

"It's just the nature of your work. As agents, you form such close bonds. It goes beyond typical coworking relationships, and for good reason. You hold the other person's life in your hands. You have to rely on each other. But in the end, that's the irony of it. It makes losing that person so much more painful."

"I guess."

"In Jason's case, the betrayal cut even deeper." Victoria sighed. "Paul wounded him deeply."

"The other option is never getting close to people," Allie replied. "You're right. Don't let anyone in if you want to go the safe route. Keep everyone at arm's length, and they can't hurt you." She stared at her glass, subconsciously running a finger around the rim. "It may not hurt, but it doesn't necessarily help you either."

"Death inevitably comes for us all," Victoria admitted.

"Whether we're ready or not." Allie felt a lump form in her throat. She had always kept up such high walls with people. She was right to self-protect. However, Jason and Victoria weren't most people. They understood Allie and her world.

But it finally dawned on her just how fragile the whole relationship was, and the realization cracked open a deeply vulnerable place inside her. The interior walls had always served to keep people out. But now that she was lowering them, what was left to protect her? She rubbed her chest with a shuddering breath.

There was a strong chance that she might lose Victoria, just like she had lost her mother and, in a very different way, her father. She suddenly felt paralyzed.

Had she made a mistake? Could she trust this friendship? Jason had trusted Paul. Look how that turned out. And how well could you really know someone anyway? Allie felt like she was walking on thin ice, unsure what would happen next.

Alarm bells went off in her head, bringing back the painful memories of her father's betrayal and the deep scars that still lingered. She never thought for a second that her father was capable of doing the things he did. But she was wrong. In her mind, it was safer to have distance between her and the people she cared about.

"Are you all right?" Victoria asked, watching Allie closely.

"I think..." Allie's thoughts were racing. She was sweating. "I think I need more wine."

Chapter Thirty-Five

Glendale Police Department
Glendale, Washington

"We don't get a lot of murders in Glendale. These days, it's the drug overdoses we're trying to curb."

The agents had traveled out to the small town to speak with the local authorities. Glendale was the closest municipality to where the calls from the burner phone originated, and they were certain enough that their unsub lived somewhere in the general vicinity. Any help they could get from the locals would be gratefully accepted.

Several days ago, Jason had emailed the station a sketch of their unsub. Now they sat in a sunny conference room with Sergeant Trey Kennedy, a sturdy man in a crisp tan uniform and a cowboy hat.

"We appreciate the follow-up," Jason said.

"Well, I honestly didn't think anything would come of it. Truth be told, I didn't want it to. I don't like the idea of a serial killer having to do with anyone in these parts," the officer drawled and leaned back in his chair. "But a promise is a promise. Call me old-fashioned, but I think a man is only as good as his word."

"I can appreciate that."

Allie was relieved for a fresh lead, even one that had them driving north out of Tacoma again. She was more than ready to find whoever was killing women in her city.

"I grew up around here," Kennedy explained, "but I've been with the department for less than a decade. Memories run long around here, and I'm still considered a whippersnapper. So I asked around. Finally called someone who knows about all there is to know about this small corner of the world. I asked him to join us. He and I have been chewing the fat this morning."

Allie vibrated with caffeine and impatience. She hated small talk. Still, she had spent enough time working on her grandmother's farm to realize the importance of relationships in rural areas. Trust was earned through hard work and responsibility. Kennedy was right about small-town memories, and she appreciated his willingness to take their request seriously.

The type of information he was cultivating couldn't be discovered via the internet. It was held in fading memories, crumbling newspapers, and family Bibles. Allie braced herself for a slow meandering trip down memory lane but started to think she shouldn't have had that third cup of coffee this morning.

"You know," Kennedy chuckled, "when I got your sketch, I thought the guy in the picture was a decent looking guy to be a killer. But then someone reminded me of Ted Bundy, and I had to admit that evil can lurk inside someone regardless of what they might look like." He looked up out of the window and saw a man striding down the hall in their direction. "Ah, here's James now."

Instead of a creaky senior citizen, Kennedy introduced them to a fit, white-haired gentleman with clear blue eyes. Everyone stood for introductions. Allie adjusted her expectations with a pleasant surprise. He wore a golf shirt and shorts but still carried himself like a police officer—upright and confident.

"This is Chief James Horowitz," Kennedy said.

Allie nodded. "Thank you for meeting us, Chief."

He waved her off and took a seat beside the sergeant. "Please, call me James. I've been retired for three years. I appreciate just being James," he said with a twinkle in his eye. "It's nice to come in occasionally to catch up with the crew, but these days, you'll find me on the golf course."

"I knew if anyone knew the people of Glendale, it would be Chief." Kennedy settled into his office chair with a laid-back grin.

"I'm not sure how much help I'll be, but when I saw the sketch, it jogged my memory a bit."

"You recognized him?" Allie asked.

"Yes and no." He raised a styrofoam cup of coffee to his lips and took a sip.

Allie squinted in frustration.

"The sketch looks like someone I used to know." James glanced out the window as if searching for an elusive memory. "Stanley Anderson. Real SOB, pardon my language."

"Anderson?" Allie scrawled the name in her notebook.

"Yep, Stan was a bum. I don't mean that in a derogatory manner, although he was that too. He was a panhandler. He'd hang out on the corner of Herndon Boulevard, next to the cemetery. Would write up a cardboard sign predicting the end of the world or some kind of nonsense. He was mean too. He'd pick a fight with any and everyone who didn't like what he had to say. I arrested him a handful of times for fights and public intoxication. It never was worth my paperwork. He never showed up for his court appearance, and I finally stopped charging him. I'd just stick him in the drunk tank until he dried out or his wife came looking for him."

Jason leaned forward. "Tell us more about her."

"Maria," James recalled. "Tiny thing. Shy, wouldn't look me in the eye. The only reason I got her name was because he beat her up so badly that she had to be hospitalized. She went to the county for a broken wrist, cracked ribs, and bruising. One of the nurses got suspicious and phoned me. I tried to talk to her, but she wouldn't press charges, and they had no choice but to let her go home." He rubbed his chin thoughtfully.

Allie liked the retired officer. Each name in his town was more than just a memory. They were souls entrusted to him for protection.

He continued. "I must have made some kind of connection though. She'd come looking for Stanley after a couple of days. I think she trusted me a little. Some days, he was with us, and she'd take him home. Often he wasn't. Those were tougher for her, you can imagine. Not sure what kind of hole he found to crawl into, but I was glad I didn't need to go poking around."

"Stanley and Maria," Jason reiterated. "But you don't think he's the man we're looking for?"

"Can't be. Stanley died about four years ago."

Allie felt the sting of the news. "Are you sure?"

"I'm sure. Signed the death certificate myself. His body turned up in Cary Lake Park. No one came looking for him that time."

"Did you have a number for his wife?"

"A number? Nah. She and Stanley were squatters out in the marsh."

Jason's head cocked to one side. "The what?"

"Trey told me you had a cell phone ping off the school bus turnaround? Out by mile marker twenty-seven?"

Jason nodded. "That's right. I went out there a few days ago, but there was nothing beyond it. It feels like the end of the world."

"That's because it is," Kennedy chuckled. "That's the end of the rural route. The county widened the road so the bus could safely maneuver without having to go a mile out of its way. Saves a decent amount of gas each year for the school district. But it's at the edge of the marshland. Nothing but an old slough beyond it."

"So that turnaround would be a good place to make a call if you didn't want it to be tracked," James picked up.

"And you said people used to live back there?" Allie asked.

James nodded. "That's right. About forty years ago, there was a community of homesteaders who moved out there fleeing capitalism or whatever cause du jour they felt persecuted by. It was early on when I joined the force. In the beginning, they were just odd. Caused an uproar in town because they didn't send their kids to school or the doctor. They'd busk on the corners or sell homemade goods. Some were real hard workers, great for hire if you need land cleared, your house painted, or furniture built. They made their own moonshine and hunted in ways that are anything but legal. But they kept to themselves, had a midwife and a preacher. They were a tight community for a few years."

"What happened?" Allie asked.

Horowitz shook his head. "No idea. I wasn't in charge back then, and it didn't pay for me to ask too many questions. The land still falls under the jurisdiction of the GPD, but it's not zoned for any school, so none of the kids out there were considered truant, and they knew it. But for whatever reason, their version of paradise fell apart. Best I can tell, the most industrious got tired of living that way and moved off. What was left behind was a cantankerous few who wanted to be left alone."

"Like Stanley Anderson," Allie said.

"Exactly. Anyway, there was a real bad fire a few years back. A couple farmers at the edge of the marsh saw the smoke. One of them picked up a young man with terrible burns. Johnson said a family appeared on the road right up by where your cell phone pinged."

"What happened to the boy?" Jason asked.

"Real sad, he died of his injuries, all alone in the county hospital. The family didn't come with him, just handed him to the farmer and disappeared back into the marsh. I tried to investigate back then, but no one would talk to me. The only way into the marsh is with boats or ATVs. Unless you were born in the marsh and know the lay of the land, it can be deadly. Every few years, a townie gets a truck stuck or loses an animal out there. It's just as dangerous as being out at sea, except that no one realizes the danger until it's too late."

Allie had busily been scratching notes. "Is it federal land?" she asked.

"Nope. Ownership goes way back to the days of the prospectors when the land was cheap, and parcels went for pennies. It's been in the same family's possession for generations."

"Do you have a name?"

"Ronald Barlow."

Jason whistles through his teeth. "The billionaire?"

"Yep," Horowitz chuckled. "The billionaire. The marsh was just a piece of his inheritance. If you listen to the Barlow estate, you'll get one version of our state history. They claim the Barlows came out on the Oregon trail and built a place down in Puyallup. They don't mention it anymore, but word is they were whalers, originally, who made their money in logging up and down the coast. When gold was discovered up in Whatcom County, they became land speculators. They bought up cheap land and made a fortune selling it for a hundred times what it was worth to greedy prospectors with gold fever."

"Was that the Mount Baker Gold Rush?" Allie asked.

"You know your state history," James told her. "When the miner would die or default, the Barlows would claim the land and sell it again." He shook his head. "I reckon the marsh was uninhabitable land that just stayed on their books over the years. It's been all but forgotten about for generations. Nowadays, the family has tried to legitimize its history and claims to be one of the early settlers of the region, big into land conservation and whatnot. But you'll hear a different story if you know who to talk to around here."

"Did you ever reach out to the Barlow estate about the squatters?"

"Absolutely. I offered to work with the family office and even recommended several good men he could hire to help run security out there. I'm a conservationist too. I'm glad that there are still large swaths of natural land. I just don't want a meth lab running outside my town."

"Makes sense. Did Barlow agree?"

"Nope. I got the run around every time. Even when that young man died. So we stopped patrolling the area. It was the eighties, so budget cuts and high gas prices. I needed to make some tough choices, and so we had to turn a blind eye. Bothers me to this day."

"How many people do you think still live in the marsh?" Allie asked.

"Honestly, I thought Stanley and Maria were the last ones."

"Why's that?"

"I hadn't seen Maria in years and was kind of shocked when Stanley showed up dead," he recalled. "He hadn't been to town much for more than fuel and provisions."

"And Maria?"

"There were rumors that she lived out there after Stanley died. She was a bit of a healer. Some of our more adventurous women talked about visiting her if they needed herbal tinctures and remedies. But I never looked into it. Figured it was just talk. Odds are she found her freedom after that SOB of a husband died. She could be down in sunny Florida for all I know."

"Forgive me, James, just so we're clear." Allie steepled her fingers. "I appreciate your information about the area, but why do you think there's a connection between our unsub and this Stanley Anderson?"

"Well, that's just the thing. I don't like hunches, but if you'd met Stanley Anderson in his younger years, maybe mid-thirties—like I did—you'd have thought he was a dead ringer for this guy right here." Horowitz tapped his finger on the sketch Vanessa Martin had described to their forensic team. "It's the dimple in the chin and the eyebrows."

Allie gave Jason a thoughtful look.

"What are the chances Stanley and Maria had kids?" Jason asked.

"It would be the natural way of things. But if they did, we never had a record of it. Whenever I saw Maria in town, she never had a child with her. No one ever saw her pregnant as far as I know."

Jason asked, "How hard would it be to get permission from Barlow to search that land?"

"Barlows have always been accommodating to law enforcement," Sergeant Kennedy said. "They'll permit you, just don't count on getting a lot of help. Getting permission is not the hard part of investigating on the marsh."

"What is?"

"Your biggest obstacle out there will be the terrain itself. That place is a no man's land."

Chapter Thirty-Six

FBI Field Office
Tacoma, Washington

Allie tacked up a large paper map on the cubicle wall of her office. She stepped back, looked at the detailed drawing, and stretched. Several pencils stuck out of the loose bun on her head, accumulated during hours of research at her computer.

"What's that?" Jason said from the doorway. Opening a protein bar, he chewed it casually. His tie was loosened and his collar unbuttoned. They had dug in all afternoon, searching for tangible evidence of James Horowitz's claims.

"A map Ronald Barlow's people sent over of the family's holdings, including Darien Marsh and Abercorn Creek." Allie pointed a pencil tip at the undeveloped section of the map. "I've been staring at satellite footage all day. I'm starting to get cross-eyed."

"I don't think I've seen a paper map in..." Jason pondered, "years."

Allie laughed. "Right? I keep looking for an X to mark the spot."

Jason squinted at it. "Look at the detail."

"It's a survey map that the Barlow family trust commissioned in the forties. It's an art form. Fascinating to see what was here back then and what's been changed, like the Puyallup levee."

"Are you looking for something in particular?"

"This area here is the marsh." She traced her finger across a large green swath of uninhabited land. "You can tell because of the lack of development over the years. This was farmland for a long time. Now it's become the suburbs. But Abercorn Creek is here, and that's the flood plain that feeds the marsh that drains into the Puyallup. See, here's the trout farm." She points. "It's been there for fifty years or so."

Jason crumpled his wrapper and tossed it into the bin like he was making a free throw. "I'm a fan of the history and all, but what does it have to do with our unsub?"

"Well, Chief Horowitz said the squatters took up residence over forty years ago? I'm trying to identify any buildings that were there or on the later map the Barlows sent over that match the satellite images from today. There are a handful of places in the marsh that look like they're habitable."

"Maybe a meth lab or homeless encampment?" Jason speculated.

"Could be. So we may need to get our own survey of the area, something current. But if Horowitz is right, we're looking for an established space that's off the beaten path. It would be bigger than a tent and would show up over the years. Maybe even a trailer?"

"From the sounds of it, no one is getting a trailer back in there."

"Okay. But Horowitz mentioned they were industrious. I'm guessing that means they built their own homes."

"Makes sense. How many spots fit that description?"

Allie tapped a key on her keyboard, and satellite imagery flooded her screen. She pointed out three distinctive sites that she had highlighted after hours of detailed scrutiny. "I would like to investigate these three spots."

Jason studied the terrain. "That's a lot of territory. We can't just waltz over and take a look."

"So we need to requisition a drone from SWAT."

Jason shook his head. "TFO doesn't have one."

"Seattle does. And I met one of their guys at Quantico."

"Look at you working the connections." Jason grinned at his partner. "Okay. Drones are a great idea. Less manpower and less risk. Less mosquitoes too."

"Less noise, and we won't spook him if he's out there." Allie chewed her lip. She couldn't stand the idea of this guy slipping through her fingers a second time.

"You hope not, but he already knows he's under surveillance," Jason warned. "And we know that he's highly skilled and intelligent. But what about permission? What have we heard from the Barlow estate? Anything?"

"Horowitz was right about those guys. They're polite, talked my ear off about their conservationism, their archives, Tacoma history."

"But?"

"Besides sending over the maps, they won't sign off on any searches without a warrant."

"I knew it," Jason winced. "It's amazing how money buys respectability but not morality."

"And better lawyers," Allie agreed. "They have a whole office of Stanford grads who just passed the bar and couldn't wait to argue land rights with me. Interestingly enough, they said we could get on the land by special request from Ronald Barlow if we're filming a documentary, or searching for mineral rights, or even hunting rare species of floral or fauna."

"But as law enforcement, we're pariah?"

"Exactly."

"No judge is going to let us near this one without some serious probable cause."

Allie took a swig from a warm Snapple sitting neglected on her desk. "The terrain is tough," she added, clicking on a few images of the swamp she found online. "You and I can do it on foot or with an ATV, but it's getting a team out there with backup that's going to be difficult. If we want to have any chance of catching this guy, we're looking at a logistical nightmare, especially with an unsub as intelligent as this one." Allie paused to confirm her idea. "That's why I think the drones may be our best bet."

"I'm listening."

"Aerial surveillance doctrine under the Fourth Amendment is on our side for this one. It states the use of a drone does *not* constitute a search for which law enforcement must obtain a warrant."

Jason scratched his beard. "That legal area is untested and

murky. Do you really want to get the FBI embedded in a legal battle with a billionaire? That could be our jobs."

"No, that's why I propose a single drone. We don't even need to record any data. The law is pretty clear when it comes to naked eye surveillance for a short period of time."

"I like it. Go on."

"We don't need to catch our unsub in the act. That takes time and manpower."

"And possibly a warrant," he said.

"We're just trying to identify if any of these three locations is currently being lived in. I can't make that call from these satellite surveys. I need a closer look."

"It would give us time to get a warrant."

Allie bounced on her toes in excitement. "And, we'd only need a warrant for one location, less red tape."

"More probable cause. Good work, rookie. I'll work on getting a warrant and some equipment if—"

"When."

"When..." he smiled. "When we find something worth investigating. What about Stanley and Maria Anderson?"

"Couple of ghosts, totally off-grid." Allie pointed out the blank spaces on her case board. "There is no marriage license, no records for Stanley Anderson except for his death certificate signed by the chief."

"Could Stanley Anderson be an alias?"

"Possibly," Allie said. "Maria did have a social security number under her maiden name. The medical records Horowitz referenced gave me a Maria Anderson at about the right age. It's one of the only places she shows up on record. She had four hospital visits over ten years."

"Anything weird about that? Did she have a baby or something?"

"If she did, there's no record of it at the county hospital. Each time she went to the hospital, it was for serious physical injuries in line with abuse, like Horowitz said. According to the medical reports, she was an accident-prone woman. Broken ribs, broken wrist, bruising. By the fourth time, that's when someone local called Horowitz."

Jason glanced over the reports with a critical eye. "Broken jaw, concussion, stitches. Like hell these are accidents, unless she's a heavy-weight boxer."

Allie grimaced. The abuse was obvious from the toll it took on the human body.

"Anything recent?"

"No. Nothing for the last five years."

"Interesting because Mr. Anderson died four years ago," Jason said.

"But none of what we've found today explains why Stanley Anderson resembles our unsub." Allie flopped frustratedly into her chair. The potential possibilities were endless.

"No, not on paper, at least. But it does confirm everything Horowitz claimed. That's good. It means we're on the right track. You set up the drone visit. I'm gonna start working on our warrant. That way, if—" Jason caught himself. "*When* we get location coordinates, we can submit them as quickly as possible. Keep your chin up. We're on the right track." He patted her on the shoulder and headed out.

Allie stared at the sketch of the unsub tacked to the case board. He stared back at her, an enigma. His profile was boyish, and his hair was trimmed into a neat clean-cut style that made him appear wholesome and handsome. She tried to imagine the story behind the innocent-looking face—a monster masquerading as a helpful neighbor, charming women and literally peeling off their beauty. Why? She could imagine all kinds of harsh realities that would come with living off the grid, but none of it led her one step closer to finding him.

Allie admitted defeat and decided she needed a run. All that time curled up over her computer staring at satellite images had left knots in her shoulders she needed to work out with a good sweat. Hopefully, a chance to let her body process all the information she uncovered today would give her some insight. She shut her computer and slipped a file in her satchel. She would look at it after dinner.

"Night, boss," Allie said on her way out.

Marze looked up from his desk. "Allie. Do you have a minute?"

Stepping into his space, she paused inside the threshold.

"Have a seat." He plopped his reading glasses on the desk, a rare show of age from a man of exceptional fitness and vitality. "Jason briefed me on your Glendale lead. Sounds like you're headed in the right direction."

"Thank you, sir." She settled into the chair across from him.

"That's why I wanted to touch base. You're making good progress on this case, and you're a good fit at the TFO. You've been a support to Jason."

"But?" Allie asked, watching subtle signs of tension flit across his face. "Why do I feel like you're trying to get rid of me?"

"I'm not. I want you here, and I want you to know it. There's no question about your fit or your work. However, each field office has a routine schedule for agents to help other field officers when they're short-staffed. The TFO is carrying a heavy caseload, but once you've wrapped up this case, I'm sending you to Boise."

The words hit Allie like a punch. "Boise? Okay..." she stammered.

"It's not personal." Marze tried to reassure her. "You're a good agent. But you're also new here and don't have any outstanding cases after you get this one closed out. You're the easiest agent for me to lend out."

Allie scanned his face, watching for signs he was lying to her. They sat in silence while the words sank in. Marze's face was open and honest. It was true she would be the easiest piece on the team to spare. She had no spouse or kids to entangle her, and she'd barely gotten settled in her apartment. "My grandmother...I..."

"I understand that it's not an ideal situation for you and Etta. That's why I want you to know you have friends here. I'm happy to swing by her place if you need me to, day or night. The same is true for Jason. I just talked to him about it."

Allie felt her body flush with the idea of Marze and Jason discussing her.

"You're family here, Allie, but Boise is desperate. They've been bugging me for weeks. They need someone easy to work with and sharp. Not someone contaminated by years of agency bureaucracy and policies. They need fresh eyes. Plus, it's good for you to see how another office works. Make some regional relationships. Jason told me you reached out to SWAT in Seattle?"

"Um, yeah." She tried to focus.

"That's excellent. Relationships are key to this work. It's not the paperwork that connects us, it's the people. My hope is that you come back to us with a depth of knowledge and experience that will serve us both well. I've bragged about you to the BFO, and they're calling in a favor."

"You *hope* I come back?" Allie stuck on the words. Was this a permanent transfer? "I'm sorry, this is a lot to process. Boise is what, eight hours from here? That's not like networking with Seattle, sir. Or even Portland?"

"That's true, but we do share a state border and you'd be surprised how many of our cases overlap," Marze tried to reassure her. "It's a short flight, Bishop. You can be back here the same day if you need to. I want this to be your home. But I have to play ball with Idaho here. It will serve you well in the end. I promise. One case with them, maybe two, and you come back home."

Allie nodded. She trusted Marze, but that didn't make it easier. "Thanks for letting me know."

She walked out of the TFO in a stupor. Without consciously realizing it, Allie had settled into the TFO and hit her stride with Jason. And then there was Victoria.

She hated the idea of leaving the two of them, remembering Victoria's frailty at their last visit. Their conversation lingered in Allie's memory. Victoria had tried to warn her it could be dangerous to get close to people in this line of work.

Maybe heading out of town for a while was good. A fresh start. Allie took a deep breath and savored the tang of the ocean air in the back of her throat. She pressed down the sadness and tried to be positive. She could focus on digging into her mother's past and really spend time combing through the case file.

At the thought of a case file, she touched her satchel. Stephanie Mercer's case was inside, reminding her to focus. Regardless of whatever changes were coming, she still had a case to solve. A killer to hunt.

Chapter Thirty-Seven

Location: Unknown

Jada blinked in the dark—at least, she thought she was blinking. She had never tried to feel herself blink before, but she had few sensations of any kind. There was a faint odor of dampness in the air and some kind of sharp chemical smell. She breathed—she was alive, right? She tried to blink again. Yes, there it was, the faintest flicker in the dark.

She was alive, she decided. She could breathe, blink, and smell.

But nothing else. The realization gave her a terrifying sense of dread. Her heart may have been hammering in her chest, but she couldn't tell because everything from the neck down was—nothing. She tried to speak. Her lips wouldn't move. A faint wheezing sound came from the direction of her mouth. Was she making that noise?

Oh, dear god.

What Jada did feel was a cold wave of terror wash over her.

She tried to feel her fingers and toes, any sensation in her body that could help her feel something. The numbness was so staggeringly oppressive.

She couldn't remember anything. How had she gotten here? Where was *here*? Then the flicker of memory returned something to her. A face, perhaps? A brown paper grocery bag. A bottle of ketchup, a box of blueberries. She had gotten groceries this afternoon and had been taking them into the house...but then what?

The memories were hollow. They flitted in and out. She remembered an apple rolling across the driveway. A face...it wasn't her husband's face. Chris was on his fishing trip with his brother. She was going to prepare a side dish for them when they returned with the fish. That's why she had been to the grocery store but—the face. It floated above her memory.

Mark!

His face brought it all back. He had stopped by the house as she was unloading, said he wanted to bring her something special to celebrate. It had been odd when he stopped her in the driveway. She looked forward to their visits. But today, when he had shown up on her driveway, he seemed frantic. Her instincts had tried to warn her when she saw him on the sidewalk. He was stooped, wild-eyed, and it looked like he was arguing with himself.

For a fleeting moment, her instincts told her to look away. Keep driving past her own house and come back when he was gone. But then he spotted her, and suddenly he looked—well, normal. Even though she felt the cold grip of dread, she ignored it. Pressed it down. She didn't want to be impolite. And he offered to help her with the groceries.

Why had she let him in the house? He brought in two gallons of water, and then there was a prick in her neck. Jada remembered everything now, all of it flooding back.

Mark caught her before her head hit the ground. She remembered that part. He was so gentle with her as he shone the flashlight in her eyes. Before she knew it, he was wrapping her in a sheet, a sheet from her own bed. She recognized the stripes and the scent of lavender. He wrapped her in the fabric and clumsily carried her outside in broad daylight.

Jada remembered the strange paralysis that made it impossible to fight him or even cry for help. She watched from inside the strange mummy that her body had become. He tossed her into the trunk of his run-down sedan. He wasn't gentle anymore. Jada had heard her body crunch against the metal with a sickening sound. But there was no pain. Just the terrifying sound of her body colliding with the wheel well. She may have broken bones or worse, but there was no way of knowing. The feeling of her limbs seizing up as she slowly lost control was the most terrifying thing she had ever experienced.

Until this moment.

Now, Jada lay in the darkness, awaiting an unknown fate with dread. Death was the only logical solution to this. Her eyelids fluttered again, and her breath came in rasps. She wondered if dying alone in the dark would be better than whatever Mark might have planned.

Chris's voice kept pulling her back to the dark, cold space. She blinked rapidly. Silence. Had she imagined her husband's voice? Images flooded her mind, her granddaughter's painted toes, her freckles, the way her head fit on her husband's chest. The way he stroked her hair as they sat in church, his rough, calloused hands that were so much larger than hers, his hand on her knee while they drove. Tears leaked out of Jada's eyes. Would her husband or Lydia, her daughter, ever know what happened to her?

A sound broke through the darkness. The click of a key turned in a lock, the scrape of metal, and a shaft of light appeared in the room as a door swung open. Jada caught a whiff of fresh air from beyond as a fluorescent light blinked on above her. She blinked rapidly, unable to shield her eyes from the sudden glare.

Footsteps sounded from the other side of the wall, and Jada felt a flutter of breath against her eyelashes. Something blocked the light, and Mark's face appeared above her. He grinned eagerly, a disturbing smile spreading across his face. He studied the details of her milky skin with his eyes. It was chilling. Jada tried to scream, but nothing.

Eyes wide in terror, she begged for her life with her gaze, trying to connect with his humanity. She prayed that he would take pity on her. But what she saw instead made her very soul shrivel up in fear. This was no human. The eyes held no life.

Only the cold, hard fascination of a psychopath fascinated by his prey.

Chapter Thirty-Eight

Darien Marsh
Glendale, Washington

Flashing lights rippled across the windshield of their car as Allie and Jason drove up to the Lovingoods' home. Several police cruisers clustered around the front of a tidy ranch home a few miles from the old school bus turnaround. A tall form in rain gear approached the car. Officer Kennedy's face appeared in the window, and Jason rolled it down. The rain came in sideways, pelting Jason, but he didn't flinch.

"Status?" Jason asked.

"Husband came home three hours ago. He wasn't supposed to, but he injured himself cleaning a fish and came back. Inside, there are signs of a struggle. Door ajar, groceries all over the floor. Jada, his wife, is gone. Keys, phone, and purse were all there. He called us immediately. I'm sure you saw that Jada matches the profile you sent over, so we mobilized our people.

We've combed every corner of the town. Receipt from the grocery gives us a window of time, and the neighbor remembers seeing a young man in an older dark sedan haul something large out of the house and dump it into the trunk. They didn't recognize him from around here, but I showed him your sketch."

"And?" Allie asked.

"It's our guy," Kennedy said soberly.

Allie's stomach clenched. The clock was ticking.

"Please tell me you guys found something out at the marsh?" Officer Kennedy yelled above the storm.

"We have a location," Jason confirmed. His phone buzzed, and he glanced down at his lap. "And a warrant."

"Good," Kennedy pounded on the car roof. "I've got my men all over the county. I'll round up everyone I can and send them into the marsh behind you." He checked his watch. "It will take us at least an hour."

"It's better than nothing," Jason said. "But it's going to take time to get across the marsh on foot."

"You said the neighbor saw our guy in a car?" Allie asked, her mind trying to take in the information.

"Yep."

"If he's got Jada and he headed back into the marsh, he'll need a way to move her body."

Jason picked up the idea. "We may need to look for a road that goes into the marsh."

"Did we see any tire tracks on the drone feed?" Allie asked.

"No, but we weren't looking for any." Jason pounded the steering wheel. "Horowitz made it sound like no one got in there with a vehicle. We'll head back and see how far we get with the car."

"I sent you the coordinates from the warrant," Allie yelled into the rain. "Get as many people out there as you can. ASAP."

"What are you guys going to do?" Kennedy asked.

"Try to find Jada before it's too late," Jason said.

"Wait." Kennedy reached into his raincoat and handed over two radios. "You're gonna need these. There's no cell service out there. We're all on channel seven point five." He waited until Jason had switched it on and heard the sound of static broken by law enforcement coming across the airwaves.

"Got it, thanks," Jason said. He rolled up the window and pulled away.

"Marze," Allie barked into her phone as they drove back to the surveillance spot. She clicked the call over to speaker, and they filled in their boss on the rapidly changing situation. "Jada Lovingood has been missing for over four hours." Urgency was thick in her voice. She knew if they waited for the storm to let up, it might be too late.

"I've got a team headed your way now," he replied. "I'll have them rendezvous with you at the turnaround at mile marker twenty-seven."

Minutes later, Jason pulled into the roundabout and crept toward the treeline. Allie glanced at a picture of their map on her phone and studied the topographical detail.

"Wait here," she said. As soon as he had come to a full stop, she popped out of the car. The rain battered her face, forcing her to pull her hat low. Hurrying to the edge of the marsh, she clicked on her flashlight and scanned the edge of the tree line.

She ran the flashlight beam across the dirt at her feet, looking for anything that might signal a pathway in. The ground was wet and muddy, nothing that would work for a trek across the marsh.

Finally, she recognized a landmark—a large pine tree stood off the road. Allie placed her hand on its rough bark and looked up. Inside a flash of lightning, she could see the outline of a large bird's nest high above. It was the same tree where the osprey had perched. She glanced back at Jason, who was sitting in the car, the beams of his headlights broken by the shredding rain. Another lightning strike lit up the ground below her feet.

She bent and noticed two sticks broken in half, then jammed her fingers into the dirt just to confirm. The ground here was solid. She ran her light over the beaten track of grass. Something had come through here recently and damaged the foliage. The rain obscured the tracks, but there was an old strip of gravel here, hemmed in by bushes and cloaked by tree limbs.

Allie ran back to Jason and threw herself inside the car. "Aim to the left of the biggest pine tree. There's a road there, I promise."

"Son of a—" Jason stared at the gap in the trees. "How did we miss that?" He gunned the engine, drove off the gravel down the embankment, and slowly moved toward the marsh.

They paused as the car neared the edge, and Allie jumped out again. This time, she tied a safety vest around the tree with a strong knot to help Kennedy and his team find the path into the marsh. She took a picture and sent him a quick text with the last of her remaining signal before they plunged into the wild marsh.

Slowly, they trundled forward. Branches scraped loudly

against the car, causing Jason to flinch. "I'll have to get a new paint job after this," he grumbled. They crept on for over a mile before Jason tapped his brakes. A rusty Ford sedan sat tucked in a stand of shrubbery, a green tarp whipping in the wind above it.

Allie felt the adrenaline pulse in her chest. "How much farther do you think?"

"About another mile." Any advance was blocked by two sturdy spruce trees. "Looks like we're on foot now." Jason radioed their position to Kennedy, climbed out of the car, and clicked on his flashlight. Together, they found a narrow trail that meandered into the marsh.

Night was beginning to fall over the area. Soon enough, Allie's legs were soaked past her knees from stepping into soft patches of marsh. She had nearly lost a shoe twice already, the thick, greedy mud trying to suck them off her feet. Rain had long ago soaked through her thin FBI windbreaker. It was a mental image of Jada Lovingood that propelled her forward.

The going was a slog, and several times they lost the path, not knowing where to turn. A diligent search would reveal it again, and they would march on.

Allie had just stepped over a large puddle when Jason placed a hand on her arm. He pointed to the outline of a building in the beam of his flashlight, then put a finger over his lips and drew his sidearm.

Allie's skin tingled in anticipation as she followed suit. They lowered the beams of their lights and hurried to make their way to the outlay of buildings before them. Most of the buildings were dilapidated and sagging, except for the one they had seen in the drone footage.

A lamp was burning low in the window of the yellow cottage. Allie flicked off her flashlight, and Jason followed suit. The light from the house was faint, but they didn't want to risk alerting anyone inside to their presence.

Jason whispered into the radio, informing anyone who was listening that they were approaching the homestead. The agents crept closer, traversing more mud, marsh grass, and unseen potholes. Jason signaled for them to approach the house and get a visual inside. If Jada was still alive, getting her out depended on their stealth and ability to assess the situation and respond quickly.

With their weapons drawn, they cautiously circled the perimeter of the home and approached from the rear, creeping toward the house. Frogs had begun their evening songs, joined by a strong chorus of crickets. The rain kept up, pinging on the metal roof of the house. Allie swatted a swarm of mosquitoes from her face.

From a distance, and from the cover of a healthy shrub, they peered into the small window of the living room. Allie held her breath. Inside, the cabin was sparsely furnished, with wooden walls and floors. No pictures hung on the walls, nothing cozy except for the tattered eyelet curtain and a spartan shelf next to a table. Then she noticed a woman with dark hair sitting in a wheelchair, her back to the window. Jason saw her too and gave Allie a look of uncertainty.

Was it Jada? Or could it possibly be Maria, Stanley's wife?

The agents shrunk back as a man with dark hair appeared through a wide doorway. He was a perfect representation of the sketch Vanessa Martin had provided. He approached the woman in the wheelchair, knelt beside her, and looked at her.

Then he held something up, raising it as if it were a hard-earned offering.

Allie stifled a gasp.

He was holding a mask. A mask made from the skin of a human face.

Chapter Thirty-Nine

Darien Marsh
Glendale, Washington

"Dispatch, this is Agent King, over," Jason whispered into the radio.

"GPD dispatch, go ahead." He had the volume down so low it was barely audible.

"Dispatch, Agent Bishop and I are at the coordinates of the unsub's location. Be advised the suspect is on the premises."

The radio crackled with a weighty silence. Finally, "Understood, Agent King. Do you have a visual on our victim? Over."

Jason looked at Allie, and she felt her gut twist.

"Be advised, the suspect is not alone in the house. I have visual on an unknown woman in a wheelchair. It may be our victim. No confirmation."

Another long pause from the radio. Allie kept her gaze fixed on the cabin window.

"Understood. All units, be advised. The suspect is at the location with at least one civilian—possibly more. Backup is en route to you now. Godspeed."

Jason lowered the radio and blew out a breath. "We need to get inside that house."

Allie felt a ripple of adrenaline pulse through her cold, wet body. Her thighs ached from trudging through the mud and slime of the marsh, but she shoved the pain to the back of her mind and forced herself to concentrate. This was what she had trained for. If there was the faintest shot of getting Jada out of there alive, she had to take it.

"What's the plan? It's going to take them at least half an hour to get here. Probably more now that it's almost fully dark."

"Our unsub has seen your face, right?" Jason asked. "During the Vanessa Martin sting?"

Allie felt her shoulders sag. "Yes."

"Okay, then you're going around. There's a side door next to the kitchen. See if you can get in either through the door or maybe a window."

"Got it, I'll make it work. What are you gonna do?"

"I'm going to distract this guy. I don't want him looking through the window and recognizing you."

Allie stared at him. "What?"

"What did you say to me today? It's a far, far better thing I do—something like that."

"That was a line from a book, Jason," she said in disbelief.

"Well, it was a good one. If we make it through this, you can tell me how the book ends. I'll distract him, and you get eyes on

Jada. Give me three taps on the radio if you can get her out of the house to safety. If you're in trouble, hold it down like this." He demonstrated, and the radio quietly squawked.

"That will give you away," Allie warned.

"I'll think of something." He nodded. "Dispatch, this is Agent King. Please be advised that Agent Bishop and I are approaching the location to engage the suspect."

The radio crackled, but nothing came through.

Jason holstered the radio. He nodded to his partner, and the pair separated silently. Allie ducked below a bush and crept around to the left side of the house while Jason moved around the other side to the front. Soon enough, she heard him pounding on the front door.

"Anderson!" Jason bellowed. "This is the FBI. We have a warrant to search your premises. You are under arrest. Come out with your hands up."

Allie's pulse raced. She desperately needed the seconds Jason was giving her to lure the man's attention away from the woman. Placing a hand on the knob of the side door, she breathed a prayer and turned. It turned effortlessly and popped open. Within moments, she was in the house and surveying the scene.

She was in a kitchen of sorts. A can of propane sat on a grimy stove. There were mismatched cabinets, old pots, and canned goods littering the shelves. Dirty dishes sat in a tiny sink. A stand-up freezer was jammed against an ancient, rusted fridge, all strung together with an extension cord. Beside the fridge was another door with a padlock on it. Ignoring it, Allie silently walked across the kitchen in three steps, stealing a glance around the wide door frame into a single large room.

The man was at the front of the house, on her left, having taken up a spot directly behind the door Jason was banging on. Jason was doing a fine job drowning out any sound with his yelling and pounding. Allie eyed the man as he yelled through the door, clutching a pistol.

To her right was the woman in the wheelchair. Silently, she crept into the room, disengaged the brake, and held her breath, hoping the wheelchair wouldn't make a sound.

"No!" he screamed at Jason. "You need to leave me alone." He whimpered and slapped his head with an open palm. "I need to stay with Mother. She needs me," he yelled, pacing the floor.

Mother?

Allie slipped the wheelchair into the kitchen unseen. She struggled to put the pieces together as she moved the wheelchair into the kitchen and over to the side door. Their unsub was Maria and Stanley Anderson's son? Allie ducked behind the thin wall separating the two rooms. There was no way she was getting the wheelchair down the side steps without being heard.

Moving quickly, she stepped around to the front of the wheelchair and glanced at the woman, then slammed her hand over her mouth to silence a scream of terror. Her fingers nearly released their grip on her gun.

Staring back at her were the mummified remains of Maria Anderson. A dark wig sat atop the dead woman's head, and a blue nightgown hung on the gray shriveled frame. Somehow, the eyes looked alive. The hands tucked into her lap were the withered claws of a corpse. Allie choked back a gag of shock.

The Face of Evil

The body had been preserved and stitched up like Frankenstein, the wig neatly brushed and braided.

Allie fixated on the flap of beige skin draped across the woman's face. She poked it with her gun, and it moved against the preserved remains of her face like a piece of fabric.

Allie pressed her back against the outer wall and tried to recalibrate her senses.

The situation in the front was escalating quickly.

Where was Jada?

Allie remembered the door with the padlock. She was about to cross to it when she was stopped by the violent thunder of three gunshots in the other room. She flinched, and before she could respond with confidence, another bullet screamed past her and punched into the wooden wall near the side door.

She froze in the silence that followed, the hairs on her neck standing up as she slowly turned to look into the face of the man she had been hunting.

His eyes were bloodshot. He seethed in the doorway, staring straight at Allie. But that's not what made her blood turn to ice. It was the pistol that was pointed straight at Allie's head.

Chapter Forty

Darien Marsh
Glendale, Washington

"Where's my partner?" Allie growled. Her gun was still clenched in her right hand, but she dared not point it at him. He had the draw on her. One flinch of his finger and she was gone.

The air was thick and musty in the tiny kitchen. Allie was stuck between the door and the slumped corpse of Maria Anderson. She stared into the dark, empty eyes of the clean-cut, friendly neighbor who had been preying on Tacoma's women.

"What's your name?" Allie asked.

"Step away from Mother," he ordered. Allie complied, forcing herself to remain calm. She didn't feel obliged to protect the fragile husk of a woman. Her mind was fixated on any information about her partner and Jada. Allie wondered how long it had been since they entered the marsh. To save a life, they had engaged without waiting for backup. Allie understood she was alone, just her, this psychotic man, and his dead mother.

He motioned for Allie to walk back into the living room. She gladly moved back toward the window, searching for signs of Jason. She couldn't see anything out of the window except blackness amidst the curtain of rain. The man followed her into the small space.

"Put your gun on the ground," he barked as he glided his mother's wheelchair back into its spot next to the fireplace. Allie noticed the little shrine he had created around the woman's final resting place in the middle of the bare wood floor. A basket of knitting sat next to a plain wood table, and a book was placed on the edge.

"Is your mother's name Maria?" Allie asked, playing for time.

"Yes. How do you know Mother?" he stammered, but his hand didn't waver.

"Chief Horowitz. He remembered her."

The man blinked at her with an animal fixation.

"He tried to help your mother."

"Mother doesn't need anyone else but me," he said and glanced down at Allie's torso. "Throw your gun on the fireplace."

Allie mentally kicked herself. "I can't do that." The room exploded as a shot from his pistol erupted into the wood piled on the stone hearth. Splintered shards danced in the air, making her flinch. Still, she kept her cool. "All right."

She bent at the knees and crouched down, placing her weapon near the grate of the fireplace. Studying the unsub's victims in detail over the past few weeks, there was no question in her mind that this man was capable of killing her. He may have already killed her partner.

Allie hated to relinquish control of her sidearm, but she had to buy time. The longer this maniac was focused on her, the better chance they had to get help. She tried to swallow and stood back with both her hands raised. He wouldn't miss a second time. Allie stepped surreptitiously to the side of the room, trying to put Maria's shrunken body between them.

"Where is Jada Lovingood?" she asked.

This time, the man's eyes flickered with recognition. "Mrs. Lovingood is so kind." He smiled at the corpse. "She gave me what I needed to help Mother."

"And what was that?" She had to keep him talking.

"The perfect face," he said in an eerie trance-like voice, the voice of a small child.

Allie skin crawled. "And why do you need her face?"

He waved the gun in the direction of his mother. "I've been searching for the right one to make Mother beautiful again." He took a ragged breath. "She's been sick for so long now. I've been experimenting with different ways to make her look better, to feel better. Mother just needed a little help from me." He reached out and waved toward his mother as if to pet her.

"Your mother is dead," Allie said.

"Stop it!" he screamed. He jammed his hand in his hair and rolled his eyes.

Allie took a step back. She had discovered the source of his pain.

"Mother is just sick." He careened and took a step toward Maria to adjust the blue nightgown. "I've been taking good care of her. She is so proud of her boy, she tells me every day. I can make her better, make her beautiful again like she was before Father hurt her."

"Your father is Stanley?"

He nodded and frowned deeply. "He is a bad man. Very bad."

"Did your father hurt Maria?" Allie nodded to the corpse.

"Father was a bad man. He hurt Mother, hurt me too. I knew he was making her sick, so I stopped him from hurting anyone ever again."

Allie recalled that Chief Horowitz said he found Stanley Anderson's body in town.

"Did you stop your father?" Allie asked. "And put him in the park?"

The man nodded, then glanced at her sharply as if irritated by the information she knew about his world. "I just wanted to be left alone and make Mother safe. I took care of her. I'm grown now. We don't need him anymore. It was going to be okay. Everything was going to be okay."

"Until your mother got sick?" Allie asked.

The man's face crumpled at the thought. "I tried to make her better. I made medicines just like in her books. I found the herbs, but she got so tired. 'I'm just so tired, Xavier.'" He parroted a woman's voice, and a chill crept down Allie's spine.

But she caught the name for the first time. Glancing at the bookshelf, she noticed the ancient volumes of herbal medicine. "Chief Horowitz told me your mother was a natural healer, that women would come to her for help."

He nodded and jammed a fist into his temple.

"Did you know she went to the hospital?" Her foot brushed

against the wall. She was trapped in the far corner, and she needed more time for a distraction. "Did you know your mother needed help?"

He shook his head in misery. He ran a hand through his hair, the gun gyrating in his hand.

"After your father hurt her, she went to the hospital four or five times."

"I was little..." he cried.

"You couldn't what, help her?"

He whimpered.

"You couldn't protect her from your father, and you couldn't help her when she got sick?"

"Shut up!" he screamed. "Shut up! No, it's a lie. You're lying. Why can't you just leave us alone?" He thrust the gun in her direction, and Allie braced herself. "Mother didn't believe in your medicine. She believed in the marsh, in nature. She believed in *me*."

Allie had to find a different tactic. She had gambled that getting him angry might cause him to make a mistake. "How long has your mother been sick?" she asked. "She's very beautiful."

He sniffed and ran his sleeve under his nose, then glanced at the ceiling and started to count. "About eighteen months," he finally said.

"And you've been trying to help her? Help her look like herself again?"

He nodded.

"I'm sure we can work something out." Allie tried again, taking a step toward the wheelchair. "If you just let me see Jada, I'm sure we can find a way to help Maria get better."

"*Don't* say her name!" he screamed. "*Don't* say it." He stamped his foot and squeezed a shot into the ceiling. Woods chips rained down on them. When he aimed the gun at Allie again, she knew the conversation was over, that it was time to act.

Diving to the ground behind the wheelchair, she heard another shot go off and slam into the wall behind her. Then a third shot, and a fourth. She landed hard beside the fireplace, scooped up her gun in a roll, and aimed it back at him as she stood.

A primal scream tore through the air. Allie leveled the gun at her attacker, but he dropped his weapon and ran toward the wheelchair. She followed him with the sight of her weapon, but he paid no attention to her. He was sobbing, mouth bubbling with agony and pain as he reached for the corpse.

Allie stepped back. Her ears pounded with the sound of the gunshots, and the air was thick with the smell of cordite. Maria's skull rolled across the floor and came to rest by her foot. It looked up at her with one lidded eye. Half of her face had been blown away by the blast of her son's careless shot.

Xavier slumped beside her chair, holding the wreckage of the wig in his hand and gaping at the headless corpse. His gun lay discarded at his feet. Allie trained her weapon on him and kicked the gun away. The weeping man offered no resistance as she cuffed him.

"Mother!" he sobbed, spittle running down his mouth. "I'm so sorry."

Allie slid his cuffs around the leg of his mother's wheelchair, binding them together in an awkward, grieving pile of decomposing flesh and metal. A face mask of someone else's skin stared up at Allie from Maria's lap. She shuddered as she retrieved Xavier's weapon.

"Hold on, Jada," she muttered, and then went hunting for her partner.

"Dispatch, this is Agent Bishop reporting. Suspect is restrained and unarmed in the primary residence. Be advised, he is with the corpse of Maria Anderson."

As expected, a question came through the radio, asking her to repeat her last transmission. She would explain later.

Right now, she needed to find her partner.

Chapter Forty-One

Darien Marsh
Glendale, Washington

Allie shoved open the front door of the old shack. She stared into the darkness of the marsh, searching for any sign of life from their promised reinforcements and willing flashlights to erupt out of the swamp.

But all she heard was the low rumble of bullfrogs chorusing together and cicadas joining in the harmony. During the mayhem, the rain had eased up, and the clouds rolled back, exposing a brilliant, sparkling sky above her.

"Jason?" Allie called frantically into the abandoned compound. She bit back the fear of stumbling upon her partner's body, lying lifeless in the mud. "Jason!"

"Here," he croaked from somewhere close.

Relief flooded into her. Allie flew down the steps of the ramshackle shack. Her flashlight swung in an arc across the bare ground and the old house posts. The edge of her light snagged on his face, and he blinked.

"Easy, cowboy." He lifted a hand to shield his face. He sat slumped against the side of the wooden structure on the bare ground. His body was slicked in mud, his face pale beneath his beard.

"Jason!" She crouched next to her partner and ran the flashlight over his body. "You're bleeding." She took in the bloody bandage he had fashioned out of his windbreaker. "You're hit?" She grabbed for her radio at her hip.

"I'm all right." He winced. "I'm all right, Allie."

"You need a doctor." Allie clicked on the radio and called it in.

"He opened fire on the door. Damn bullet went right through." He groaned and tried to sit up. "But there's another one...down there." He struggled to breathe.

Allie refocused the beam of her light and gasped. "No. No...no!" He gasped when she lifted his shirt. The side of his abdomen was slick with blood, covering a dark red spot where the bullet went in.

He licked his lips. "It's my fault. I—shouldn't have stayed in front of the door that long."

"My god, Jason!" She tore off her windbreaker and balled it up. He screamed in pain as she pressed it into the wound.

"I hate you so much right now," he grunted, but not without a thin smile.

"We have to mitigate the bleeding." Allie got on the radio and updated the other end on his condition, calling for a helicopter fitted with a rescue basket.

"So you got Señor Psychopath up there?" He nodded to the house.

"Yeah. Does it hurt?"

"Allie."

She ignored him, still fussing over his wounds.

"Allie!"

She blinked. "What?"

"I'm okay. Stop it."

She sat back on her knees. "But you're not. You—"

"Allie, I have a mother and a wife. I don't need you pinch hitting for them."

She nodded. "Okay."

"So what happened in there? Did you find Jada?"

Jada.

Jason's condition had momentarily caused her to forget everything else. "No." She rose to her feet. "I need to find her. Will you be okay by yourself?"

"Allie, we came here to find Jada. Now go finish the job."

She nodded. Her mind was racing. "Okay. I'm on the radio if you need me."

He winced and took in a shaky breath. "Go already."

THE HEADLESS BODY of Maria Anderson greeted her from its place on the floor. Her son was still sitting against the wheelchair, rocking and keening a mournful wail.

"Xavier," she said. "I need the key to that padlock in the kitchen." No answer. "Xavier! I need the key! Either way, I'm getting in that room." Desperate, she tried a different angle. "Your mother would want you to give it to me."

He blinked through his tears, growled at her, then lifted a defeated hand toward the mantle. Allie hurried over and found a dull bronze key sitting on the smooth stone slab. She grabbed it and shot across the room into the kitchen.

Reaching the padlock, Allie had both the lock and the door open in seconds. She froze in the doorway. The acrid scent of blood and formaldehyde assailed her. She clicked on the flashlight and stepped into the darkened space. Her eyes roved over the places touched by the beam of light. She gasped as her mind registered the horrors.

Dozens of jars containing preserved specimens lined the wooden shelves. There was a long table filled with jars of powders, beakers of solutions, a strange assortment of flower bulbs, dried herbs, tools, and all manners of taxidermied animals—squirrels and rabbits and fish. Allie was transfixed by the bizarre display of horror that filled the space.

Then she saw it. A bare foot sticking out from behind a shelf at the back of the room. Allie approached to discover a wooden table with the body of a woman draped across it. The face had been removed to reveal the delicate muscles underneath. Allie gasped. Fresh blood dripped off Jada Lovingood's wounds and pooled on the floor in a slick puddle.

Allie's stomach revolted. She placed her wrist at her mouth.

They were too late.

A sense of defeat pummeled her. She had wasted so much time tracking down clues, being precise, securing warrants. None of that mattered to this woman or her family. Instead of cooking dinner for her husband, Jada had been forced into this macabre freak show.

Allie allowed her finger to graze the woman's foot, startled to find that it was still warm. "Jada?" Quickly, she moved up the body and reached for a pulse at her throat. Under her fingers, Allie felt the faintest flicker of a heartbeat.

"I'm here, Jada," Allie said faintly into the woman's ear. To her horror and shock, Allie noticed the woman's eyeballs were still moving beneath bloodied and mangled eyelids.

Everything in Allie wanted to scream and run outside, demanding an airlift for this poor woman. But death was very close. Allie sensed it in her bones, and if she ran to get help, Jada Lovingood would probably meet her end alone.

Allie had spent hours studying the poison Anderson used on his victims. It numbed their senses enough for him to carve away their faces. The autopsy reports had identified that most died before he mutilated their bodies. The lab hypothesized that Xavier slowly perfected his solution to prolong their death, to better preserve the masks of their faces without the sudden halt of blood flow. He carefully worked out a technique for stunning his prey, immobilizing their limbs and vital organs until slowly their hearts stopped and their lungs filled with fluid.

The helicopter wouldn't get here in time.

Nothing prepared Allie for the emotional toll of being near a human soul in their final moments of life. Allie swiped a tear from her face and took Jada's hands in her own. No one deserved to be alone at this moment. It was a universal truth.

"Jada," Allie bit back the tremor in her voice. "If you can hear me, I want you to move your eyes to the right." Jada did, and the movement made Allie's chest tighten. "My name is Allie Bishop. I'm with the FBI. I'm holding your hands right now. I'm here, Jada. You're safe."

She tried not to blubber. She wanted to pour her energy into this woman and give her the dignity she deserved.

"I'm so sorry I wasn't here sooner. Please forgive me. But I want you to know it's over. Xavier Anderson will never hurt anyone again. Help is on its way. You're safe, and you're very loved. I'm not leaving you. The entire town has been looking for you. We're going to get you home."

Allie mourned all this terror that had been inflicted on this woman. The poison, ironically, was probably the only thing keeping her alive. She was numb to the trauma responses her body would naturally be having, which was prolonging her death as if she had been put on heavy anesthesia. But Allie could tell that she wouldn't last long. She was losing a lot of blood, and the poison would take its final toll at any moment.

Allie spoke softly to Jada as her eye movements slowed. She was running out of words. She found that she couldn't lie to this innocent woman, tell her half-truths, or give empty promises. The weight of death drove out anything but the purest of words from its presence.

Finally, Allie tenderly began to sing a gentle lullaby that her mother had sung to her whenever she had a nightmare as a little girl. It was a simple tune, but Allie had forgotten its power over fear. She offered it as a meager gift of gentle comfort, and as she sang the last refrain, Jada's eyes stilled and went blank.

Allie checked her pulse. Everything had stopped. She glanced at her watch and made a note of the time. Looking around the makeshift laboratory, she noticed a blanket nearby and covered the body, feeling cold and numb all over.

Focus.

Allie held her eyes closed for a long moment. The chemical fumes in the room made it difficult to think.

Facts first.

Jason's phrase floated through her mind. Jason was alive out there, bleeding from two gunshot wounds. He needed her now. There was nothing else she could do for Jada.

Allie quickly scanned the rest of the room, gathering enough medical supplies to make a tourniquet, and rushed back outside. Her partner's head bobbed as her light found it again. He blinked, trying to hold his eyes open as she lowered herself to his side.

"Stay with me, Jason." She didn't know where to start but decided to begin with his leg. His body was going into shock from blood loss and exposure. Cutting off his pant leg, she secured a makeshift tourniquet over his leg and began to tighten it with all the force she could muster. She needed to slow the bleeding.

"I'm here," he said, but his words were slurred with fatigue. "Where's Jada?"

"Gone," she said bitterly. "Anderson killed her. I—I couldn't do anything." She felt her words flood with emotion. "I stayed with her until she passed, but—"

"It's not your fault, Allie." Jason tried to comfort her. "You didn't hurt her. He did." He faded but came back when his chin bobbed on his chest. "She wasn't alone, at the end." He looked Allie in the eyes. "Hold on to that. It's not nothing. It's everything."

She noticed the gray color of her partner's skin and the sticky wetness of his shirt. A new fear demanded all of her attention. She froze, listening. "Do you hear that?"

Out of the darkness came a low chopping sound, gradually getting louder. Allie grabbed the radio. Switching on both lights, she waved them in the air above her head.

Marze's voice sounded over the radio. "Allie, that you?"

"Yes!" she shouted into the radio as the wind from the incoming helicopter swirled the tops of the trees and whipped her hair. "We're here!"

The helicopter's blinding light locked onto Allie's face, and she was swallowed up by the enormous relief of its thundering presence.

Chapter Forty-Two

Riverside Memorial Park
Glendale, Washington

"We, therefore, commit this body to the ground, earth to earth, ashes to ashes, dust to dust, in sure and certain hope of the resurrection to eternal life."

The priest in snow white robes scooped up a handful of dirt and gently tossed it atop the final resting place of Jada Lovingood. Allie watched from the edge of the proceedings as the family filed past, tossing in flowers at the graveside service beneath the towering oak trees of the quiet cemetery.

Her attention followed a butterfly that danced across the heads of the gravestones and meandered through the somber farewell to a beloved mother, wife, and friend. Allie had made a promise to Jada. She promised that she would stay with her until the end. Today, she was keeping that promise.

Finally, family members and friends slipped away from the graveside in ones and twos, holding onto each other in their grief. Jada's husband nodded to her before he followed his daughter to the car.

But Allie stayed behind, lingering under the shade of a maple tree until the casket was lowered and completely interred. Only then did she approach. The butterfly was the only witness to her words to the woman. Then, with a final prayer for the woman's peace, she returned to her car and started back to Tacoma.

The ride was quiet without Jason. He had finally been released from the hospital to recover at home. But Allie didn't mind silence. It gave her time to think and process all the emotions that flow through a person at a funeral. One couldn't help but contemplate the brevity of life—the regrets, the joys, and the importance of relationships—when remembering a soul.

Now alone with her thoughts, Allie circled the questions around her mother's old case. As an investigator, she understood how one person's life could simply become a file in a box. But each of those files represented someone's loved one, someone who gave their life meaning.

Her mother's files were waiting unanswered in a file of their own. And they were so much more than a puzzle to Allie. They were a part of her life that bore a gaping wound. The central relationship of her young life that had simply evaporated like fog in the sunshine.

On the ride back toward the TFO, Allie made peace with the fact that her hunt for answers would haunt her until, like the Lovingoods, she could put her loved one to rest. It was part of the reason Allie had felt such guilt about Stephanie Mercer's death. The two shared a common bond, the ache of having a mother ripped away suddenly without explanation. Allie was only seven when her mother disappeared, but it marked the rest of her days and shaped the purpose of her life. Stephanie gave her life in pursuit of justice and answers about her own mother.

And ironically, it was the love of a mother that drove Xavier Anderson to kill his father. After hours of interrogation, Allie and Marze uncovered the man's brutal upbringing. Alone in the marsh, Xavier and Maria were at the mercy of his father's violent whims. He would hit or strangle them when provoked by the smallest things. As a result, Xavier and Maria formed an unhealthy bond.

Xavier never had a birth certificate or a social security card, leaving him with little option but to survive in the harsh conditions. Stanley's abuse had fractured his son's fragile mind into strange trains of thought, left unchecked in his isolation. Maria's autopsy confirmed what the medical report and Xavier had identified—years of traumatic abuse, broken bones, and fractures that had taken their toll on both mind and body.

Xavier's love for his mother and his ignorance about the outer world forced him to take the law into his own hands. He slipped poison into his father's canteen and followed at a distance while Stanley went about his business, falling dead in the center of Cary Lake Park.

Xavier shared a couple of happier years with his mother before Maria fell ill. Then he went to work, pouring over his mother's herbal medicine books, spending hours foraging, distilling, and trying out his experiments on local animals. Saving his mother became his life's mission. He had saved her once before, from his father. He was certain he could do it again.

A clinical psychiatrist had confirmed what Allie suspected. Maria Anderson's death had caused her son's dissociation, which was when his killings began. The face was what Xavier believed truly kept his mother with him. He confessed that he had killed more women than they first thought, directing them to search the marshes near the homestead.

The FBI processed the Anderson homestead for evidence of human remains. Along with Xavier's detailed admission, Allie and the Glendale Police Department employed cadaver dogs to locate the bodies of seven more women. Six of the seven they unearthed represented a stagnant missing persons case from somewhere in the greater Tacoma area.

Only one, Xavier's first impromptu poisoning, was a Jane Doe. He described her as a homeless woman who had approached him for help in a grocery store parking lot and reminded him of his mother. With the help of Dr. Winters, Allie traced the woman's DNA and identified her as Patricia Mathews, a known addict from Vancouver who often moved nomadically up and down the West Coast, traveling with lonely truckers.

Xavier's story was painfully sordid. Raised alone, cut off from the world, he had no cultural concepts of death. He fished and hunted his land for food, killing and taking pelts for what he needed. He treated the world beyond the marsh much in the same manner—a hunting ground for everything he needed to help his mother. He confessed to developing his toxin out of the spinal fluid of a fish that flowed in abundance up Abercorn Creek.

In Xavier's strange, broken reality, a human face was key to personhood. It was central to his mother's vitality, the sole source of life that kept his mother with him. The Glendale PD, the FBI, and a team of forensic anthropologists assisted in the removal of the bodies for proper burial.

The specialist hypothesized that Anderson's experiments failed to preserve the bodies, and as they began to rot, the bodies decayed, causing a stench that attracted predators. Anderson altered his technique and began dumping the bodies in the Puyallup, hoping the current would dispose of the evidence for him. It was determined that the decayed, maggoty body found in the skate park had slipped from the marsh over time and entered the waterway.

Anderson also explained that Stephanie had called his phone the day after he had dumped Helen and told him she knew what he had done, that she was going to hunt him down and gouge his eyes out. Stephanie's physical profile didn't match Anderson's connection with his mother, so he frantically devised a different way to dispose of her body.

Allie couldn't help but wonder how this meeting would have ended if Robert Hall had agreed to assist Stephanie or had notified the authorities of her intentions. Allie's professional training made her wary of ad hoc investigations, but she couldn't help but wonder if her desperate search for answers about her mother would have led her to take the same action. It was a chilling warning.

Arriving back at the TFO, Allie parked her rental car in the garage and stepped out. A loud engine rumble reverberated off the concrete. Allie stepped back as Brandy came in on her motorcycle, parking beside her.

"Allie, glad I caught you," Brandy said as she pulled off her helmet and dropped her bike's kickstand. Brandy was dressed in her signature Ferrari red racing jacket with white boots and crisp-white shorts under a black sweater. "How was the funeral?"

"Sad, but beautiful, in its way."

"I brought you a boba." Brandy opened her seat to reveal an oversized cup of her high-octane green tea mix.

Allie stammered at the sight. "I think my heart might explode."

"Oh, this one's mine," Brandy laughed. "This one's for you." Out of the storage compartment, she withdrew a small cup of bright red watermelon tea. "Funerals always drain me, so I figured you could use something today."

"You're wonderful. Thank you." The two fell into step, walking toward the office building. "Thank you for all your help by the way." They entered the building and started down the hall to the lobby.

"We're a good team," Brandy said. "It was a blast working with you. You're heading to Boise tomorrow?"

Allie nodded. They reached the elevator and stepped inside. Brandy punched the button. "You're still good to take care of my flowers?" Allie asked her.

Brandy smiled. "My betta fish loves the African violets. And the grow light. Thanks for setting that up. It's nice to have a little color in my space."

"Something to remember me by." Allie gave a wistful smile. She could feel the buzz of caffeine hitting her bloodstream.

"Remember you? You're coming back, Allie. I will put up a royal stink if you don't. Don't go getting comfortable in Boise, you hear?"

The Face of Evil

Allie cracked her first genuine smile all day. "Understood. Thanks for having my back."

"We need to stick together, and don't hesitate to call if you need any help out there in the boonies. I'm always up for a challenge."

They stepped out onto their floor, Allie in her understated agent funeral attire and Brandy in her unapologetic, totally unofficial uniform. Allie received Brandy's warm embrace and headed toward her cubicle.

The bare, beige walls of her cubicle greeted her as she dropped her satchel. Gone was the collection of Snapple bottles, sticky notes, and broken No. 2 pencils. She glanced around the space. The case board was blank, and the bust of Abraham Lincoln was tucked into a cardboard box next to her coffee paraphernalia, along with several packets of Jason's signature electrolyte water. On his insistence, of course.

Allie picked up the completed stack of case reports on Xavier Anderson's victims and made her way toward Marze's office.

"There she is." The SAC motioned for her to sit. "It's not every day we close twelve cases in one afternoon." He smiled as he received the stack from her.

"I'm not sure I can feel pride about it when they represent twelve dead women."

"And that's what makes you a good agent." Marze lowered his voice. "We're gonna miss you around here, but I know you will represent the TFO well out there. Show those Boise folks how to run a clean operation."

Allie accepted the compliment with a nod.

"I heard Jason's doing well at home," he said.

"Yep, Victoria's cooking up a storm, always a good sign. And she's enjoying making him sit in her hospital recliner. He's going nuts, and she's loving every second of it."

"That's good," Marze laughed. "He won't be running any marathons anytime soon, and I know he's got a long road back. We'll work on getting him ready for you. I'll let you know when he's ready for the field. I know he wouldn't settle for anyone else as a partner. You two work well together."

Allie tried to absorb the praise. It was true, they did work well together.

"Jason has overcome a lot in his career already. I was cautiously optimistic about you. I'm glad to see I was right. Your strengths complement each other, and your experience has made you resilient and teachable."

"Resilient is code for broken?" Allie asked plainly.

"Resilience is code for resilience, Bishop." Marze didn't flinch. "Life will try to break you, regardless of the career. You learned that young. It shouldn't be a surprise. You and Jason have each faced difficult challenges. You could even argue that you've been dealt a rough hand in life. But I believe that's part of why you're good at this work. You understand how circumstances can affect the human condition. You've witnessed the dark side of life up close. Most people would crumble under what you two have faced. Crawled into a bottle or some kind of socially acceptable addiction and checked out of life."

Allie contemplated his perspective.

"I need to thank you," Marze continued.

Allie cocked her head, perplexed.

"Jason was…struggling. It wasn't a surprise. First Paul, then Victoria's cancer. It hasn't been easy on the man. I was hoping he'd come around in time. But he was struggling to find his footing. He had plenty to feel sorry about, and not much else. You were the perfect antidote to his misery. You've overcome a lot to be here. Your history isn't a secret, but you use it to fuel you. That's apparent."

Allie blinked at the honesty.

"You set the bar for Jason," Marze continued. "Demonstrated what it looks like to embrace your past and let it drive you forward. You find a personal connection in all of your cases, and your focus is admirable. Not only that, but you need Jason. He tries to hide his empathy under his well-cut suits, but he's excellent at reading people. He thinks he did well in the FBI because of Paul, but it was the other way around. Paul and Jason's success was largely due to Jason's skills. He excels at developing assets and understanding people's motivations."

Allie nodded. "I've learned a lot from him already. I was thankful that he told me about Paul."

Her boss huffed. "He didn't see it coming. No one did. But it made him question everything. He lost his internal compass until you came along. I've watched him find his footing again next to you. Paul's deception didn't just wound Jason as a friend. It undercut his professional reputation, set his career back years, and unraveled hundreds of cases. All the people who trusted Jason with the worst parts of their lives watched their cases get dismissed simply because Paul's name was associated with their paperwork. It's one of the reasons our office has been so underwater. We had to reinvestigate years of back work."

"Sir, why are you telling me this?" Allie asked. "Not that

I'm unappreciative. But no one other than Jason has broached the topic with me yet."

"You've worked hard for me, worked hard to be a part of a team even when you didn't know the history or the lay of the land. You deserve to hear it from me. I also want you to trust me when I say I'm not sending you away as a punishment. I want you here. I'm glad you're a part of the Tacoma Field Office."

Allie was uncomfortable with the lavish praise. Admittedly, she had gotten used to being underestimated. It was a big part of her drive. She thrived on the doubt of others and wasn't sure of herself without the motivation to prove others wrong.

"Thank you," she said quietly. Allie stared at the scar on her wrist and ran her thumb across the smooth skin. She hated goodbyes and could feel Marze's scrutiny in the silence.

"Ready for a new case in a new town?"

"Ready for anything, sir."

"Good, I just spoke to the Boise Field Office. They're looking forward to having you. They just opened a new case and could use some regional support. They'll provide accommodations and a partner. I forwarded the information to your email. Have a safe trip, and give me a call when you get settled."

"Absolutely." Allie stood and shook his hand. "Thank you for everything."

"Don't be dramatic, Bishop. I'll get you back here sooner than you think."

Back at her desk, Allie sent Jason a simple text promising to stop by when she came back to visit Grams over Labor Day. Allie searched for Eastman in the office and tried not to feel disappointed when she couldn't find him. Finally, she glanced at her watch and made a decision.

"Hey, Hagan?" Allie wrapped her arms around Grams's potted bleeding heart. "Can I ask you a favor?"

"What's the matter, Bishop?" His eyebrow cocked in disbelief. "You need a babysitter for your houseplant?"

She shrugged. "It was my grandmother's."

"Do I look like a guy with time on my hands?" he asked defensively.

Allie didn't want to answer the question. She was trying to extend an olive branch.

"Why me?" he sneered.

"You have the best light," she said, nodding to the bank of windows that lined the back wall. He stared at her. Allie shifted the pot uncomfortably on her hip. She didn't move.

"Fine." He rolled his eyes.

"Thanks, Hagan." Allie tucked the plant in the corner and handed him a piece of paper.

"What's this?"

"Watering instructions, in case you're too busy to remember."

He nodded. "Good luck, rookie. And don't get comfortable with me doing you favors, all right?"

Allie dusted the dirt off her hands and exited the office, ready for whatever came next. She liked to travel light, and leaving a piece of herself at the TFO felt right, like a promise to herself.

This wasn't goodbye, just the next step along the path.

Epilogue

7-Eleven, Interstate 84
Outskirts of Tacoma, WA

> *Good morning heartache*
> *You're the one who knew me when*
> *Might as well get used to you*
> *Hanging around*
> *Good morning heartache*

Allie crooned along with Billie Holiday as she pulled into the gas station on her way to Boise. The moon hung over the neon sign. Outside the city, the stars were magnificent, tugging at Allie's nostalgic heartstrings.

It was later than she anticipated. After leaving the TFO, she had stopped off at her grandmother's for a visit. She should have known she would lose track of time, considering they never managed a quick visit.

Allie hated to leave Grams alone, but it wouldn't be any

different than when she left for Quantico. Except this time she wouldn't be on the other side of the country, and she was bringing several loaves of Grams's bread and jars of butter pickles to tide her over until she could return for a weekend.

Allie glanced at her gas light. It had clicked on after the last exit. She should have stopped in the nicer area a few miles back, but she had been caught up in the music and trying to make up time down this desolate stretch. She needed gas and caffeine, seeing that she would be driving through the night.

Allie hummed as she pumped gas. The space between cases always left her spirit a little lighter. She wondered if this was how normal people felt every day, without the responsibility of an open case hanging over their heads. Soon enough, tomorrow's problems would fill up every corner of her mind. Tonight though, she enjoyed the heat coming off the cement as she cleaned her windshield.

She was scheduled to get her car back in a couple of weeks. For now, this rental would continue to serve her just fine. Somehow, the scent of fuel and the heat of the engine reminded her of the car bomb that killed the young family of Jason's informant. The story had haunted Allie ever since he had confided in her. Victoria had been right. The FBI, by nature, forged close relationships that were painful to lose.

Allie leaned against the trunk and thought back to the night she arrested Xavier Anderson. The memory still felt intense as it tried to untangle itself from her mind. The panic of not knowing if Jason was dead or alive still burned at the back of her throat.

But if watching him bleed out in the marsh made her feel anything, it was only to confirm her fears of getting too close.

People betrayed you, hurt you, died on you. When did the fear of all the associated pain become too much?

Her first instinct was to withdraw and observe. She was probably more like Dave Hagan than she liked to admit, and that made her clench her teeth. This job demanded rapid assessments of people, and they were life-or-death decisions. But if she didn't engage with a new team—if they couldn't trust her—then how would they work together?

Allie crossed her arms and blew out a breath. Change sucked, no matter how much she liked the distance between her and other people.

The gas pump clicked off, and Allie stepped around her car to disengage it. She casually noticed a truck pulling into the spot next to hers, not thinking much of it, except that it didn't seem to be aligned with a pump.

Allie's defenses were always high as a single woman in the middle of nowhere. But her phone was in the center console of the vehicle, and her gun was in the glovebox. She quickly punched the button for the receipt and waited impatiently for it to print.

"Come on," she urged, her heart pulsing with sudden adrenaline. The driver stepped out of his car and immediately made eye contact with Allie.

She recognized him.

It took a moment to place him, but as she glanced at the pump to grab the slip of paper, it hit her. He was the man in the restaurant when she dined with Sadie—the handsome man with a beard watching her while she ate.

Allie's spidey senses went on high alert.

When she started walking toward her car door, her

defenses went into overdrive. She glanced at the cameras, at the lonely storefront, the empty parking lot. Allie moved to her passenger door and opened it. Surreptitiously sliding her handgun from the glovebox, she held it low next to her thigh. She didn't like the volatile mix of firearms and gasoline, but better to be safe than sorry.

The man tugged on his hat in greeting and stepped toward her car.

"Stop right there," she demanded, keeping the gun at her side and the car between them. She had every right to her personal safety. "Why are you following me?"

He raised both hands and paused next to her driver side door. His green Seahawks cap matched his eyes.

"Easy. I'm trying to help," he replied. "We're on the same side." His voice was gentle, very different from the strange scenario. "I'd never hurt you, Allie."

"Same side?" she snapped. "And how do you know my name?" Allie placed her gun on the roof of the car and kept her hand on it, not pointing it at him in confrontation but letting its presence shift the conversation in her favor.

"You and I want the same things," he said, unbothered by the weapon.

"What do you mean?"

"Look." He glanced to the right and the left. Allie felt the hairs on the back of her neck stand up straight. Her senses were screaming at her. Something was not right. But she was drawn toward the man, hanging on his words for some reason she didn't understand.

"Look," he said again, "you need to—"

Before he could get out another word, a second car

screeched into the parking lot—a gold Mercedes. It turned in a wide arc, tires squealing behind her in a flurry of smoke and gravel. The dark window rolled down, and as soon as Allie saw a pistol emerge, she crouched behind her car.

Three shots rang out in rapid succession. She screamed as the man stumbled backward, clutching his chest.

Allie broke cover and started for him. "No!" he yelled, and pulled a gun from the back of his jeans. He started to return fire. "Go!" he shouted, then coughed and stumbled to the ground, his blood staining the pavement. His eyes locked on hers for an instant. "Get out of here!" He fired two more shots over her shoulder.

Allie's training refused to let her flee a crime scene, but when another gunshot whizzed by her head, she knew she didn't have a choice.

She jumped into the car, crouched low behind the wheel, and sped off.

Fresh gunshots rang out behind her, mimicking the questions ricocheting through her mind...

* * *

THANK you <u>so much</u> for reading *The Face of Evil*! I hope you enjoyed it as much as I enjoyed writing it.

Allie returns in **The Candidate**, the third installment of the *Allie Bishop FBI Mystery Thriller Series*, now available for pre-order!

About the Author

🩶 Dearest Reader,

Thank you *so much* reading *The Face of Evil Daughter*. It's been a lot of fun getting to know these new characters!

If you enjoyed spending time in Allie's world, would you be so kind as to recommend the book to other mystery lovers as well? As a self-published author, recommendations can go a long way to getting my books in front of other readers, and I'm working hard to write stories that you will continue to enjoy.

I'm off to work on Allie's next thrilling investigation, *The Candidate*. Make sure to sign up for my newsletter so you don't miss it.

If this was your first time reading one of my books, please check out the Darcy Hunt series. If you loved Allie, you're sure to love Darcy too! Happy Reading!

Love,
Eva

P.S. If there are areas of improvement that you would like to suggest, or if you noticed any typos, would you email me directly and let me know? I reply directly to each and every email I receive: evasparksbooks@gmail.com. 🩶

Sign up HERE to get notified of every new release!

Follow Eva on Facebook

Also by EVA SPARKS

Darcy Hunt FBI Mystery Thriller Series
The Girl in Room 16
Her Final Wish

The Girls They Kept

One More Grave

The Killer's Son

The House Down the Lane

A Cry in the Woods

The Girl Who Woke Up

Get Notified

You may not be automatically notified of my next release. ***So sign up for my newsletter HERE to get notified of every new release!***

Made in United States
Cleveland, OH
16 February 2025